A Catalogue record for this book is available from the British Library

ISBN-13: 978 0 340 91744 2

Typeset in AGaramond by Avon DataSet Ltd,
Bidford on Avon, Warwickshire

Printed in the UK by CPI Bookmarque, Croydon, CR0 4TD

The paper and board used in this paperback by Hodder Children's Books
are natural recyclable products made from wood grown in sustainable
forests. The manufacturing processes conform to the environmental
regulations of the country of origin.

Hodder Children's Books
a division of Hachette Children's Books
338 Euston Road, London NW1 3BH
An Hachette Livre UK Company

# DAVID GRIMSTONE

# DAVEY SWAG

*Hodder
Children's
Books*

A division of Hachette Children's Books

For Andrea & Mark Webb, Lee Stoddart and
Mike Robinson. Thanks for all the
Thursday mayhem – and the glass table.

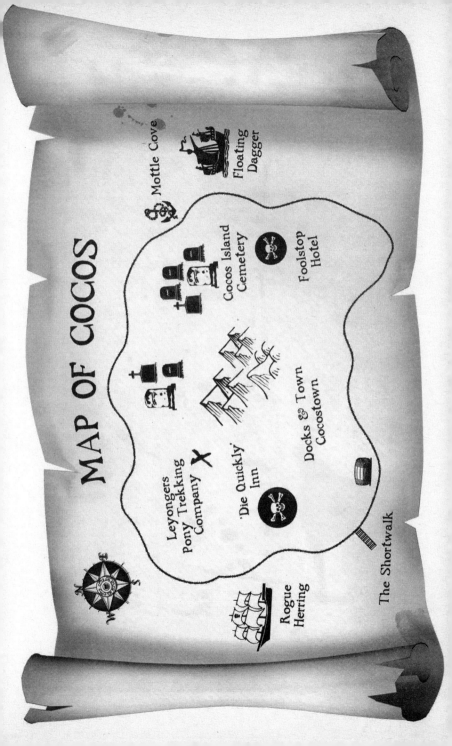

# Prologue

The ship anchored on the dark side of Jade Island, in a tiny cove sheltered by a bank of weeping trees. A few seconds passed before half a dozen shadowy figures appeared on the port side of the deck and three rowing boats were lowered into the waters.

A series of rope ladders were unfurled over the side of the ship, and a steady stream of pirates began to crawl down them like so many spiders released from a jar.

Despite the scene taking place in the cove, the only audible noise came from the rustling of the trees and the lap, lap, lapping of the cool water.

For a time, nothing happened.

Then, slowly, carefully and above all *noiselessly*, the boats were detached from the ship and rowed ashore. When the first of the three neared the sand, it was swiftly abandoned as the silent horde rushed up the beach, quickly disappearing between the trees. As they moved through the moon's unblinking spotlight, it became clear that several of the men were armed, some brandishing sabres and cutlasses while others had knives clenched between their teeth.

The last of the men to put a foot on the shore was roughly twice the size of most of his companions, and carried no weapons at all, but he moved with a grim determination that made him all the more frightening for it. Weapons, it seemed, would be mere decorations on this pirate.

Jade Island basked under the moonlight, oblivious to the darkness that had just breached its borders.

The island look-outs, two men who had worked together for most of their adult life, were playing cards. One had taken more than half his friend's wages, and the other was determined to even the score.

'Three fives,' said the first look-out, laying his hand on the grimy tree stump they'd fashioned into a table. 'Beat that.'

The second look-out studied his own cards, and groaned.

'I don't think I can,' he began, and froze.

'Well?' said his friend, not looking up. 'You laying down or what?'

When no reply was forthcoming, he muttered under his breath and, finally, glanced across the makeshift card table.

There was a thin trickle of blood lining his friend's neck. As he looked on, with mounting horror, the trickle became a flood and the man keeled over.

The look-out dropped his cards and made a grab for his belt, but a blade edge suddenly appeared from his stomach and a terrible coldness stole over him.

'Tha's righ', mates,' hissed a voice beside his ear. 'Jus' you die quiet-like.'

Two pirates grinned at each other in the moonlight. As much as they'd have liked to finish the look-outs' card game, a sound of distant music reminded them that they still had work to do . . .

A shrill whistle soon coaxed their friends from the trees, and together the horde moved on towards the large building that towered over the cliffs.

The party at the governor's mansion was in full swing and everyone who was anyone on Jade Island was there. In one corner of the enormous hall, the butcher and the baker were having an argument with the candlestick maker about some bet he'd supposed to have lost and wouldn't pay up on. Elsewhere, members of the island's carnival consortium were trying to prove that they could each stand on one leg and arm wrestle, while at the same time attempting to empty the contents of their ale mugs into their mouths; one had seriously hurt himself in the attempt.

As parties went, however, it was a good one.

In the centre of the hall, Governor Jordel Swag was unwittingly entertaining several of his closest friends with his total inability to cope with a screaming baby. The governor's wife, who'd refused to entrust her son to the servants, had deposited little Davey with her husband so that she could join the erratic and (mostly) drunken dancers, who were throwing themselves around enthusiastically in a cleared space beside the stairs. The quality of the display was largely poor, as people were jiggling, diving and shimmying to the accompaniment of a wailed chorus from one of the island's most celebrated but least talented singers.

It was a jolly room, full of happy people laughing and joking. This was mainly due to Governor Swag, who was generally thought of as the last compassionate governor left in the Caribbean. He was a family man, content with life and his place in it, and was consequently much loved by those around him. Jordel might have been considered something of a laughing stock by the power-hungry governors of neighbouring islands, but his inexhaustible kindness among his own people had won him an immense amount of loyalty over the years. The islanders often remarked that Governor Swag would be remembered for his charitable nature long after other governors in the Caribbean had been forgotten.

Unfortunately, in *this* opinion the islanders were wrong. Jordel Swag *would* be remembered, but – sadly – not for his charity. The kind and gentle governor would be remembered only for his horrific death, and the terrible events that were to take place on Jade Island this very night.

Sadly, it was the very *celebration* of the island's peace-loving ruler that left it open to its most devastating invasion . . .

. . . For the singing, dancing and general merriment at the mansion had drowned out the cries that had erupted from the guardhouse nearby.

Eventually, however, the revellers at the party *did* hear something.

A single, frenzied war-cry rose above the din of the party, and the mansion's great double doors came crashing down . . .

Several gasps went up from the crowd, which was

quickly swept away from the wreckage as pirates began to pour into the opening and, cutlasses flashing, started to hack, slash and lunge their way through the hall.

One group of terrified islanders took to the stairs while several others made for side rooms, only to find that more of the wily, toothless marauders were waiting for them. This crew was unlike any the islanders had seen before: most were bleeding profusely from recent wounds, and several were baying like mad hounds as they mercilessly cut down anyone in their path.

Jordel Swag had retreated to the top of the stairs, clutching his baby in one arm and dragging his wife behind him with the other.

'Help us!' the governor's wife screamed, though it wasn't clear to whom she was calling. 'Somebody! Please help us!'

Jordel tightened his grip on his wife's wrist and, reaching the final step, shook her suddenly, wrenching her off her feet in an effort to calm her down.

'Take Davey,' he snapped, thrusting the baby into her arms and grasping both her shoulders.

The governor's wife simply stared wide-eyed at the carnage below.

'LISTEN to me!' Jordel shouted, slapping her across the cheek. 'Take Davey NOW and run. Get out of one of the upstairs windows and go across the roof – just do whatever you have to do. Do you hear me? Now! GO!'

He shoved his wife back with such force that she almost stumbled, but the near-fall served to shake her from her trance, and she quickly hurried off through a nearby door.

Jordel returned his attention to the fray below, and quickly drew his own blade. He wasn't a fighting man – swordplay was not in his nature – but he couldn't stand idly by and watch his loyal islanders butchered in front of him. He drew in a deep breath and charged down the stairs, slashing at the pirate swarm as they tried to force an advance.

A few of the beasts had fallen in combat, though many more of the islanders lay sprawled on the floor in various parts of the hall; the attack on the mansion had quickly become a sudden and unstoppable slaughter.

The governor's wife stepped out on to the roof of the mansion, clutching the tiny bundle in her arms. Trying desperately not to look down, she scrambled up on to the crest of the roof, tears streaming down her cheeks as the baby began to wriggle.

How could they *do* this? *Why* did they do it? Why

not just loot the island and leave? *Morgan*, she thought. *It had to be Morgan's men.*

The governor's wife carefully negotiated the roof, raising up the baby on the chance she might slip. But she soon realized that falling from this great height would be a mercy. To her horror, she saw that two pirates were crawling over the roof towards her. She glanced down, then behind her and to either side; there was no possible chance of escape.

Jordel Swag had broken through the first wave of attackers, slashing at two of the men and narrowly avoiding a cutlass thrown by a third. Driving his own sword forward at a new attacker, he tripped and stumbled on the steps and was swiftly disarmed by a horrific-looking pirate with a gaping wound where his eye should have been. Seizing the opportunity, his crewmates swiftly snatched hold of the governor's arms and cast him down the remaining stairs. Jordel tumbled head over foot and collapsed at the bottom of the flight. There he lay in a dazed state, trying and failing to raise himself up again. Several of the pirates dived after the governor like birds swooping on downed prey, but before they could do any damage, a pistol shot rang out and they quickly retreated again, their eyes peeled for the source of the noise.

A shadow had fallen over the hall, cast by a figure so immense that it had blocked out the pale wash of moonlight that illuminated the wreckage of the great double doors. The pistol that had fired the shot was thrown aside.

Nobody moved.

The figure stepped forward, and was revealed as nothing less than a mountain of a man. His face, or what little of it there was to be seen under the matted black hair that surrounded it, was a picture of pure hatred. His tiny, pinprick eyes seemed to gleam red at the sight of so much bloody conflict, and a smile split his lips. His beard looked ragged and burnt, his skin blotched and patchy, as if in a sudden fit of rage he'd set alight to his own face just to see how the pain felt.

A few remaining islanders, mostly wounded or dying, trembled at the sight of the mountainous man . . . and all who looked upon him knew at once that this could only be the legendary Morgan himself, for death seemed to walk with him. What other pirate could command such an evil crew?

A thin and somewhat meek looking boy stepped out from behind the giant, while the vicious looking pirate with the savage gash on his face quickly retreated from the stairs to stand beside him.

The rest of the crew remained motionless, their cutlasses poised to sink into the throats of the remaining islanders.

'Do we kill 'em all, Cap'n?' snapped the fiend with the face wound, who was evidently the ship's first mate. 'Or shall we leave one alive to tell the tale?'

Henry Morgan's smile lengthened and he seemed to make an unseen gesture to the first mate, who quickly turned back to the assembled crew.

'Leave a couple,' he instructed. 'Ol' 'Enry is feeling merciful.'

The slaughter that followed was indescribable. Blades flashed and blood flowed. Men, women and children ran for their lives. Few were spared.

Amid the ensuing carnage, Morgan stepped forward and snatched up the semi-conscious form of Governor Swag, thrusting a sword into the poor man's shaking hands.

Then he drew his own blade.

'You'll kill me or die tryin',' he muttered. 'Now fight.'

Jordel found the new sword heavy in his hand. Still, the thought of his wife and child even now fleeing for their lives lit a fire within him. He feigned a greater exhaustion than he was feeling, then lunged at the great man with all the strength he could muster.

Morgan glanced the blow aside and slashed a wound in Jordel's neck, grinning as the governor staggered back in shock. A roar of laughter erupted from the audience.

'Again. Only this time, try ta 'it me.'

Jordel didn't waste a second. Before the pirates could applaud their captain again, he leaped forward and brought his sword up in a wild arc. This time, however, Morgan didn't simply block the attack: he swung his blade with breathtaking strength, blasting the sword from the governor's hand. Then he produced a second, smaller blade – seemingly from mid-air – and drove it straight into Jordel's stomach. The governor staggered, his face contorted with pain . . . but Morgan moved to catch him before he could fall.

Closing his giant hands around the poor man's neck, the dread pirate lifted Jordel Swag into the air. Jolted into shock, the governor kicked and struggled madly in a desperate attempt to escape the choke-hold, but Morgan's strength was insurmountable. To the few islanders fortunate enough to be spared that night, it seemed to take an eternity for the governor to die.

Eventually, though, Jordel's body fell limp and he was cast aside like a rag doll.

'Take the corpse an' hang it from the front windows,' Morgan boomed.

'D— do we leave the usual message, cap'n?' the first mate asked, as the body was dragged away behind him. 'Do we use Blackb—'

'Nah, tha' ol' legend ain't takin' the credit for this. Leave *my* name; 's the only one 'as counts.'

A round of applause broke out from the captivated pirates, but it soon died away when Morgan again raised his hand. A door at the top of the stairs had flown open and a fat pirate had staggered into view. He was carrying a screaming baby. A second, equally rotund, supported the unconscious body of a woman.

'Captain!' yelled the first. 'We got us a pretty, here . . . an' a baby 'n' all.'

'S' the governor's wife,' spat the wounded pirate. 'I seen 'er before . . . betting that's the governor's whelp, too. A son, so I've 'eard.'

Morgan's eyes gleamed again, and he motioned for the two captives to be brought down.

The first mate took the governor's wife from his colleague's stout arms and presented her to Morgan, as if he was holding up a prize turkey. There was a collective intake of breath.

Morgan stared at the lady for a time. Then, very gently, he lifted her lolling head and seemed to study her face more closely.

For a moment, even the dread pirate's own crew thought he might show the woman mercy; she was beautiful, after all, and Morgan was occasionally known to have a weakness for beauty. Therefore, it came as a surprise to the gathered pirates when he suddenly twisted his hands and broke her neck. One pirate, who'd been standing at the back of the hall, let out a gasp of shock ... which Morgan repaid by drawing a second pistol and shooting the man dead. A cheer exploded even before the unfortunate wretch hit the ground.

'Take this wench and hang 'er 'side 'er 'usband. Where's Mallory?'

The question drew a series of sneering, resentful looks from the pirate crew.

'MALLORY,' he said again. 'Where are you, ya li'l wretch?'

The boy at Morgan's side winced at the sound of his name. He looked as if he wanted the ground to swallow him up, but he knew better than to ignore the most sadistic pirate in the Caribbean.

'Y— yeah, Cap'n?' he managed.

'Take that whelp.'

Mallory's eyes widened. 'Th— the baby? What for? I . . . er . . . what . . . what would you like me to do with him, Cap'n?'

Morgan snatched hold of Mallory's ragged shirt and lifted the scrawny youth off his feet.

'You'll take him to the ship,' he growled.

'Is . . . is he to be part of the crew, Cap'n?' Mallory asked, some of his trademark twitches kicking in at a frantic pace.

Morgan's grin displayed a mouthful of rotting yellow teeth.

'No . . . he's gonna be fired outta the cannon . . . and iffen you ask another riddle of me, 'e'll 'ave some company.'

Mallory was forcefully thrown back. He flew into the base of the staircase, breaking several banisters on the way.

The fat pirate carrying the baby turned and tossed him at Mallory, who hurried to catch the cloth bundle before it hit the floor.

'Do as you're told, boy,' he advised, with a nasty smirk. 'You'll live longer.'

Mallory struggled to his feet and, with a pained expression on his face, staggered past the assembled pirates and out into the night.

'Why does the cap'n put up with tha' idiot?' one of the crew whispered to another. 'Everyone knows he ain't right in the 'ead.'

'Aye,' said a stern voice, and the small group turned as Morgan's disfigured first mate stepped between them. 'And he's a snitch at that. The cap'n'll kill 'im eventually; he kills 'em *all* eventually.'

It had to be said that Mallory's presence aboard the ship was a severe annoyance to the rest of the crew. Ever since that awful night at the Curvale Island Inn when Morgan had woken to discover the boy stealing his purse, their lives had been hell. Some thought the dread pirate tolerated the lad because he was the first person ever to try to thieve off him, or because he knew the whereabouts of some long-forgotten treasure hoard. Some thought it was because the monster had taken pity on him. They were all wrong. Morgan kept Mallory on board for other reasons.

Firstly, the boy was entertaining, suffered terrible cabin-fever and was prone to bouts of absolute madness at times. Most of all, however, he was a rat who had regularly and shamelessly betrayed *everyone* on board at one point or another. Whether it was a crew-hand palming some silver or the first mate tearing a strip of meat from the captain's table, Mallory brought every little indiscretion out into the open . . . and he was thoroughly hated for it. One day, of course, Morgan *would* tire of the boy . . . and kill him, but Mallory had consistently managed to delay that day by doing endless menial chores for the captain: cleaning his cabin, washing his clothes and even polishing the pirate's most treasured possessions. All this made him far too convenient to be given the damn-good hiding the crew thought he so thoroughly deserved.

Mallory ran, muttering an old sailing rhyme under his breath so that he could focus on that rather than the screaming bundle in his arms; it wasn't working. Dark and terrible visions kept popping into his mind, and they wouldn't pop out again.

Kill the baby. They were going to kill the baby. Would they really do that? Mallory checked himself for even wondering – of course they would, they were pirates. They'd fire the poor little thing out of the cannon.

He'd seen them dispatch many men and even a few women . . . but a baby? How could even the most evil pirates in the world *consider* doing something like that? Moreover . . . how could he stand by and watch? Wouldn't that make him as evil as them?

Yes, but if he ran, he'd have to keep on running . . . and if Morgan ever found him, he'd be executed for sure, possibly run through with a sword, or strangled; perhaps that witch-doctor Morgan traded with would take out his teeth or put a hex on him . . .

Mallory stopped dead, his eyes darting from the ship to the mansion and back again. He could feel a new fear creeping over him, and he quickly shook his head to try to dislodge it. He looked down at the baby. If terror got a hold on him now, only the gods of the sea knew where *either of them* would end up. He had to focus his mind on the problem . . . and the problem was that he absolutely could not let this child be slaughtered. He *had* seen Morgan murder defenceless people for years, but he'd never been in a position to do anything to help *them*. This was different; all he had to do was run in another direction. He'd never disobeyed the captain before, so Morgan really had no reason to doubt him. By the time the crew realized he'd run, he could be . . .

. . . Where? Where could he be? He was on an island, and one far too small to hide on for long. He couldn't run to the town, because the pirates would be raiding the houses. He *had* to find a boat . . . and fast.

Mallory turned on his heels and ran towards a rough patch of woodland, determined to keep the fear out of his mind and the baby out of the cannon. Once he was off the island, he could start thinking about the little one and where he could leave him in the black heart of the Caribbean . . .

Morgan would be angry for a time, but he would forget this night. After all, what was one child in a lifetime of murderous activity? Nothing more than a trinket, he supposed.

He was wrong.

Davey Swag, only son of Governor Jordel Swag, became the first individual ever to escape Henry Morgan. In years to come, his name would form a focus for all the dread pirate's hatred and malice.

The cabin-boy, Mallory, wasn't so lucky.

# Personal diary of
# Davey Swag, aged 16¼

I've been on Cocos for just three days ... and already I'm
beginning to regret my decision to come here. I had only put
three steps on the beach before I was swamped by a group
of dodgy-looking merchant traders. Upon learning my desire to
become a pirate, one of the men offered to sell me a parrot
as 'a quiet companion'. The bird in question was twice the size
of a normal parrot and looked magnificent; it nuzzled up to me
with warm affection when I put it on my shoulder. He wanted
ten for it; I paid five.

The bird didn't say anything until lunchtime, when it suddenly and
inexplicably announced that it had never belonged to the man who
sold it and proceeded to insult my coat. For a moment, I thought
the voice might be a result of my imagination, so I called the
creature into question. Now it will NOT shut up and has talked
more or less constantly for the last few hours.

Apparently, its name is McGuffin and it belonged to a pirate called Short Jack Plat'num. Jack, it claims, was the greatest man ever to hold a cutlass, but for reasons the parrot will not go into, recently decided to hang himself from a tree. I'm pretty sure I know why ... the bird has only been with me for a short time and I'm already looking up at the beams with longing. Not only was the 'quiet' description a lie, the bird isn't much of a companion, either. In fact, it seems to spend half of each day flying off and doing its own thing ... Some pet!

# The First Day

In a small and pokey guest room above the Die Quickly Inn on Cocos Island, sixteen-year-old Davey Swag stood before a full-length mirror and examined himself critically.

Everything appeared to be in order. The black coiffure curled attractively over his forehead, whilst the remainder of his hair had been pulled into a tight ponytail and secured with a length of twine. Admittedly the moustache lacked definition, but this, he felt, would improve with time; most boys Davey's age didn't have a moustache at all.

They did tend to have parents, though. Davey's mother and father had died when he was a baby, murdered by dread pirate Henry Morgan and his filthy henchmen. His own escape from the slaughter, aged just ten weeks, was still a mystery, but he'd arrived safe and sound on the doorstep of Uncle Jake's Home For

Pirate Orphans, a tiny scroll explaining his identity. One day, when the time was right, Davey determined to even the score and kill Henry Morgan. Uncle Jake had taught him all about the business of revenge . . . and patience was the key, especially since Morgan seemed to be as dangerous a threat these days as ever he had been; remarkable for a man who *had* to be well into his seventies.

The first thing about becoming a pirate, Uncle Jake had told him, was to look like one. If all else failed then at least play the part like a true professional. The attitude would develop with experience.

Davey allowed his eyes to wander across the various items of clothing that lay strewn across the bed. He spent a few moments roaming through his head, mentally ticking off the items of pirate clobber Uncle Jake had mentioned.

First requirement: a headband. Jake had said something about keeping feathers in it and, as Davey had no feathers that he knew of, he decided to steer away from that one. Next up was a loose cotton shirt; yes, he had one of those and the baggy trousers to match. Hmm . . . a wooden leg: not yet thank goodness, maybe later. The same went for number four: an eye-patch. A leather belt with a brass buckle had been provided, courtesy of Uncle Jake. Glass eye and hook both occupied the same category – unnecessary at this early stage. Nose-rings were out, but he did possess a rather smart silver earring that he diligently fastened to his left lobe. It was a clip-on, of course, but Jake confided that *he* had worn a clip-on for years and none of his crewmates ever noticed. Spyglass: check. Neckerchief: check. Cutlass: check.

Davey grimaced; he needed a better weapon before he could begin to apply for work . . . and applying for work was a necessity when you came from Uncle Jake's. Jake Raskin was a gentle man with an incredible capacity for kindness and a love of children. Having none of his own, he'd started an orphanage to give hope and care to the Caribbean's lost and abandoned youngsters. He nurtured, taught and provided for every child left on his doorstep, and only asked for one thing in return: upon leaving the school, a pirate had to send back two gold pieces from every raid, ship-take, treasure haul or island attack he became involved in, for the rest of that pirate's natural life. Davey supposed it was fair, and evidently so did the others; Jake lived in a house that looked as if it was *built* out of gold. This was quite remarkable considering that the only real obligation was a pirate's word, and in the Caribbean a pirate's word, generally speaking, stood for nothing; most would betray their own grandmothers for a bottle of the dark spirit.

As Davey laughed at the thought, his newly acquired parrot flew through the open window and landed on the bedpost, dropping a scroll on to the mattress.

'What's that?' Davey asked, reaching for it.

'Document of ownership: you have to keep it with you at all times. Well, until I'm sold on, that is.'

'Oh, right.'

The bird, which called itself McGuffin, eyed him cautiously. 'Aren't you going to read it?'

'No.' Davey tucked the parchment inside his coat and winced as he felt it slip through a ripped pocket and into the lining.

'You going out dressed like that, are you?' McGuffin prompted.

'I am.'

'Your funeral.'


The layout of Cocos Island was curious to say the least. A thick wood covered three quarters of the surface area and important locations, it seemed, were positioned haphazardly in order to make trips between them as difficult as possible. The docks and town were to the south with the only reputable hotel in the far north-west. A path amusingly known as the Shortwalk garlanded Cocos in a perfect circle, but since all the pony-trekking businesses had folded along with the island's government, people preferred to stay where they docked. The Die Quickly Inn served this demand by commanding a position not twenty paces from the quayside. It was the oldest establishment on the island apart from the infamous Foolstop Hotel.

The Foolstop (named not out of choice but simply because mud sticks) had the dubious honour of being the least visited resort in the Caribbean. It boasted only six paying guests a year, and two of those were employed by the owner.

This lack of custom could perhaps have been due to its position on the furthest corner of the island from the town, but a more likely reason was the hotel's appearance: the Foolstop stood alone atop a sharp rocky outcrop and tended to put visitors in mind of an overweight man balancing on a three-legged stool. Consequently, even though the building had stood for a hundred years, guests were inclined to walk in the middle of their rooms and no more than two people ever sat at the bar. These minor quarrels aside, the rooms were pleasant enough and every summer the hotel enjoyed three days of piping hot water.

Pirates, on the other hand, usually headed straight for the Die Quickly Inn.

Currently, the Quickly had only one guest, Davey Swag. Unfortunately, Davey had recently acquired a guest of his own, one that didn't seem to know when it wasn't wanted.

McGuffin landed on his shoulder, causing Davey to slip slightly on the cobbles.

'Off to town, are you?' said the bird, its claws pricking his flesh. 'Better kit yourself up, boy. Only, I can't see you taking to the waves with this load of old shonk you've collected . . .'

Davey glared straight ahead.

'Why don't you just FLY AWAY!' he growled.

'Oh, I can't do that; a parrot is for life, not just for Christmas.'

'Is that what you told Short Jack Platinum? You know, just before he hung himself?'

'Ha! Very funny. Did I ever mention that I know a great song about a pirate who wore clip-on earrings? It's a bit *loud* to sing in the street, but I could give you a quick rendition . . .'

'Er . . . no, no you're all right. Just don't keep pestering me, that's all.'

The town was relatively quiet as Davey made his way along its twisted streets. He passed a cheese shop on his right, smiled nervously at a pair of eyes just visible above the counter, and headed across the street to Samuel Cutter's Supplies. Fortunately, McGuffin seemed more interested in the prospect of cheese, so alighted on the shop window as Davey strode for the building opposite.

A little brass bell tinkled as he pushed open the door, announcing his arrival. Then a curtain moved aside at the back of the shop and Samuel Cutter lurched into view, supported by a gnarled crutch that looked more like a weapon than a walking aid.

'Good evening, Mr Cutter,' said Davey, smiling.

'What of it?' the old man snapped, eyeing his customer suspiciously. 'Haven't seen you around here before. You're *young*.'

Davey swallowed – the shopkeeper was pointing at him as if he'd wet himself.

'Yes sir, I am,' he said.

Cutter seemed to calm down at this.

'You shouldn't be out by yourself, lad. Lot of evil walkin' the streets, these days.'

'I'm trying to get into pirating!' Davey proclaimed with pride.

'Ha! Then more fool you.'

The boy looked deflated. This wasn't exactly the reaction he'd been hoping for.

'Ah, well. What will you be wanting then, Mr Pirate Wannabe?'

'Arms, sir. That is, a good weapon for a buccaneer. I've already got a cutlass.'

Cutter leaned heavily on the counter, stroking his beard with vigour. Finally, after what seemed like an eternity (but was in fact just a few seconds) he spoke: 'Go over to that cupboard by the door and bring me the brown case inside.'

Davey did as instructed and Cutter flipped the lid. Inside lay a little shard of heaven.

'This here's a flintlock pistol; it's not quite as grand as its pappy, the musket, but just as lethal. It fires one shot at a time, and takes about a minute to reload. It's yours for twenty pieces.'

'I'll take it!' Davey announced, unable to conceal his excitement any longer.

A stern expression seized the old man's features and he removed the pistol carefully from its case.

'OK, boy . . . but listen up and watch very closely.'

Davey attempted to look as mature as his heartbeat would allow.

'To use this,' Cutter continued, 'you must first uncork the powder flask in there, then pour some powder into the barrel and stuff it down with this ramrod. After that, you drop in one of these little lead balls and ram it into place. Then you lift the flash-pan cover and pour some powder into the flash-pan. That done, you replace the flash-pan cover and pull back the cock. Then you take aim, and fire. I've already loaded this one for you, at no extra charge. You got all that? Now, you take that there pistol . . . and I've a free gift for ya.'

However, rather than approaching the special weapons box or the sword display, Cutter staggered over to a small curtain beside the counter . . . and pulled on a thick cord.

'Avast! I give you . . . the Caribbean's first – and only – fully functioning hat-cage!'

The curtain was drawn back to reveal something that Davey knew instinctively was nothing short of a mangled monstrosity. His face fell.

'What's that look for?' Cutter snapped. 'It's one of a kind! There are harnesses to fix it to your neck and shoulders so you don't even *feel* the weight on your head!'

'I . . .' Davey couldn't think of anything to say. 'It's, er . . . it's very nice . . . but I'm afraid I don't have a bird.'

'No?' Cutter hazarded. 'I thought I saw a parrot on your shoulder, out in the street before you came in?'

Davey froze. 'You mean McGuffin?' he muttered. 'Oh, no, he belongs to a friend. Besides, I think it's a bit cruel to keep a bird in a cage, especially if the cage is attached to your head.'

Cutter's tiny eyes twinkled. 'Oh well,' he said, crossing over to the counter and muttering something offensive under his breath. 'You know where I am if you change yer mind. Now, let's see if we can find yer any other good freebies . . .'

Davey sauntered through the streets of Cocos, the pistol case nestling snugly under his left arm. For his twenty pieces of eight, he'd managed to purchase one flintlock pistol that he hadn't the slightest clue how to operate, one complimentary glass eye inscribed with the name and address of the store (a curious item extended to all customers of Samuel Cutter), and a medium-size boarding axe which the old man had thrown in at the last minute, either out of compassion or cunning (he wasn't sure which).

'Cor blimey – look at you!' said McGuffin, as he landed on the boy's shoulder once again. 'Anyone'd think you were half a pirate.'

'Thanks. At least I'm starting to feel like one. Where did *you* go?'

'I was on the swinging sign over the cheese shop. I got talking to two other parrots. We were swapping stories about the heroic adventures of our latest masters. Fortunately you came out of the shop before it was my turn . . .'

Davey's return to the Quickly was everything he could have hoped for. All heads turned as he entered the bar, fully armed, and picked his way through the crowd. Reaching the stairs without incident, he glanced briefly behind him, then marched purposefully up the stairs and along the corridor that led to his temporary accommodation. Even a few of the serious pirates had ceased quaffing long enough to pay him some attention. *Look the part*, Uncle Jake's words boomed in his ears. *That's as much as any ship's captain can ask of an apprentice.*

Unfortunately for Davey, he hadn't quite reached his door when McGuffin cried out, 'He's not a patch on my old master, but I'm making do. You know how it is;

needs must when the black wind blows you beak over feathers . . .'

There was an explosive roar of laughter from the floor below, and Davey slammed the door behind him.

# Signing Up

Davey waited until early the next morning to visit his prospective employers, partly because he wanted to be fresh and alert, but mostly because McGuffin had been hanging around all night and he definitely didn't want the parrot on his shoulder while he was trying to get a job.

At first, the pickings on Cocos were slim: plenty of ships and no vacancies, or plenty of vacancies on the sorts of ships any decent pirate would do well to avoid. Then, crucially, he overheard some useful gossip.

The crew of the *Rogue Herring* were recruiting for a voyage: famous ship, legendary crew, golden opportunity.

Davey arrived at the harbour within seconds of hearing the news. Some of the regular crew were already busy loading supplies on board and singing notorious dirges at one another. A small boat had been provided to take any would-be applicants out to the ship for an interview.

Davey eagerly clambered aboard and tried to hide his excitement beneath a nonchalant expression, something that became increasingly difficult as the little boat was rowed closer to the grand galleon that occupied most of the distant horizon.

Eventually, the boat drew near to the *Herring* and its occupants all hurried up a rickety rope ladder to scramble aboard.

The recruiting officer was a burly rogue with a black moustache, dressed in full clobber and wearing several golden rings through each ear. His name, it transpired, was Gullin.

Davey stood before him and coughed politely when a few minutes had passed in silence.

'Yeah?' barked the pirate, spitting over his shoulder before he looked up at Davey's chin. Apparently, eye contact was something you had to earn.

'I'd like to become a pirate,' Davey managed, meekly.

'You and everyone else. Gangrene?'

Davey waited a few seconds. 'I'm sorry?'

The officer rolled his eyes.

'Have you ever had gangrene, boy? You know, rotting of the flesh?'

'No!'

'What 'bout malaria?'

Davey shook his head.

'Yellow fever? Typhus?'

'No, I've never had anything like that. I had a swollen foot last summer . . .'

Gullin eyed him suspiciously. 'What happened?'

Davey shrugged. 'It got better. Uncle J— er . . . I put some ointment on it and it just sort of . . . healed up.'

The pirate glared at him. 'Armed?'

'Yes, sir! I've got a cutlass, a boarding axe and this pistol.'

He produced the flintlock and handed it to Gullin who, to his surprise, looked genuinely impressed.

'Nice pistol,' he said, nodding approvingly before handing the weapon back. 'Right, let's get down to the brass. What's your name?'

'Davey.'

'Right you are. Surname?'

'Swag.'

He sat back and stared Davey directly in the eyes. 'And why in the name of Blackbeard should we have you aboard? What special qualifications have you got that'd help the ship in times of trouble?'

Davey thought long and hard.

'I'm quite tall,' he said, after a time. 'And I can swim a bit . . . er . . . and I don't mind hard work.'

The pirate didn't look too convinced. 'Anything else?'

The answer jumped into Davey's head, and he was unable to stop himself blurting it out.

'Well, I *am* actually Calico Jack's . . . er . . . fourth cousin, twice removed,' he admitted, 'and my father was none other than Governor Jordel Swag, formerly of Jade Island.'

'Hmm . . . I haven't seen Calico Jack in many moons, and I've never even *heard* of your old man.'

Davey looked down at his feet. 'Yes, well, he died a long time ago.'

There was a brief pause as Gullin turned over a new scroll.

'Well, I can't promise you anythin', Swag,' he muttered. 'We set sail tomorrow, if the cap'n thinks we're ready. He doesn't usually take raw recruits with no experience, but I reckon he'll make an exception if I put in a good word; we haven't had that many applicants for *this* trip.'

'Thanks!' said Davey. 'That's fantastic! I'm staying at the Die Quickly Inn, if you need me before tomorrow!'

The pirate nodded. 'Don't count your chickens yet, but I'll certainly see what I can do for you,' he said.

Davey turned, sporting a gormless grin, climbed back down the rope ladder and dropped happily into the little rowing boat.

It was turning into a beautiful morning: the sun was bright, he had a potential new job and McGuffin was absolutely nowhere to be seen.

As he wandered away from the quayside, Davey bumped into a weathered-looking, one-eyed pirate who was loitering lazily along the path outside the Quickly nursing a bottle of Kill Devil. The man burped apologetically and offered Davey a swig.

'Er . . . no thanks, I don't drink.'

'Ah, just joined up, 'ave ya?'

'That's right,' Davey said, turning back to examine the ship from a distance. It was an inspiring sight and seemed well suited to the soft waters of the Caribbean. Davey noted that the ship had a bronze ram at one end, used for battering enemy vessels before boarding them.

'I think I've got a pretty good chance of getting taken on,' he said, optimistically.

The drunkard nodded an acknowledgment at a

passer-by and then pointed over Davey's shoulder at the *Herring*. 'It carries the second biggest cannon on the seas,' he observed.

Davey shook his head in amazement.

'It can reach twelve knots at full speed and it's more 'an forty yards long.'

'Gosh,' said Davey. 'I bet that's . . .' He trailed off, then straightened up and frowned. 'Wait a minute, how do you know all this?'

The drunkard shrugged. 'I used to be a crewman; didn't last long at the job, though. Frank Corsham's the name.'

Davey's eyes widened like a couple of cannon-balls.

'A crewman? You? On there? Really!'

'Yep.'

'Well I never! When did you leave?'

The drunkard studied the freckles on his left arm.

'Um . . . tomorrow morning; early, I reckon.'

'Oh! I— I'm sorry to hear that.' Davey tried to fake a solemn nod, but he couldn't keep a lid on his own curiosity. 'Will they throw you overboard?' he asked, maintaining a serious expression.

'What? Hah! No, no, no.' The drunkard shook his head. 'They . . . er . . . my leaving will probably come as a surprise to 'em.'

'Oh, I see.' Davey nodded. 'Didn't you like it on there?'

'Me? I loved it. I was first mate on the *Herring* for nearly three years. Then a new captain arrived, murdered the old one and basically took over the ship. He's been a nightmare to work with for most o' the lads, as we're all terrified of 'im, but ... er ... fortunately, he likes me.'

'So why are you leaving, then?'

'Hmm ... good question. Why am I leaving ... are you kidding me? Don't tell me you don't know where they're headed?'

Davey's face dropped like an anchor.

'Where?' he asked, nervously.

'The Triangle of Death, the old headquarter islands of The Perilous Three.'

Sudden realization dawned in Davey's eyes.

'I s— see,' he stammered, clambering slowly to his feet. He began to back away, never once taking his eyes off the ship. 'D— don't think I'll be j— joining up then.'

A million thoughts collided in his head. He certainly needed no explanation when it came to The Perilous Three. Blackbeard, Henry Morgan and Bartholomew Roberts were by far the most feared names haunting the waters of the Spanish Main. While Morgan would eventually pay for the slaughter he'd handed out on Jade Island the night he'd robbed him of his parents, Davey knew enough about Henry Morgan to know that he wasn't *anywhere near* good enough to meet him in combat. Still, although Morgan was a key member of The Perilous Three, his equally despicable contemporaries were fast becoming dark legends.

Blackbeard hadn't been sighted for a good few years and was presumed dead, which was just as well. A giant of a man with arms that reached down past his knees and filthy waist-length hair curled into rat's tails, he was no better than the monster responsible for the death of Davey's parents; he'd learned quite a bit about the man at school. It was said that, during a battle, Blackbeard always wore burning fuses in his hair to make himself look like the devil. One infamous story told of the man extinguishing all the candles during supper and shooting pistols under the table at his unfortunate crewmen. In his day, Blackbeard was thought to be impossible to kill, having famously died several times in different parts of the Caribbean, only to spring up again elsewhere.

'Black' Bartholomew Roberts was an unholy terror upon the seas. Davey had heard it said that Black Bart had destroyed over four hundred ships since starting out. Apparently, he drank tea instead of alcohol and captained *Royal Fortune*, the most impressive vessel ever built.

Davey sucked in some air. The Perilous Three, eh? Well, that was one trip he could certainly do without. He'd just have to get a place on board another, less dangerous ship, if he could find one.

Just when he felt that nothing could depress him further, he noticed the familiar shape of McGuffin hopping along the path towards him.

Davey was a slightly different shade when he returned to the inn later that morning. His excitement at being hired by a *real* pirate crew had been dampened (to put it mildly) by the horrible news that the *Rogue Herring*'s ex-crewman had dropped on him like a ten-ton anchor.

It was at this juncture in the day that Davey decided he might accept some of the Quickly's sample rum, although the liquid was tinted blue and actually smelled more like rotten bilge water. Still, it was free and Davey wasn't too proud to accept charity (although he drew the line at the rat sorbet that was offered up afterwards). However, McGuffin had temporarily abandoned him yet again, so he accepted one last thimbleful of the sticky liquid before bidding the barman farewell.

Tired and miserable, he resigned himself to spending a last peaceful night alone in his room, before Uncle Jake's money ran out. He was just preparing to struggle up the inn's rickety staircase, when fate extended a hand towards him.

Davey stared down at the grimy palm, and traced it along a freckly arm to its owner.

'You!' he gasped.

A considerably more sober Frank Corsham grinned at him.

'I have some advice for you, young'un,' he began, grabbing Davey by the arm and leading him over to a small table in the smoky depths of the Quickly. 'I don't reckon you should go aboard the *Herring*.'

'Ha! Don't worry. I don't intend to! I might be young and a bit naïve, but I'm not suicidal.'

Corsham nodded as the innkeeper brought him an ale, and returned his attention to the young pirate. 'Good to hear it, lad, good to hear it. Now, of course, if you was smart you'd set up on your own . . .'

There was a moment of silence in which Davey tried to work out the meaning of this suggestion.

'On my own? Doing what, exactly?'

'Piracy.'

'What, you mean freelance?'

Corsham nodded.

'Lot of money in it nowadays. I'm thinking of starting up, myself.'

The saloon door of the Quickly swung open and, for a second, Davey gazed out at the azure waters of the Spanish Main and felt the cool wind on his face. *Davey Swag*, he thought to himself, *freelance pirate*. He had to admit that the title had a certain ring to it.

'You'd need a boat, mind,' Corsham went on.

'Oh yeah,' Davey said dismally, leaning back on his elbows. 'That's *that* then. I can't even afford an oar.'

'Shame,' the pirate admitted. 'Unless . . .'

Davey sat up again, quickly.

'Unless what? You know where I can get a boat?'

'Maybe . . .'

'What, for nothing?'

'Aye.' Corsham had a smile like a demonically possessed jackal. 'Matter of fact, I've got one you could use,' he muttered. 'It's moored up at Paragon Peninsula, northernmost point of this very island.'

'And you'd lend it to me? For free?'

Corsham nodded. 'I suppose so, if you'd be kind enough to do an old man the smallest of favours . . .'

'Anything,' Davey replied smartly, eager to learn the price of his new venture.

Corsham nodded, and took a swig of ale from a tankard that had been left on the table.

'You know the Foolstop Hotel?' he asked.

'Yes!'

'Well, I've got a small package up there; it's being guarded by my bloodhound, Lucifer.'

'Great! I like dogs.'

'Good. So, anyway, if you can collect the package for me and take it to a friend o' mine, I'll tell you where you can find your new boat.'

'You'd do that for me?'

'Aye. After all, a favour deserves a favour.'

Davey smiled. That was it? Just walk from one corner of Cocos Island to the other, for a life on the ocean wave and a chance to become his own master?

'Consider it done,' he said.

Corsham extended a hand and the two friends shook on the deal.

However, as Davey left the bar and headed to his room, McGuffin flew down from the inn's shadowy rafters and dug his claws deep into Davey's shoulder.

'Ow!'

'Serves you right, idiot! My entire life, I never saw a

more dodgy-looking pirate than *that.*'

'You think?' Davey glanced back at Corsham as he climbed the stairs. 'He seemed all right to me.'

'Yeah, but you're thicker than a hangman's noose. I mean, the bloke's obviously on the sly. I tell you, if a pirate like that had come up to Short Jack Plat'num and asked him— Arghhhh!'

Davey swiped the parrot off his shoulder, marched into his room and slammed the door behind him.

'Don't trust him!' echoed the squeaky voice. 'He'll get you into all sorts, that one!'

# An Unfortunate Coincidence

Davey awoke the next morning with a splitting headache. Either the Quickly's free rum hadn't agreed with him or else McGuffin had returned and attacked him in the night. It was probably a mixture of both.

He tried to swallow, but his mouth was as dry as a pirate's flannel. Looking around, he found that his vision was blurry. The dingy little room that passed for his accommodation took a long time to swim into focus.

In the distance, a bird twittered annoyingly, but at least it wasn't McGuffin.

Davey sat up like an old man trying to surprise a relative who'd just declared him dead. The bed was soaked with sweat, and there was a nasty smell lingering in the room. Davey checked his armpits in order to make sure it wasn't him. It was.

Aiming for the door, he struggled to his feet and

lurched forward, zombie-like, until he found a wall to lean against.

'Morning,' said a voice.

Davey looked up. At first he thought the room was empty but, then, looking closer, he saw a dark shadow in the corner furthest from the window . . . and nearly jumped out of his skin when it detached itself from the wall and winked at him.

'Mister Corsham!'

'The same.'

Davey quickly relaxed and slumped back down on to his mattress with an exasperated sigh of relief.

'Why are you wearing a fake beard?' he enquired.

Corsham looked both ways before answering, which was pretty peculiar behaviour in a small room with only one window. 'I'm trying not to attract any unnecessary attention,' he said.

'By wearing a big ginger beard?'

'Yes, well . . . it might look ridiculous, but it was all the costume shop had left.'

'Right. Er . . . I see. Who exactly are you hiding from?'

Corsham suddenly became all hunched up and for a moment Davey thought he might make a move to leap for the window. Eventually, breathing in long, slow breaths, he prepared himself to speak:

'It's the new captain of the *Rogue Herring*,' he managed. 'He's trying to find me, and if he *does* I'm a dead man.'

'What? I thought you said he liked you!'

'Shhh! Keep your voice down!'

Davey frowned, his eyebrows colliding like a couple of tiny thunderheads. 'But I don't understand; why would the new captain be trying to kill you now, suddenly, when you said he liked you before!'

Corsham sighed.

'To tell you the truth,' he whispered, 'there was a bit of trouble on the last trip and the new captain blamed me for it. I didn't exactly leave on the best of terms, this morning . . .'

'So the new captain wants you dead because he *thinks* you're to blame for some trouble?'

A nod.

'But what about yesterday? You were talking to me as plain as day! Everyone saw you! Why didn't he try to kill you then?'

Corsham looked suddenly nervous, even more so than he had done before.

'It's complicated,' he muttered. 'But I can tell you this. For the last few weeks, the crew of the *Rogue*

*Herring* haven't been all that bothered about me, and I've been secretly planning to quit the ship. Then, early this morning when I left, something happened on board and now they want me dead. I'll say no more.'

Davey took a moment to consider this.

'Something happened on board the ship,' he said, eyeing the pirate carefully. 'And at first they didn't pay you much attention, but now they're after you. Hmm . . . that doesn't really make any sense, unless . . . did you steal something?'

'WHAT?' Corsham looked as if he'd just seen a ghost. 'What on earth makes you say that?'

'Well, if the captain of the *Rogue Herring* wasn't after you yesterday and he *is* today, then it could be because you took something from the ship and they've only just noticed it's missing.'

'I thought you were an idiot . . .' Corsham muttered.

'What was that?'

'Oh . . . nothing. I was just mumbling to myself.'

The expression on Corsham's face put Davey in mind of a cat licking mustard off a nettle.

'Who did you say you were again?' the pirate managed.

Davey shrugged.

'I'm Davey Swag, son of the thirty-first governor of Jade Island. Calico Jack's one of my cousins.'

'I'll remember you for a long time, lad,' Corsham admitted.

'Thank you, sir. I'll be sure to remember you, too. After all, it will be thanks to you that I have a bo—'

'Don't worry about that, lad, just make sure you collect my parcel for me.'

'No problem!' Davey said, getting to his feet and drawing himself up to his full height. 'I'm aiming to go the day after tomorrow. Then you can tell me where the boat's moored. Ha! I'll be a freelance pirate yet!'

Corsham nodded.

'I reckon you will,' he said.

Davey gave the *Herring*'s former first mate a thoughtful look.

'When I have the parcel, should I still take it to your friend? Where will he be, exactly?'

'Mister Gra—' Corsham almost bit through his own tongue. 'No, no. Actually there's been a change of plan,' he said quickly. 'I need you to take the parcel to . . . er . . . the end of Paragon Peninsula, just past Glad's Wood and the Beached Whale. I'll get my . . . er . . . *friend* to collect it from you there.'

'Great. Great! Will he tell me where the boat is moored at the same time?'

There was a slight pause.

'Yes,' said the pirate, carefully. 'Yes, he will.'

Davey stepped forward and grasped Corsham's hand, shaking it so hard that the pirate could feel his bones rattling.

'Nice doing business with you, sir!' he finished.

'And you, lad . . . and you.'

Corsham bid Davey goodbye, then made his way to a dank and largely abandoned corner of the inn's basement, where he packed his belongings, donned a new disguise and very quietly left the building.

Back in the room, Davey was explaining his exciting news to McGuffin, who had flapped in with little explanation for his absence and was now staring balefully at his new master.

'It still sounds like a load of trouble to me,' he squawked, when the young pirate had finished updating him on the deal. 'And if this bloke's running around dressed in five different disguises, you really have to ask yourself *why*.'

'We've been through all that! Besides, I don't *care* about his reasons . . . I just care about getting a boat!'

'Then more fool you. I tell you, one wrong move on an island like this and they'll be fishing you out of the sea with a pike . . .'

'Yeah, yeah . . .'

'Don't listen to me, then,' the parrot snapped. 'It's your look-out, boy. I just need a shoulder to sit on, and I'm not too fussy whether there's a head attached to it.'

Davey had to plan his trip to the Foolstop Hotel very carefully. After spending most of the day asking around, he'd discovered that the journey was likely to take him about three days on foot.

Worse still, Davey had nothing to eat and absolutely no money. In fact, he quickly realized that he had little alternative but to sell something. The question was *what*? He had no jewellery, no clothes worth buying and he couldn't bring himself to part with either of his weapons.

Davey sighed, and mooched over to the window to peer down at the beach below. It was a particularly busy evening in Cocos Harbour. Davey let his gaze wander until it fixed on the shoulders of a lone sword-fighter. The man was obviously a professional; he was performing before a large audience comprising pirates and a few islanders. Davey noticed, with envy, that he handled his sword as if it were a feather, swishing it through the air in a series of perfect arcs and bringing it to bear on the shoulders of a trembling cabin-boy, who erupted in fits of laughter when he realized that his head was still secure.

Davey turned away from the window with a disgruntled frown. If only he had a skill like that, he could earn an absolute fortune from it! He shook his head and tried to think of the few skills he did possess: he couldn't sing, couldn't dance, couldn't even stand on his head. He *could* play the piano (as long as people liked to hear 'Jolly Jack Tar' forty-seven times a night – it was the only song Uncle Jake had ever taught him) and he *was* a whiz at telling stories, but— Hey, that was it! He could tell stories! The Beachers – a group of particularly lazy pirates – loved to hear stories and, even if they didn't pay him, they might have some food to trade for a good yarn.

'Ha, ha! I can tell stories! Hell, I can *sell* stories.'

'You?' McGuffin flapped up on to his shoulder. 'What stories can *you* possibly have? You don't even have any face fur, yet!'

'Not this time, bird. I've *always* been able to tell stories. Me – I'm a naturally gifted spinner of yarns.'

Davey smiled to himself. Then he made a quick

search of the room, located his pistol and cutlass and marched through the Quickly en route to the streets of Cocos. Now, at least, he had a plan. First he would find a really good map of the island and then he'd make for the beach to try to glean some reward from the most tale-hungry group of pirates ever to shiver a timber: the 'Beachers'.

It was approaching midnight.

As he made his way on to the sands, Davey could already make out a number of small cooking fires on the beach. Some pirates sat alone but most huddled together in groups of four or five. Davey headed for the smallest of these, a trio of friendly-looking buccaneers toasting chicken on a hand-made spit. To his horror, McGuffin seemed intent on sticking around for the entertainment. It was time to make a sale . . .

The early signs were not all that encouraging; the Beachers abruptly stopped their conversation as Davey approached. Two of the pirates, the two perched on either end of the log, were behemoths. One was dark with a beard like a rhododendron bush and the other was just as dark but merely stubbly. The pirate in the middle was balding and considerably smaller than his

companions, but something about the glint in his eye
made him out to be the shark of the group.

Davey shuffled to a stop on the far side of the fire
and gave the men a pathetic wave.

'Ahoy there,' he said, in his friendliest voice. 'My
name is Davey Swag, and I'm a freelance pirate. Any
chance I could join your group?'

The pirates exchanged glances and, at length, the
shark gave a shrug.

'It's a free island, young'un,' he said. His voice
reminded Davey of someone attempting to saw
through a tin can.

'You'll have to sit on the sand, though,' added the
stubbly pirate. 'This log's full.'

'No problem,' said Davey, lowering himself on to the
sand and crossing his legs. 'This is my parrot, by the
way. He's called—'

'Hungry.'

Davey glared at the bird. 'It's McGuffin, actually.
Please try to ignore him – it's difficult, I know.' He
made a threatening face at the bird before turning back
to the group and smiling wanly. 'So, fellow swashers,
how's the pirating game this week?'

The shark-like man grinned.

'You tell us,' he said. 'You're the freelance pirate.

Krilly, Le Croix and myself – we're just your normal, everyday sea-dogs on shore leave.'

'Ah, well, I'm not actually what you would call a pirate, *yet*,' Davey admitted. 'I'm more a sort of pirate wannabe, but I'm hoping to change all that over the next few days.'

'You've signed up for a ship, then?' said Krilly, the pirate with the rhododendron beard.

Davey took a moment to think about this.

'Yes and no,' he said eventually. 'That is, I signed up for the *Rogue Herring*, but I'm not actually going to join the crew.'

'Well, bless my barnacles!' Krilly gasped.

'That's desertion, that is,' explained Le Croix. 'You can get yourself tarred an' feathered for desertion.'

'Tarred and feathered?' Davey looked from one to the other. McGuffin remained quiet on his shoulder, but he could tell the parrot was enjoying itself. 'You're not serious?'

'He's deadly serious,' echoed the Shark. 'I knew the young pirate who deserted the *Flyin' Serpent*, Cap'n Avery's ship. You must've heard about him, surely?'

Davey shook his head. 'No, I haven't. What happened?'

'Oh, they caught up with him right an' proper, gave

him a week's worth of keel hauling.'

'That's where they drag you behind the ship,' added Krilly, when he saw Davey's blank expression. 'Literally.'

'Oh, that was only the *start* of it,' the Shark continued. 'Once they'd hauled the boy up, they slit his nose and ears with a bread knife, then they went an' marooned him on a desert island.'

'B— b— but that's evil! All those punishments just for running away?'

'Aye,' mumbled the trio, in unison.

'How do you know all this?'

Krilly leaned forward and ripped a piece of chicken from the spit.

'Goreblade did his first year o' service on board the *Flyin' Serpent*,' he confirmed, indicating the shark character beside him.

'Aye, I did. Best year o' me workin' life and no mistake. There wasn' a sailor on the seven seas as could've touched old Avery and his band of skullbusters.'

'Sure 'n' you're right,' agreed Le Croix. 'Though I'll say this: Henry Morgan's no slouch when it comes to hard punishment. Cross old Henry and a cross is what you'll get . . . over your grave.'

Davey froze. 'Henry Morgan is no pirate,' he

growled, a dark look flooding his features. 'The man has no right to breathe the same air as decent people. That evil swine murdered my parents and left me an orphan. One day, even if it takes me a thousand years, one day I'll make him answer for his crimes.'

The trio looked frankly astonished. Even McGuffin quietened down.

'Henry Morgan killed your parents?' Krilly repeated. 'He actually *orphaned* you?'

Davey was momentarily caught off guard by the pirates' surprise, and was slightly disturbed by the looks of sympathy and (in one case) puzzlement they were now giving him.

'What? Morgan has killed hundreds, probably *thousands* of people. I can't be the only boy that scumbag has orphaned.'

Davey stared at the group determinedly, but he certainly wasn't prepared for the response he got.

'Er . . . you're probably *not* the only boy he's orphaned,' Goreblade admitted. 'But I'd wager you *are* the only boy who then signed up to a ship captained by him! Your plan must be no less than to face him on his own turf! Astounding!'

'I think maybe you heard me wrong,' Davey said, the truth not quite sinking in. 'I didn't sign up to

Henry Morgan's ship. I signed with the *Rogue Herring*.'

Goreblade was the first to speak up.

'Well, I'm afraid I've got some bad news for ya,' he said. 'You might know a lot about Morgan, but you can't know much about current affairs! Old Henry's been captain of the *Rogue Herring* for more 'an a month now – took it from Edward Stewart.'

'WHAT?' Davey exclaimed. 'The *Herring*? Are you sure? Are you absolutely sure?'

Goreblade nodded. 'About as sure as I am that I'm sober.'

'Yeah, an' he ain't touched a drop o' rum all night.'

Davey couldn't think of anything to say. Instead, he sat as still as a statue, opening and closing his mouth without actually speaking.

*Henry Morgan*, he thought. *Henry Morgan captains the* Rogue Herring.

Davey had been longing to meet the pirate all his life, longing to look into the eyes of the man who killed his parents – and strike him down. Why would the gods of fate do *this* to him? Why would they allow him to stumble right into Morgan when he hadn't even trained with a sword, when he just wasn't *strong enough* to fight. It was so terribly unfair . . .

Davey's head continued to swim with thoughts:

some violent, some frightening, most of them hateful. *So Frank Corsham did something to spite Henry Morgan – stole from him, wronged him. It doesn't matter what. Frank Corsham is Henry Morgan's enemy.*

Davey stared at his feet. He suddenly felt a lot more determined to help the old man out, but a terrible voice was repeating the same warning over and over in his head. *You told them you were Governor Swag's son. Even if you run now, Morgan will find out . . . and he will come after you.*

Davey grimaced. If that was the case, then at least by completing Corsham's task he might end up holding something to bargain with . . .

A sharp tap on the shoulder awoke him from his nightmares.

'You got any decent stories, young 'un?' Krilly demanded.

A little over two hours later, Davey strode away from the beach. His story had been a disaster well before the bit with the zombie squirrels, but it was the forty-six questions about the phantom nut-hoarding scene that had finally made him lose his temper and storm away. After all, who in their right mind *cared* if a zombie squirrel hell-bent on the end of human civilization was left-handed? It was absolutely infuriating; they didn't want a story at all, they just wanted to annoy someone!

However, he couldn't complain too much. McGuffin hadn't said a *word* throughout the entire tale . . . and three pieces of eight would get him enough rations to last the week! Clinking the coins together in his pocket, he made straight for the food store.

He hadn't gone more than a few steps, however, when he realized that the parrot hadn't flown off for the night. It was also quite unusual for McGuffin to be on Davey's shoulder and not take the opportunity to insult him.

'Are you all right?' he said, trying to focus on the Quickly's welcome sign rather than turn his head to look at McGuffin.

The bird said nothing, just quietly clung to his shoulder.

'What's wrong with you?' Davey persisted. 'Why aren't you speaking? Have you been struck dumb?'

McGuffin flapped on to the Quickly's sign and fixed him with two beady eyes.

'If Henry Morgan really did kill your parents,' it squawked, 'you must hate him. You must *really, really* hate him . . .'

Davey wasn't expecting the question, and he certainly wasn't expecting a rush of emotion . . . but his eyes filled with tears.

'There are no words for how much I— I— Why? Why do you ask? What's it to you, bird?'

McGuffin took a long time to answer, but just when Davey was about to walk away, it said, 'I know all about Henry Morgan. I used to belong to him, you know . . .'

There was a moment of terrible silence, then Davey lunged forward like a possessed ghost and snatched the bird out of the air.

An eruption of squawking ensued.

# Into the Jungle

Captain Henry Morgan, arguably one of the most hated pirates in the Caribbean, sheathed his cutlass and produced a fat belt dagger instead.

'Let 'im go,' he boomed.

The thin, trembling prisoner was released and shoved forward by the two hulking brutes on either side of him. He staggered a little, then fell on to his knees and began to sob.

Morgan produced a second belt dagger, dropped it on to the ship's deck and kicked it across to him.

'Pick it up,' he barked. 'Now!'

The terrified prisoner reached out a hand and his fingers closed around the weapon.

'Now tell me, Mister Gray,' Morgan bellowed. 'Do you reckon me a stupid man?'

The prisoner looked up from the deck.

'N— no, Cap'n. O'course not.'

'Then why're you treatin' me like one? I reckon I'm educated; right, mates?'

There was a chorus of approval from the crew.

'Y— you are, Cap'n. Ver' educated,' added Gray, a pleading edge to his voice.

Morgan nodded, but his eyes had narrowed to slits.

'Then I'll ask you one more time,' he spat. 'Where is me box?'

The prisoner sniffed back a stringy length of snot, and attempted to wipe his eye with the back of his filthy hand.

'It was Frank,' he managed. 'F— Frank took it.'

'I reckon we know that,' said Morgan, slyly. 'But Frank is nothin' more than a slippery tar, and he 'ad the good sense ta slither inta the shadows when he done wrong by me, leavin' your sorry carcass to take the blame f'r it.'

Before the prisoner could argue, Morgan pitched his dagger at the bedraggled form. The weapon flew true, sinking into Gray's knee and causing him to scream in agony.

A cacophony of filthy laughs erupted all over the deck as the crew of Henry Morgan's flagship cheered their ruthless leader.

Amid the noise, Gray attempted to tighten his grip on the dagger Morgan had given him, but another pirate's boot came down on his hand before he could close his fist. Bones crunched under the pressure, and Gray sobbed again.

'Oh, Frank's away like the wind, right enough,' Morgan snapped. 'You, other 'and, I have here in me clutches, to speak. So tell us, 'trayed friend o'Frank, where's me box?'

'H— he told me where he was taking it for safe keeping!' came the yelped reply. 'I'll tell you *everything*. I'll tell you where I planned to meet up with him *right now* and you can catch him red-handed! Please, Cap'n. I didn't know what I was doing! Please, be merciful!'

Morgan smiled, crossed the deck and crouched down beside the prisoner.

'Whisper,' he commanded. 'Whisper it all in me ear.'

Gray made a pained effort to bring his mouth level with the pirate's greased lughole, and mumbled for a few seconds.

Morgan listened carefully, then clambered to his feet.

'Good man, Gray,' he said, turning to the rest of the crew and raising his dagger. 'Now throw this stinkin' 'spirator ta the sharks. I'll eat whatever they leave.'

As the crew hauled the unfortunate prisoner away,

several of them risked a few casual glances at their legend of a captain. It was strongly rumoured that Henry Morgan was in his seventies, yet here he was, as tough as ever with not one hint of a sign to show that he was ageing in any way. The man's hair was still jet black and his eyes still glowed with the same fiery malice that had always occupied them. Henry Morgan was a dark and horrific miracle.

Yet there were a few among the ship's crew who knew old Henry well; well enough to know the secret that kept the man living way beyond his years, oblivious to the myriad cliff-top falls, blazing infernos and mortal wounds he'd suffered.

'We'll deal wiv Corsham soon enough,' he boomed, addressing the trembling horde. 'Nade an' 'arper can 'ave the honour. Then we set sail, crewed up an' all.' He glared around the deck. 'Gullin? Gullin! Where are you hidin' up, you scally?'

The crew parted to reveal a heavy pirate with a black moustache, who quickly moved across the boards to stand beside his captain.

'If you got ol' 'Enry a full crew o' the next voyage, I reckon you is as good as a new firs' mate. If you 'aven', you can keep Ol' Gray comp'ny as the sharks take 'im . . .'

Gullin's expression didn't betray the fear he felt. He'd served with Henry Morgan long enough to know that fear didn't buy a man mercy.

'In order of recruitment, Cap'n!' he cried. 'Mackasay, Jones, Davok, Porter, Gilliam, Westfall, Chigley, Tammerin, Palin, Foster, Swag, Arnham!'

Morgan nodded, then turned to stride away. He'd only taken a few steps, however, when he suddenly reared around like a dragon.

'Go back one!' he screamed. 'Go back one!'

'From the end, Cap'n?'

'If I 'ave to ask ye again . . .'

'Swag, Cap'n! Davey Swag. I joined him up myself, Cap'n! He didn't seem much of a pirate, but his father was a governor and his—'

Morgan snatched at the parchment and scrutinized it. Then a terrible smile spread across his face.

'So . . .' he growled, his eyes filling with malice. 'The fates shine on ol' 'Enry once agin. Mallory's whelp returns to me clutches . . .'

'Mallory, Cap'n?' Gullin left the question hanging, as Morgan seemed to have drifted off into a world of his own.

'Survived 'fter all these years an' now 'e's here. Could be Mallory's foun' 'im agin . . . I wonder. Ha! It'll almos' be a shame ta kill 'em, them 'avin escaped ol' 'Enry once an' tol' the tale.'

Morgan suddenly appeared to shake himself from his reverie, and turned his attention to the staring faces of the crew.

'The baby whelp what got away fro' ol' 'Enry!' he announced. ''As come back for 'is doom.'

The crew, who knew when applause was required, burst into several bouts of false laughter. Most of them were trying to conceal puzzled expressions, while waiting for their master to continue.

'Gullin,' Morgan went on, dragging the ship's newly crowned first mate to one side and whispering conspiratorially in his ear. 'If the boy doesn' show in the mornin', we'll be sendin' out *two* search parties. When we set sail on the morrow, I wan' Corsham drowned and youn' Swag dragged 'ere bleedin' aplenty. You 'earin' me?'

Gullin, still expressionless, nodded. 'I hear, Cap'n,' he muttered. 'Nade and Harper will finish Corsham, and I will find the boy personally. So say we all.' He turned and roared at the crew. 'So say we ALL!'

There was a unified cry of obedience from the crew, and several complimentary cheers aimed at the captain. Fortunately, all of them drowned out the screams of

Mister Gray, as the poor wretch was eaten alive in the waters below.

The next morning, Davey awoke so early that it was still dark outside. He ignored the screams that seemed to be coming from beneath a blanket at the far end of the room, washed from a water barrel in the corridor, dressed as swiftly as possible and returned to pack his things. It was only when he had completed his travel preparations that he strode over to the blanket and threw it aside.

'Let me out!' screamed McGuffin. 'This is torture, this is! This is cruelty to animals! This is— this is— this is—'

'My new hat-cage,' Davey finished. 'I thought it was cruel, myself, at first . . . but then I also thought you were nothing but an annoying nuisance. Now I've changed my mind; I'm keeping you around.'

'Locked in a cage?'

'A hat-cage, yes.'

'Let me out! Let me OUT! I haven't done anything to you!'

'True.' Davey nodded as he picked up the contraption. 'But you told me you know all about Henry Morgan; you said it yourself. That means you can help me find the best way to defeat him, tell me all his weaknesses, you name it. That fact makes you invaluable to me. Therefore, I can't just let you fly off whenever you feel like it. I've got to be *sure* you'll stick around.'

'I was lying! I don't know anything about him! I just belonged to him, that's all! He kept me locked in a cage at the bottom of his ship, most of the time! I hated him; he didn't give me a single cracker the whole time he had me! Just let me out, please! I'm claustrophobic!'

'Yeah, right.' Davey fixed the cage to his head, feeling a little foolish at first. However, the shoulder straps and supports were quite handy, and he soon found the hat-cage surprisingly comfortable.

'You look like a stupid moron!' McGuffin squawked. 'What kind of a useless, bum-brained pirate walks around with a cage on his head?'

'Carry on. I'm not changing my mind.'

'If you don't let me out this INSTANT, I'll never tell you a *thing* about Henry Morgan. Do you hear me? Henry Morgan's name will never pass this beak while I'm caged up like this. Are you listening, kettleteeth?'

Davey didn't dignify the question with a response.

Instead, he turned and headed out of the Quickly.

The waters of the Caribbean lapped gently up the shore and he could just make out the vast shadow of the *Rogue Herring*.

His pack slung over his shoulder, he set off along the coast road. The pistol he'd purchased from Cutter was wedged into his belt, but he held the cutlass firmly in his hand. It was dark, after all, and bad things could happen to a pirate who ventured out in the small hours with a birdcage attached to his head.

The road that ran alongside the harbour soon wound up into the cliffs and, at length, bled into the Shortwalk. A battered wooden sign beside the track announced:

### The Cocos Island Shortwalk
#### May Your Stamina Never Fail!

Davey sat down on a sawn-off tree stump behind the sign to eat his breakfast.

The sun had yet to rise over Cocos Island when Frank Corsham crept along a narrow jetty sheltered from the main docks by an old and very dilapidated shipyard.

Arriving at the end of the jetty, Corsham peered out

over the sea and was somewhat surprised not to see a ship waiting for him. Fear suddenly snatched at his throat, but the shivers quickly died away when he chanced to look down and saw the little rowing boat drift out from beneath the jetty.

A hooded figure was manning the oars.

'Thank the devil's goose for that,' Corsham muttered, starting down the rope ladder that spilled from the end of the jetty. 'You're early, Gray. Makes a nice change.'

The boatman said nothing, but extended a hand as if for payment.

Corsham shook his head at the gesture.

'Afraid we've come a cropper, old mate. Listen, I chickened out; Morgan is just too dangerous to cross. I don't know what I was thinking to be honest. I reckon the thrill of the treasure addled my brain. Anyway, we've both wanted to get away from him for long enough; at least now we can go.'

The figure nodded, and put both hands on the oars.

'A lucky escape if you ask me,' Corsham continued. 'I've passed the box on to some stupid kid I met and now *he's* got the burden – at least he will have when he follows my directions and finds it. The innkeeper's going to pass a note on to Morgan begging forgiveness and telling him where the boy's headed—'

'And where might that be,' said the boatman, as his hood was pulled back to reveal the face of Harper, a particularly spiteful pirate who served on the *Rogue Herring*'s cannon crew. 'You treacherous, double-dealing maggot?'

Corsham's eyes filled with horror, and he leapt for the rope ladder – only to see Nade, another of the crew, descending it.

'I c— can explain,' Corsham stuttered, looking from one man to the other and trying to weigh up his options. 'I never meant no harm by it. Surely the captain knows that. Tell him—'

'Captain Morgan's not interested in anything you might have to say,' Nade growled, producing his sword.

'Besides,' added Harper. 'As you've already spilled your guts in the letter you've admitted giving to the innkeeper, what does the captain actually need *you* for at all?'

Nade raised his sword, and smiled down at Corsham through broken teeth. 'Frank, you always were a spineless wretch. Gullin will make a far better first mate for the cap'n. He's twice the man you are.'

The sword came down in a sweeping arc. Corsham didn't live long enough to scream.

* * *

It was turning out to be a very murky morning.

Davey had come upon a tumbledown shack set quite a way back from the path. From what he could make out, the place was boarded up. There was a donkey outside, grazing on a small patch of grass. It looked half starved and *smelled* half cooked.

Davey slowly approached the shack. It was, as he had first thought, completely deserted. A lengthy banner stretched over the front door and window, pronouncing it to be the home of 'Leyonger's Pony Trekking Company – Travel All the Way Around Our Fair Isle Without a Blister To Show For Your Trouble'. There was also a chalked message on the door: 'closed due to lack of'.

The rest of the message had been erased, but what remained was enough to make Davey angry. If this pony business was still up and running, he could have travelled around the island without breaking a sweat!

There was no doubt about it, Cocos certainly wasn't the place Uncle Jake had made it out to be. The people were strange, most of the services had closed down and, from what he'd overheard during his stay at the Quickly, the governor's mansion was an abandoned, burnt-out mess. The entire island was going to the dogs!

'What's that over there?' McGuffin squawked.

'What? Where?'

'By the path – three stones. Look east, nutbrain!'

Davey followed the parrot's directions and came upon three gravestones beside the path.

One read:

Here lies Palo Leyonger, Loving Husband & Father

One read:

Here lies Kiaka Leyonger, Devoted Wife & Mother

One read:

Here lies Threeday Leyonger, Much Loved Son

The ground around the final gravestone looked disturbed, as if something had been clawing at it.

'An entire family,' Davey muttered. 'How awful. I wonder what happened to the son's grave?'

'Tomb-robbers.'

'You think?'

'Yeah. Islands are full of 'em.'

Davey headed back to the shack and circled it three or four times, announced his presence in a very loud voice and ended up hammering on the door just to make sure nobody had fallen asleep inside. Then he strode up to take a look at the donkey. A leather cord ran from an iron hoop in the ground to a metal collar around its neck. Hanging from the collar was a tiny wooden disc with the name Musket scratched on both sides.

Davey crouched down and tugged at the hoop, but it was stuck fast. He felt around the collar but there was no hint of give there either. He took a step back, clicked his fingers and tried to get the donkey's attention instead. After the third or fourth attempt, it looked up at him.

Davey thought for a moment, then drew his cutlass and swung out with it. Musket gave him a hopeful look but there was a fair amount of doubt in there as well.

The cutlass arced through the air, severing the leather cord in one swift motion.

Davey stepped back to survey his handiwork.

'Not bad, if I do say so myself!' he exclaimed.

'You're letting it go?' McGuffin exclaimed. 'Lucky ba—'

'Shh! I want to see what it does!'

Musket looked from the hoop to Davey and back again. Then it trotted off in the direction of the wood.

'Hey! Come back here! I didn't let you free so you could run off!' Davey closed up his pack and bolted after the beast, trying to ignore McGuffin's derisory squawks as he went.

'Come back! Please!'

Davey ran on, the cage rattling around on his head, waving his arms in the hope that the donkey might change its mind and trot back to the shack. On the contrary, it paid absolutely no attention to him whatsoever, and continued on its determined course.

'Come on, Musket!' Davey shouted, making a grab for the beast's tail and missing by a mile. 'Don't go in there, boy! It's really dangerous!'

'That's why we're following him, is it?' McGuffin squawked, flapping around inside the cage like a demented lunatic. 'Of all the pirates to get lumped with . . .'

Musket increased its pace from a brisk trot to a canter, and hared off down a dirt track that ran between two overhanging trees.

'Wait up, Musket! There're probably cannibals down that way! Cannibals! Did you hear me, boy?'

Out of breath now, Davey slowed to a stop. Then he staggered off the track and, hacking aside a cluster of hanging vines with his cutlass, collapsed against the gnarled bole of a wild palm tree, jarring McGuffin's cage as he did so.

'Ah! You clumsy moron. I'm holding on to this perch with my *beak* – you do know that, right?'

Noon arrived on Cocos Island with little ceremony, and the weather was getting worse.

Onboard the *Rogue Herring*, Gullin paced back and forth as a short and rather ugly deckhand raced up to speak with him.

'We've boarded them all now, boss,' said the pirate, scratching his stubble absent-mindedly. 'The Swag boy definitely isn't among them, but that's not all. There's more. Er . . . maybe you should get the cap'n. Is he awake yet?'

Gullin shook his head. 'No, and if you want to go wake him up, be my guest.' He leaned against the side of the boat, folded his arms, and grimaced. 'No? Right, then. You're stuck with me. Spill your guts.'

The deckhand swallowed a few times, rubbing his chin in order to steady his nerves. It didn't look like it was working.

'Nade and Harper just got back. They got the drop on Corsham and dispatched him.'

'And the captain's box?' Gullin froze, an odd expression on his face. 'TELL me we've got it back.'

The deckhand faltered for a moment, as if he were

too afraid to continue. 'N— not exactly, Sir. It appears that Corsham struck up a deal with Swag and now *he* has the box.'

Gullin took a moment to digest the news, a pained expression on his weathered face.

'Where is Swag now?'

'Th— that's the thing, boss. Corsham said he'd written a special note to the captain telling of Swag's whereabouts, and that he'd left this note with the innkeeper. So Harper and Nade killed him, because they knew the captain wanted him drowned an' all. Only . . .'

'Only,' Gullin finished with a growl, 'now they've been to the inn and there *isn't* any note *because Corsham was a filthy liar.*'

The deckhand was raising a hand as if trying to interrupt a sacred sermon.

'Th— there is one piece of good news, boss. Nade and Harper roughed up the innkeeper and got some information out of him. It seems that Swag is still on Cocos. He left the Quickly before first light this morning, headed up the Shortwalk.'

Gullin thought for a moment, his mind racing.

'You think he has the box on him now?'

The deckhand smiled weakly, but he looked far too

scared to commit himself to an opinion. Several smiles came and went.

'If he does,' Gullin went on, 'it actually halves our problems. We have to find Swag, anyway – if he's got the box on him, that's a bonus.'

Gullin smiled, suddenly, and clapped a rough hand on the ugly pirate's shoulder. 'Go wake the cap'n,' he roared. 'That's an order.'

Davey sighed.

What in the name of seven bells was he thinking of? He'd just followed a runaway donkey into a jungle. To make matters worse, he had a terrible feeling that he'd come too far in to find his way out again. Terrific. Just terrific! Some freelance pirate he'd turned out to be; an idiot with a parrot-cage strapped to his head wandering around in a deadly environment! Priceless!

He closed his eyes and counted to ten, something Uncle Jake had told him to do whenever he was feeling stressed or panicky. When he opened them again, the situation seemed a little less hopeless. After all, he thought, it could have been *worse*. He could've been under attack from a wild jungle tribe or Henry Morgan could've caught up with him. Hah! Things were never as bad when you thought about them logically.

'What the hell?' McGuffin squawked suddenly, flapping around noisily. 'Look! Over there!'

Davey darted frantic glances left and right. 'What is it?'

'Something moved! A shadow just ran between two trees!'

'Are you sure?'

'As sure as I am that you're a poor excuse for a pirate . . .'

Davey squinted into the middle distance, but he still couldn't see anything.

'Look, are you having me on? I—'

Sheeooooow! Kadunnk.

An arrow whizzed past his face and thudded into the tree trunk, mere inches away from him. Davey gasped, frozen to the spot with sheer terror.

Sheeeooooow! Kadunnk.

'See! I told you, but did you listen to me? Did you?'

Sheeeooooow! Kadunnk.

The third arrow was even nearer. Davey tentatively put a finger to the lobe of his left ear and, when he took it away again, there was a speck of blood on it. The arrow had skimmed his ear, it had actually skimmed his ear!

'Run, you idiot!' McGuffin squawked. 'You want to

get shot by a poisoned arrow? Do you? Ruuuuuuun!'

Davey suddenly shook off his terror and, as he estimated that the next shot was likely to pass between his ears, he decided for once to take McGuffin's advice. He ran like hell.

Trees flashed past on either side of him, and the cage rattled around on his head. Inside, the parrot was a blur – it had been slammed against the sides of the cage so many times that it was actually beginning to lose consciousness.

'Ahhhhhhhhhhhhh!' Davey screamed, running headlong through the jungle and waving his cutlass around him as if it were a feather duster. Arrows whizzed left and right. One came perilously close to skewering McGuffin and another would have finished firmly in Davey's back had he not tripped over a protruding tree root and plunged headlong towards a soggy pit at the base of an overgrown clearing. The straps securing his hat-cage had snapped during the mad dash through the wood, and the contraption now flew off, along with his boarding axe, as the young pirate rolled head over heels down the incline and came to land in an awkward and very uncomfortable heap at the bottom. Davey muttered to himself for a few seconds – and then passed out.

Henry Morgan strode across the deck of the *Rogue Herring*, his crew parting before him like frightened animals.

'I want tha' boy brough' 'ere alive – torture 'im all you wan', but I wanna be the one who snuffs him out. Got tha', 'ave ya? Tha' boy is my prop'ty.'

'Yes, Cap'n!' Gullin screamed, as the rest of the crew all mumbled obediently. 'How many should I take?'

'No more 'an four. He'll be easy pickin's.'

'Very well, Cap'n.' Gullin glanced around him. 'In that case I'll take Spang, Jaggs, Nade and Harper. They were all up on deck yesterday, so they know him by sight.'

The four named crewmen quickly armed themselves, while Morgan dragged Gullin over to the far side of the boat.

'Long ago I rid the boy o' 'is parents. Weakling scum, 'at they were.'

Gullin swallowed, hanging on the captain's every word, not daring to interrupt.

'The boy should o' been me kill 'o the bargain. A baby 'e was. Stolen fro' ou' me grasp by a cabin wretch call' Mallory. He paid a price for 'is treach'ry, tha' one.'

'I'll get Swag,' Gullin muttered. 'One way or another, I'll get him.'

When Morgan nodded and turned away, Gullin quickly assembled his team and departed the *Rogue Herring*.

Morgan watched them from the deck of the ship, and a dark smile settled on his ancient lips.

Davey sat up, quickly realizing that his feeling of light-headedness was due to the absence of a hat-cage. McGuffin's temporary prison was nowhere to be seen and he'd lost his cutlass, too – the blade had wedged in the bark of a huge oak and, despite several attempts to retrieve it, Davey eventually had to leave the wretched thing behind. True, you couldn't really call yourself a pirate unless you had a cutlass but, then again, you couldn't really call yourself a pirate if you were nailed to a tree, and the people who had fired the arrows were still out there somewhere, waiting in the undergrowth to kill you. He didn't have *time* to retrieve his weapon. Fortunately, he managed to grab the weapon when he arrived in the clearing a second time, even more lost than he had been before.

'McGuffin,' Davey whispered, hurrying around the clearing and not daring to keep still for more than a few seconds at a time. 'McGuffin! Where are you, bird? McGuuuuuuuuffin.'

He couldn't see the cage *anywhere*. Oh, well, he had no choice but to keep on going . . .

Taking just one more moment to peer around, he bolted off again, rushing between the trees like a deer, and peering out from behind them like a very paranoid squirrel.

Just when Davey thought things couldn't possibly get any worse, they suddenly did. He'd been running flat out, which he felt certain was a *good* thing. He'd also been looking over his shoulder every few seconds and it was during one of *these* little drops in concentration that he careered face first into another ditch. He landed with a sickening squelch, mud spraying up all around him. Then there was silence.

Davey rolled over, but struggled to find his footing. He quickly realized that this was because he'd lost a boot. He spotted it a few feet away from him and, yanking it out of the swampy ground, attempted to work his foot back inside. Then he headed for a patch of solid-looking sand in a small clearing to the west of the mud pool.

Hmm . . . there was a wooden sign fastened to one of the trees that surrounded the clearing. Davey couldn't see what it said from where he was, so he traversed the clearing in order to read it. Unfortunately, most of the sign had been obscured (a trend in these parts, it seemed) and all he could make out was:

e    ar
ui        n

Strange. Obviously, the message didn't make any sense, but Davey found himself trying to say it aloud anyway.

'Earuin,' he said to himself. 'Ear-u-in? Earareuin? Hey, maybe it's "here, are you in?"'

He had to admit it sounded highly unlikely. Then an idea occurred to him. Perhaps he could trace the letters with his finger. The message might have been obliterated but perhaps the engraving was still good. He yanked the board off the tree – it came away with surprising ease – and traced his finger along the letters. Fantastic. It was working! He read:

## Beware
## Quicksand

Clutching the board to his chest, Davey looked down. He could no longer see his boots, or his knees, or even his waist. The sign had been a warning of imminent danger. He swore under his breath. What was the point of a dire warning, if you had to spend ten minutes deciphering the thing before you understood what it was you were in danger of! The whole jungle was an absolute death-trap, a nightmarish hell-hole filled with hostile archers that embedded you up to your elbows in quicksand! Could it possibly get any worse than this?

Gullin knelt by the side of the road and studied the path, carefully.

'You see these?' he said, indicating some tracks in the dirt.

Spang and Jaggs, two murderous-looking brothers with twin scars on their left cheeks, plodded over to where their boss was crouched. Neither man said anything, but they both nodded.

'They look fresh to me,' Gullin continued. 'Out of place *fresh*. I want you two to follow the road and keep your eyes *firmly* on 'em.'

As the pair mumbled to each other, Gullin unhooked a chain around his neck. There was a silver whistle on the end.

'Take this,' he advised. 'Follow the road like I said

but – and listen carefully here – if those tracks deviate and go into the wood at any point, I want you to plunge straight in, blowing the whistle as you go. The rest of us will hear it and we'll come find you.'

Nade and Harper, two of the more able swordsmen among the crew, suddenly moved over to join the group around the tracks.

'Where are *we* going, then?' Harper asked, a confused expression on his face.

'You two are going into the woods right here,' Gullin muttered, pointing off the path. 'In case the brat got smart and decided to double back. *I'm* going into the woods on the other side.'

'On your own, boss?' Nade exclaimed, looking genuinely doubtful.

'Of course on my own! I can take damn good care o' myself . . . and we can't afford to take *any* chances here. We need to get back with Swag AND the captain's box, or we're all dead anyway. Now MOVE!'

The voice was thin and raspy, and didn't sound at all welcoming.

'You!' it said. 'Pirate! Don't move a muscle.'

Davey craned around to see where the voice had come from, and quickly wished he hadn't.

Standing on the edge of the clearing was a tall, dark-skinned boy, holding a longbow. That in itself would have been bad news, but there were several other things that struck Davey as immediate problems, like the fact that half the boy's skin had rotted away and the rest hung in loose folds from his bones, which were actually visible in several places. His eyes glowed a dark, dark red and his teeth looked as though they had been sharpened into points. To make matters *even* worse, the boy had obviously taken extra offence at Davey's stare and had subsequently drawn the longbow back and was now ready to fire an arrow *at* him.

'W— w— wait a minute! You don't need to shoot me! I haven't done anything to you!'

The boy shook his head. 'You're walking in *my* jungle without permission.'

'Your jungle?' Davey managed. 'B— but I didn't have a clue. I just followed a stupid donkey and ended up lost in here! Can I ask how I was supposed to know this was *your* jungle? I mean, there aren't any signs up or anything . . .'

'Everyone on the island knows that this jungle belongs to Threeday Leyonger. You obviously didn't bother to ask anyone . . . that makes you stupid.'

Davey sank deeper into the quicksand.

'I'm new to the island! I'm new to the island!' he cried, snatching pointlessly at the air as the swamp claimed even more of him. 'No one told me anything about a Threeglade . . . er Threefold . . .'

'ThreeDAY Leyonger,' repeated the boy, slowly and deliberately, as though he was chanting. 'ThreeDAY Leyonger.'

'Right . . .' Davey frowned suddenly, as a wave of recollection washed over him. 'That was the name on the gravestone!' he gasped. 'Y— y— you're d— d— dead!'

Threeday lowered his bow suddenly, and the glow in his eyes seemed to shine even more brightly.

'I was, for a long time,' he said, seemingly half to himself. 'Now, I'm only *mostly* dead.'

'HELP!' Davey screamed, taking the opportunity to cry out. 'Somebody help me! I'm trapped in quicksand and there's a zombie trying to shoot me with an arrow! HEEEELP!'

Threeday suddenly put his head on one side, a move that exposed a missing layer of flesh from his jawbone. He appeared to be listening to some distant, otherwise inaudible sound.

Davey was about to scream again, but he was quickly interrupted.

'If you want help, be quiet,' Threeday snapped. 'You're not the only stranger out on the Shortwalk today.'

Nade and Harper charged through the wood, slashing aside vines, crushing twigs and generally proving their lack of sympathy for nature's wonders.

'You reckon we can cut the kid up a bit?' said Nade, slapping at the myriad of mosquito bites rising on his arms.

'I don' reckon the boss'd blame us fer that,' Harper hazarded. 'I still can't believe he gave Spang and Jaggs that whistle. I don't reckon Jaggs even knows how to *use* a whistle . . .'

The pair had reached a fork in the jungle path. A rather crude and unhelpful sign on the tree in the centre of the path displayed an arrow with two heads.

'Should we go east or west?' said Harper, uncertainly.

Nade shrugged.

'East looks easier.'

'Let's go check it out, then.'

The two pirates ploughed their way along another seemingly abandoned path until they arrived, at length, beside a small and very shabby-looking shack among the trees. Both men instinctively drew a second blade.

'Shhh!' Nade whispered, stalking up to the front door. 'There might be somebody inside.'

'Agreed.' Harper crept towards the door of the shack. 'You wait here. I'll go in, and if anybody runs out, you can take 'em.'

'Deal.'

The pirate readied his sword, then leaped around with a heavy kick that separated the already half-destroyed door from its tired hinges.

Nade looked on, both swords readied, as Harper rushed into the shack. There followed a few seconds of silence, before Harper re-emerged, staggering slightly, with one hand clapped over his mouth.

'What's wrong?' said Nade, side-stepping slightly to get a look inside the shack. 'Is there something—'

'There's flies everywhere,' Harper managed, almost retching as he took his hand away from his face. 'And it stinks – really, *really* stinks.'

'Worse than the *Herring*?'

'A whole lot worse. There's bedding on the floor, and a pile of pictures, scrolls and other old junk. It's been used recently, I reckon, but I tell you – it smells like somebody just *died* in there.'

'Anything of value?'

'Nah. A few arrows, but nothing really salvageable.'

'Should we burn it, d'you think?' Nade asked, eyeing the flies that were swarming in the doorway. 'I've got me a tinder.'

Harper glanced back into the shadowy interior of the shack, and then around at the trees.

'A big enough clearing,' he admitted. 'Let's do it, at least we'll be able to see where we've come from with a decent fire behind us.'

Gullin was proceeding through his part of the woods with more caution. Where his men might slash at a branch he carefully ducked to avoid it, where they would have ripped down hanging vines, he gently swept them aside. Gullin was an altogether more instinctive hunter. He knew that a patient man would inevitably succeed where an impatient man would fail.

He allowed himself a crafty, indulgent smile and was just about to reach out towards another collection of vines when the whistle went: loud and clear.

'Thanks for pulling me out of the swamp. I really owe you one.'

'Quiet.'

'Right, sorry.'

High in the trees, Threeday Leyonger turned to

Davey Swag and put a rotten finger to what remained of his lips.

'You brought others into the jungle with you . . .' he whispered.

'I didn't,' Davey mouthed back. 'I was travelling alone. Well, unless you count McGuffin . . .'

'What is a McGuffin?'

'It's the name of my parrot. I had him inside a kind of cage thingy, but then you started shooting at me, and I lost him when—'

'You fell into the first ditch.' Threeday smiled, a terrifying sight full of broken teeth and ragged gums. 'I know. I found him. He is safe.'

Davey rolled his eyes. 'Oh joy,' he whispered.

'He made a lot of noise – I had to put him inside a purse.'

'Good job, too. What about the cage?'

'I threw it away.' Threeday pointed down at two distant shapes moving through the woods off to the east. 'I take it *they* are no companions of yours?'

Davey strained to see where the zombie was pointing, but could only make out a very indistinct blur.

'Could they be wanderers, like me?' he hazarded.

'No,' muttered Threeday, shaking his head. 'They are hunting for something . . . and as you are the only person to enter this wood in the last few hours, I would guess that that something is *you*.'

Davey gulped a few times and stared harder at the approaching figure.

'P— p— pirates,' he managed. 'If those are Henry Morgan's men, I'm dead meat.' He took a second to think about what he'd just said, and added, 'No offence.'

Threeday took in a deep, oddly expansive breath and again put his head at an unsettling angle. 'There are . . . more of them,' he continued, as a whistle sounded in the distance. 'At least three, possibly as many as five. Why do they search for you?'

Davey cast a pleading look at his strange new friend.

'It's a long story,' he whispered. 'But I'd be glad to tell you, if you can just see your way clear to helping me a bit. I know you're not exactly top-notch with that bow, but I bet you could hit them from here!'

Threeday made no move to unclasp his weapon.

'Why should I help you, jungle intruder?' he spat. 'You are, after all, very evidently a pirate – just as they are – and equally unwelcome in my jungle.'

Davey gritted his teeth and tried to look the possessed boy directly in both of his foetid eyes. 'Once again, I didn't know this was *your* jungle, otherwise I would have steered well clear . . . and you should help me because, well, because those pirates work for a man who killed my *entire* family and made me an orphan! Do you have any idea what that's like?'

Threeday returned his attention to the shapes below.

'Yes,' he whispered, his eyes now alight with flame. 'I know *exactly* how that feels.'

For a moment, Davey could only stare at the wretched creature, but he quickly pulled himself together. 'Then help me, please!'

Threeday slowly seemed to reach a decision.

'Very well,' he said. 'I will help you. I can only deal with one at a time, though. You will have to help *yourself* a little.'

'M— me?' Davey boggled at him. 'What, you mean fight them? I can't do that – I'm not *trained*.'

Threeday turned to Davey and his eyes blazed anew.

'I wasn't *asking* you,' he growled.

Jaggs clambered to his feet and threw down a rough handful of dirt.

'These tracks are all over the place, now,' he muttered. 'The boy must be around here somewhere, though. You think we should blow the whistle again, you know, just in case they didn't hear it the first time?'

'Do it.'

Jaggs reached around his neck, but the chain was suddenly strangling him. Spang looked on with mounting horror as a rotted arm pulled the chain into the trees, dragging his half-throttled brother with it.

'Jaggs? Jaggs!'

'Help me! Hlp me!'

Spang leaped forward and tried to reach up to strike at the thing in the tree, but he saw a pair of glowing red eyes staring down at him and quickly dropped his sword.

'Gkgjgjgj!' Jaggs choked. 'Hlp me! Plse!'

Spang dropped to his knees and began to scramble in the mud for his sword. His fingers had just found the hilt when a boot slammed down on them, accompanied by a sickening crack. Spang cried out in pain, and peered up into the face of . . .

. . . a young boy? *The* young boy.

'You!'

Spang gritted his teeth and made to swing round with his good hand, but Davey thrust up with the tree branch he'd been carrying and knocked the pirate to the floor.

In the trees, Jaggs' violently shaking legs had suddenly gone limp, and he was dropped on to the ground like a sack of potatoes. Davey started when he realized his grim friend had actually strangled the pirate. He'd never seen anyone killed before . . . not like that.

Threeday quickly swung out of the tree and landed in a crouching position on the dirt. It was only as the zombie rushed towards him that Davey realized he had taken his attention off Spang, who had jumped to his feet and was even now sprinting away through the woods.

'I see you are armed with a pistol,' Threeday muttered. 'Yet you don't seem to use it?'

'I don't know how! The man who sold it to me went through the instructions too quickly!'

'Hmm . . . I suspect that you are not much of a pirate.'

Threeday reached down and, snatching hold of Jaggs' collar, dragged the corpse into a nearby bush.

'I didn't realize I was being followed!' Davey protested, hurrying to keep up when he saw that Threeday was making off in the opposite direction. 'I mean, I might have guessed Morgan's men would come after me, what with me signing up to his ship and all, but I didn't actually realize those pirates were hunting me until you pointed them out! Where are we going?'

Threeday didn't pause or turn his head, and Davey noticed that his ragged flesh seemed to glisten in the half-light of the wood.

'There is no *we*,' spat the zombie. 'There is only you. I'm going to return your bird . . . and then I want you out of my jungle.'

'They'll kill me, though!' Davey put on an extra burst of speed in order to keep up with his strange companion.

'That is your problem, *pirate*, not mine.'

Spang's frantic dash from the clearing saw him run straight into Gullin – literally. The two men collided and both crashed to the floor.

'What in the name of seven hells—'

'Arghgh! We've got to get out of here! Quick! Argghh!' Spang leapt to his feet again, but Gullin quickly swept the pirate's legs out from under him. When the big man tried to find his feet a second time, Gullin swung out with a left hook and almost broke his nose.

Spang staggered back, his vision blurred, and collapsed against a nearby tree.

'Right,' Gullin snarled. 'Now pull yourself together and speak.'

Spang's eyes seemed to wander about the jungle before they settled on Gullin's unimpressed face.

'J— J— Jaggs is dead,' he managed.

'Is he?' Gullin's question sounded more like a resigned statement. The pirate nodded. 'Tell me what happened . . .'

'We were attacked . . .'

'By Swag?'

'Not just Swag . . . there was s— something with him. Red eyes, it had, glowing bright like embers. It dragged Jaggs into a tree and th— th— throttled him.'

'Red eyes, you say?' Gullin paused for a moment in thought. Then he drew his sword, marched over to one of the closest trees and hacked off a stout branch. Discarding his sword, he produced a tinder-pistol from his belt, struck up a flame and set the branch alight. The pistol went back into the belt and the sword was quickly reclaimed.

'A zombie, by your description,' Gullin muttered, motioning for his companion to follow him. 'Fear not, my friend. Even the dead shrink from flame.'

He marched off into the wood, pausing only to kick away a branch that blocked his path.

'If you're not at my side the next time I look, Mister

*Spang,* you can explain your cowardice to Captain Morgan, in person.'

Davey's arms felt like they were being ripped from his sockets as he slowly and rather desperately hauled himself up the final section of rope and managed, puffing and panting, to heave his skinny frame on to the wooden platform that rested between the tops of two of the tallest trees in the jungle.

When he could finally breathe again, he saw that Threeday was staring down at him with a quizzical expression on his tatty face.

'This isn't much of a tree-house,' Davey spluttered. 'I expected at least a roof.'

'I don't sleep here,' Threeday assured him. 'This is my watching platform. I use it to . . . observe the life below.'

'Right.' Davey forced himself up on to his elbows. 'You don't still sleep in your . . . er . . . grave, do you?' The young pirate smiled weakly at Threeday, wondering if the zombie might actually try to throttle him for asking the question.

'I have a shack, nearby. I sleep there.'

'Bet it's a right old dump,' squawked a familiar voice.

Threeday turned suddenly and, reaching up into a

hollow, produced a large, stringed purse. It was bulging all over, as McGuffin valiantly attempted to make his escape.

Davey took the bag from the zombie and quickly freed the opening, turning his face away from the hole as McGuffin flew free. The bird flapped around for a time, squawking and moaning, before fatigue evidently got the better of it and it came to land on the young pirate's shoulder.

'I dunno; I thought *you* were cruel to animals, but stuffing me in a bag reached a new level of spiteful. I'd wish him dead, but it looks like somebody got there fir—'

Davey snatched at the bird and clamped a hand over its beak.

'Don't mind McGuffin,' he said. 'He's harmless, really – all beak and no claw.'

Threeday wasn't paying attention. The zombie had padded over to the edge of the observation platform and was scouring the jungle floor.

'Keep the creature quiet,' he said, suddenly turning his head and glaring at Davey with such malice that McGuffin instinctively nuzzled up to his neck.

'More pirates?' Davey hazarded, straining to see over the zombie's shoulder.

'Yes,' said Threeday, grimly. 'And now they bring *fire*.'

If anything, Gullin was moving even more cautiously than he had done before.

'Zombies,' he muttered, as he moved aside a network of vines and raised his flaming torch in order to see beyond them. 'I'd wager gold on it.'

'Aren't you s— s— scared, boss?' Spang hazarded. 'I mean, I never even believed in zombies until that *thing* attacked Jaggs.'

'I'm scared, well enough,' Gullin muttered. 'But not of zombies. I've seen a few in my time. Besides, at least they *die* if you burn 'em. At least when you slash a wound in a zombie, the wound stays. I've seen Captain Morgan run through with a dagger, and I've seen the gashes heal up before my own eyes. Yes, with my own *eyes*. I've seen him lose an arm, and I've seen him pick that arm up and watched as the skin knitted together again. You're frightened of zombies? All they are is the dead brought to life by voodoo magic, animated corpses who walk until they're cut down or set alight. I don't know *what* Captain Morgan is. I've never seen anything *like* him.'

The shaking pirate looked up at his superior with

rheumy eyes. He'd only been aboard the *Herring* for a few weeks, and even in that short time he'd heard the rumours about Morgan, but he'd taken them simply as pieces of invented *gossip* for the new blood. Gullin sounded *deadly* serious.

Spang grimaced, then raised his flaming torch and moved to stand in front of his companion.

'Let's find this kid,' he muttered. 'Before Mr Morgan thinks we've let him down . . .'

Gullin nodded, and the two pirates moved on.

'We're running?' Davey gasped, as Threeday swung across the treetops and swept the vine back to him.

'They have fire,' Threeday called. 'And they outnumber us. We would lose.'

'But—'

'Listen to your dead mate,' McGuffin squawked. 'It's obvious he's got a fair amount of experience when it comes to mortal peril. Besides, I'm all feathers. If they light me up, I'll be grilled an' served before I can squawk.'

'Shhh!' Threeday warned, his eyes blazing. He pointed down at the jungle floor. 'They will hear.'

The zombie yanked on another vine, and swung to a new tree. Davey waited for the return of the vine before he followed suit, McGuffin flapping after him. When he reached the other side, however, he noticed the observation platform about three trees over.

'We're back where we started!' Davey hissed. 'Look, that's the platform we just came from, isn't it?'

'I have many look-out points,' Threeday explained, before flying off on another vine.

Davey and McGuffin pursued the zombie through what seemed like forty trees' worth of jungle airspace. However, when Davey had finally found purchase on yet another stout branch, Threeday suddenly rounded on him.

'You will stay here,' he snapped, unclasping his bow and a pack of arrows and thrusting them both into the young pirate's arms. 'I'm going to leave you with these. The pirates will soon reach the edge of the jungle and then they will double back. I don't have much time. You are safe here. On *no* account should you fire this bow unless you are actually in danger. I would rather the pirates tired of looking for you and left my jungle of their own accord. Do you understand?'

Davey frowned slightly.

'W— where are you going?' he managed.

'I am going to see if these *infiltrators* have found my

shack . . . and also to see if there are more of them on the road. I may be some time . . .'

'Right.'

Threeday took hold of another vine, and glanced back, his inflamed pupils piercing Davey's soul.

'Remember what I said. Do NOT fire that bow unless you have no other choice.'

Davey nodded an acknowledgement, and watched as the zombie disappeared between the trees.

'Right,' McGuffin squawked, suddenly flapping from his shoulder and alighting on a branch beside his face. 'Now, you've got ten arrows there, so even if you make a couple of mistakes you still get two shots at each one. That's assuming there are only two of 'em down there in total.'

Davey boggled at the bird.

'Are you *mad*? Didn't you hear what he said? I'm not to fire at *anything* unless I'm in *real* danger.'

McGuffin hopped along the branch.

'Yeah, I 'eard 'im, but the boy's *dead*.'

'So?'

'So, despite what I said earlier, he's obviously not the best judge of what to do in a dangerous situation . . .'

'He's helped us out, so far.'

'Fine. We'll go with *your* plan – you know, the one

that got you into a dodgy deal with a man in a bad disguise, chased by pirates and lost in a jungle populated by zombies. Excellent. You're doing well, so far.'

McGuffin hopped back on to Davey's shoulder.

'I just hope he doesn't eat flesh; most of 'em do, you know.'

Davey ignored the parrot and squinted into the distance. Afternoon had arrived, and the weather was beginning to look bleak. *Still*, he thought, *the darker the jungle the more difficult it's going to be to find me.*

There was certainly no obvious movement from the jungle floor.

'Do *you* think those pirates were Morgan's men?' he whispered.

'It's likely,' squawked McGuffin. 'Either they clocked your name when you signed up to the ship or you drew their attention by signing up and *then* doing a runner. Either way, it's a fair bet that Morgan's recognized your name. Either that or . . .'

'Or?' Davey suddenly froze, waiting on the bird's next utterance.

'Or else they caught up with Corsham and he blabbed. If that happened, Morgan probably thinks you've got whatever it is Corsham half-inched. Add that to the fact that you escaped him when you was a baby, and you've got a world o' problems . . .'

Davey gritted his teeth and grimaced at the parrot.

'It's really nice having you around to remind me of all this stuff,' he spat.

'I know,' McGuffin squawked. 'Don't mention it.'

Davey sat bolt upright, almost toppling off the branch as he did so. Despite McGuffin's disturbed flapping, he managed to snatch back some purchase and steady his breath. He'd definitely heard *something*.

Peering down at the jungle floor, he could just make out two shapes picking their way through the undergrowth. Both men carried swords, and both looked decidedly unafraid.

'Do you see them?' Davey whispered, hoping McGuffin's reply wouldn't be accompanied by any overly exertive squawking.

'I see 'em,' the bird confirmed. 'A different lot, though: no torches.'

'Hell's teeth! How many of them are out there?'

'I dunno. The whole crew?'

'Don't even *suggest* that.'

Davey squinted at the two pirates, who were getting *very* close to the base of his tree.

*You know*, Davey thought, *I could probably hit them from here . . . if I really tried.*

'You ever fired a bow?' McGuffin asked, as if reading his mind.

'A bit,' Davey whispered. 'Uncle Jake let me practise with one a few times.'

'Go on, then. Have a go.'

Davey was about to admonish the bird, but a sudden wave of confidence overwhelmed him and he unclasped the bow from around his neck. Leaning in a comfortable space between two of the tree branches, he notched an arrow . . . and took aim.

'Don't miss,' McGuffin advised him. 'Or you'll mess up my part of the plan.'

'*Your* par—'

Davey didn't have time to question the parrot further, as McGuffin took this opportunity to dive off the branch and plunge towards the pair at the base of the tree.

Suddenly panicked by the parrot, Davey took aim . . . and released his first arrow.

The scream erupted through the jungle. It was heard by Threeday Leyonger, standing at the smouldering wreckage that was now all that remained of his home.

It was heard by Gullin and Spang as they negotiated their way through the jungle. The person who heard it loudest, however, was Harper.

The pirate had almost gasped with shock when his friend had first let out the agonizing scream.

Nade staggered a few feet and fell to his knees, an arrow planted awkwardly in the space between his neck and shoulder. The pirate scrambled frantically to retrieve the arrow, but the pain was evidently causing him to scream even louder with every attempt.

Harper quickly drew his sword and circled the clearing. He immediately cast his glance toward the treetops . . . and was hit full in the face by a scratching, squawking, screaming parrot.

The creature flapped frantically, tearing at Harper's face with beak and claw. The pirate smacked the bird aside, toppled over and quickly rubbed the blood from his eyes, only to see Nade collapse to the ground with a second arrow in his back. The pirate twitched a few times, and was still.

Harper rolled over and scrambled up to the nearest tree, keeping himself low while at the same time readying his sword for combat. Blood still leaked into his eyes from a deep wound in his forehead – *the cursed bird would pay for that.*

He peered up into the trees from his new position, but could see no movement. Then he spotted the parrot. It flew around the clearing a few times, circling higher and higher, and came to rest on . . . a boy's shoulder.

Harper looked up at Davey Swag, watching the boy carefully as he cast furtive glances down at the clearing. Then, moving with extreme care, he slid on his stomach and pulled himself to the next tree across. Now he was *behind* the tree in which the boy was hiding.


'We got 'em, we got 'em!' McGuffin squawked, hopping up and down on Davey's shoulder. 'I told ya you could get a decent shot from this height!'

'Yeah.' Davey was scrutinizing the clearing, an uneasy look on his face. 'I don't see the other one though.'

'He probably ran off. I clawed him up like a good 'un.'

Davey nodded. 'I saw – thanks for that. Where did you learn—'

'I been around a long time, I have. I'm not yer average bird.'

'Did you actually see him run off?'

McGuffin flapped on to a nearby branch.

'Well, no. I got in and out as quick as I could.'

'That's what I thought.' Davey shouldered his bow and put a hand on the hilt of his sword. 'I don't think he ran. I think he's hiding down there . . .'

'You want me to—'

The young pirate shook his head. 'No,' he muttered. 'You stay out of this unless I call for you. It's *my* fight. I'm either a pirate, or I'm a boy pretending to be one.'

He nodded at the bird, then swung around the branch and began to climb down the tree.

It took Davey several minutes to reach the ground, and he immediately hurried over to check on the fallen pirate. He was dead, but unfortunately he carried nothing of any immediate use.

Stepping back from the corpse, Davey drew his sword and glanced once again around the clearing. All was silent.

'Show yourself, pirate,' Davey muttered. 'If you *are* a pirate.'

A twig snapped behind him, and he spun around. The man now standing opposite Davey was twice his size. He was also armed.

'Give it up, kid,' Harper muttered. 'You may have got lucky killin' a pirate when his back was turned, but you're totally outmatched here. Drop your sword.'

Though shaking with fear inside, Davey was determined not to let his weakness show.

'Drop *yours*,' he said.

Harper acknowledged the reply with a curt nod of his head. 'Brave, kid. Brave but stupid.' He dashed across the clearing and drove the blade towards Davey, who managed to side-step at the last minute. The young pirate tried to knock the blade aside, but found it held with such strength that he ended up toppling himself.

Davey quickly rolled back and scrambled to his feet.

'Now you've felt my strength, lad, I'll give you *one* more chance to put your weapon *down*. If you don't, I swear I'll take a limb.'

Harper grinned, his teeth flashing as the first drops of rain fell on his cheeks, signalling the arrival of a shower.

'You'd do well to heed his word,' said a voice, and Davey almost jumped with shock as another pirate, taller and decidedly more menacing, emerged from between the trees. He was carrying a flaming branch in one hand and a sword in the other, and it was a few moments before Davey recognized him as Gullin, the pirate who'd almost recruited him for the *Herring* crew.

'Harper's a very good swordsman. He'd find it just as easy to hack off your arm as he would to kill you, and believe me, boy, we don't want to kill you. At least, not until Captain Morgan decides it's time. Frank Corsham wasn't so lucky, but he's dead now – his troubles are over. Tell me – did ol' Frank give you the box or did he merely advise you where it was? I'd really like to know.'

Davey took another step back, trying to keep both pirates in his eye-line. He was suddenly feeling small, foolish and very frightened.

'It's no good backing off,' Gullin continued. 'You'll observe Mister Spang moving along there, and seeing as you and your *jungle* friends murdered his brother, I don't advise backing into *his* blade.'

Davey took a quick glance back and noted, with mounting horror, the arrival of a third pirate. He was surrounded by steel.

McGuffin circled high above the clearing, his beady eyes fixed on the situation below. *Don't interfere*, he thought to himself, flapping on the air as the trio slowly circled his young master. *He's got to do these things on his own and, besides, he'll only end up resenting you.* The parrot's conscience added: *He'd have a job resenting you if he's dead, though.*

Far below, the three pirates were closing in for the kill.

'The sword,' Gullin repeated, carefully. 'Put it *down*. I'll not tell you again.'

Davey looked crestfallen. His face was reddening, his eyes were watering up and he was beginning to shiver in the rain.

'All right,' he muttered. 'If I have no other choice.'

The young pirate dropped his sword hand . . . and quickly raised the other. There was a pistol in it.

'Your move,' he snapped.

McGuffin swept into the clearing and alighted on a low branch. Harper eyed the parrot with pure hatred.

'I doubt you even know how to *use* that,' Gullin ventured, looking from Davey's face to the pistol, and back. 'Besides, your zombie companions have evidently abandoned you, so even if your weapon has *been* prepared – and I very much doubt that – you'd only muster a single shot. Who will you spend it on?'

Davey grinned at the pirate.

'You,' he muttered, side-stepping as Spang entered the clearing behind him. '*You're* the mouthy one.'

Gullin threw down his torch and made a slight, almost imperceptible movement with his jaw.

Spang and Harper began to creep in.

'Watch it, lad,' McGuffin squawked. 'They're on the move . . .'

Davey straightened his gun arm before him, and raised his sword arm to cover his back.

'Somebody kill that bird,' Gullin snapped, motioning to Harper who speedily produced a belt dagger and pitched it at the tree. The dagger hit the branch on which McGuffin was perched, but the parrot had flown.

Distracted by the action, Davey dropped his guard . . . and Gullin took the initiative. Leaping forward like a tiger, he struck out with a high kick that knocked Davey's pistol hand aloft. Then he drove his head into the young pirate's chin and knocked him to the floor.

Davey crashed into the damp mud, but managed to hold on to his sword and roll aside seconds before Gullin followed him up. Dragging himself back to his feet, Davey used a low branch to swing himself out of the danger, but Spang caught hold of him and quickly forced his arms behind his back.

Harper rushed across the clearing, planting two savage fists into the young pirate's stomach.

'Always show respect to your elders, boy,' he muttered. 'Always show respect to your el—'

The pirate was suddenly silenced by two rotted hands that reached around his chest and lifted him into the air.

'Burn my home, would you?' Threeday screamed, his ruby eyes molten in the pouring rain. 'Burn everything I own? Every memory I have!'

Davey watched in horror as the zombie threw his victim against a tree with such force that the man's back snapped like a twig.

Seizing the initiative, Davey ran his legs up the side of the tree and kicked away from it with violent abandon, sending both he and Spang crashing into the dirt. Then he threw back his head and connected with the pirate's nose.

'Arghh!' Spang released the young pirate and rolled around in the mud, clutching his face and moaning in pain.

Gullin had watched the scene with mounting interest, but he made no move to join the fight. Instead, he'd quickly rummaged through Harper's coats for his tinder-pistol and now held the weapon out in front of him, but it apparently failed to discharge even the smallest gout of flame. The same malfunction had claimed his own tinder, negating his ability to attack with fire.

Gullin looked from Harper's pistol to Threeday, and appeared to reach a decision. He tossed the weapon aside.

Spang, still clutching his wounded nose, tried to find his bearings, but Threeday dispatched him with a swift crack of the neck. The pirate collapsed into the dirt.

'Impressive,' Gullin said, his voice echoing through the jungle clearing. 'But you'd best stay back, *creature*. I've fought your kind before . . .'

'Yet I notice you're not attacking,' Davey pulled himself to his feet, sheathing his sword and reclaiming his empty pistol from the mud. 'You're outnumbered, Gullin. This pistol is pointed *right* at you and without your fire you're obviously no match for my friend. Why don't you turn tail and run back to Morgan?'

Gullin didn't take his eyes off Threeday.

'Mixing with the dead is no way for a pirate to make his name,' he warned, suddenly moving back at greater speed. The zombie made no move to pursue him.

'You've punched above your ability today, Swag,' Gullin continued. 'Henry Morgan never forgets a debt, and now you've shown your face he will not *rest* until he's even.'

'Even for *what*?' Davey screamed, stepping forward with Threeday at his side. 'He murdered my *entire* family – it should be me getting even with him.' Davey raced forward as Gullin receded into the shadows, feeling his anger beginning to overcome his fear. 'You go back and you tell Henry Morgan he'll never get back what Corsham stole from him. You hear me? NEVER!'

Davey could feel his eyes welling up with tears, but he stomped on, through the rain. It was only when McGuffin flapped on to his shoulder that he realized he was soaking wet and that Gullin was no longer in sight. He reached up to wipe his face with the sleeve of his coat.

'I've decided that I *will* tell you everything I know about Morgan,' squawked the parrot. 'But only if you don't try to put me in a cage again.'

Davey managed to smile through his tears. 'Thanks,' he said. 'No more cages. I promise.'

Turning on his heel, he padded back to where Threeday still stood – motionless – among the corpses.

'I appreciate your help,' Davey said, extending his hand, hopefully. 'I'm sorry they destroyed your home.'

The zombie didn't move, merely regarded Davey with an oddly curious expression.

'Henry Morgan will hunt you until you die,' he said. 'A man of his reputation will not allow one such as yourself to walk free.'

'Yes,' Davey agreed, withdrawing his offer of a handshake. 'I guess I'll just have to keep running until . . . until I get tired. What will you do? Build a new home? I'd help, only I think I should keep moving, at least until I can find whatever it is Morgan is after and get off the island with it.'

Threeday appeared to look past the young pirate, into the dark heart of the wood. Davey followed his expression.

'They will come back,' said the zombie. 'The man with the fire will seek us both. They will burn my jungle.'

Davey didn't know what to say. He merely ran a hand through his hair, sighed deeply and shook his head.

'Like I say, I'm really sorry. I made a terrible mistake yesterday and I'm *still* paying for it.'

Threeday turned as Davey started to walk past him.

'Where *are* you going?' he said, his eyes dimming somewhat as the rains intensified.

Davey sniffed, and gave a slight shrug.

'The thing Corsham took from Morgan is at the Foolstop, so I suppose I'm heading there.'

Threeday took a long time to speak again, and Davey was almost convinced that their conversation was over when the zombie suddenly announced: 'I will come with you.' The words were spoken in a matter-of-fact way, leaving little room for argument.

'You will?' Davey gasped, half in shock. 'Er . . . why would you do that?'

'He doesn't have much choice, does he?' McGuffin squawked. 'Seeing as you've gone and brought seven different kinds of destruction straight to his front door. Besides, we *need* all the friends we can get.'

'Th— that's true,' the young pirate admitted, nodding at Threeday. 'Th— thanks. I'd appreciate that.'

The zombie moved forward and took his bow and the arrow pouch from around Davey's neck.

'I know the way to the Foolstop,' he proclaimed, moving off towards the far side of the jungle. 'My family spent a lot of time up there . . . with Mister Paprika.'

'Mister Paprika,' Davey repeated. 'Is he the owner of the Foolstop?'

'Yes,' said the zombie, with a slight hint of anger. 'He was.'

The two companions progressed through the wood, McGuffin flapping noisily around them. Davey felt distinctly uneasy about his new companion, but at least he wasn't travelling *alone*.

# The Foolstop

*Uncork the powder flask, pour into barrel and stuff down with . . .*

Davey suddenly became self-conscious when he felt both McGuffin *and* the zombie looking over his shoulder.

'I'm trying to operate this pistol,' he explained, casting a nervous smile at his strange new friend. 'You know what a pistol is, right?'

The zombie maintained his silence. They'd left the main body of the jungle behind them and were now en route to the Foolstop Hotel. Threeday seemed to know exactly where he was going, so Davey didn't bother to question him (not that doing so would have done much good, as the zombie seemingly ignored most of his attempts at conversation).

*Perhaps he's not very bright*, the young pirate mused.

'I know exactly what a pistol is,' Threeday muttered,

suddenly breaking the silence. He reached out, snatched the weapon from Davey's hands and proceeded to fiddle with it. 'I have only been dead for a short time.'

'Oh . . . right.' Davey just stared at him. 'Er . . . b— but if you don't mind me saying, your skin is—'

'Dropping off? Yes, a strange side effect of the spell I am under. Ramrod, please.'

Davey nodded and rummaged in his coat for the rod. 'You're under a spell? I didn't think magic existed; not *really.*' *On the other hand*, he reminded himself, *I didn't think zombies existed until today.* 'Who put a spell on you? Was it something to do with your parents?'

'Lead,' Threeday requested, apparently oblivious to the question.

Davey thrust another hand into his pocket and produced a handful of tiny balls. Threeday took one and dropped it into the barrel, ramming the rod down after it. Then he lifted a small cover at the end of the pistol and poured some more powder into the flash-pan. Finally, he pulled back the cock and handed the loaded weapon to Davey.

'Fire it,' the zombie advised. 'Then you can reload it again to see if you are able.'

Davey took aim at one of the lower branches of a

tree beside the path, and pulled the trigger. He hadn't expected quite such an explosion of sound in the open air. The birds nesting above the branch apparently felt the same way, as all but one of them took off in fright.

'Nothing like announcing your presence,' McGuffin observed. The parrot had taken off a couple of seconds before Davey fired, but now it returned to its place on his shoulder. 'That entirely wise, was it? I mean, if Morgan's man was still in the jungle, he'd definitely know where you are *now* . . .'

'The weapon is useless if it cannot be used,' Threeday said, his mouth moving soullessly.

'Yeah,' Davey agreed. 'Besides, this island isn't exactly a labyrinth. They'll find me soon enough as it is.'

Threeday nodded . . . and the pair moved on.

Gullin scrambled up the rope ladder and leapt on to the *Rogue Herring*, a furious expression on his face and his sword still shaking in his hand.

The crew looked on as their new first mate marched straight into the captain's cabin and slammed the door behind him.

Inside, Morgan was smoking a strange-looking pipe and muttering to himself. He barely even glanced up as the pirate half-slumped, half-fell into the decrepit chair opposite him.

'I f— f— found Swag,' Gullin managed, trying to catch his breath and spit at the same time.

'Ya don' return wi' 'im, tho' – I can' sees no Swag, nor me box ona ship.'

'Harper, Jaggs, Spang and Nade are all dead,' the first mate explained, a little taken aback when the announcement drew no reaction from the brooding captain. 'Swag has somehow managed to get the undead to aid him – zombies. I only saw one myself, but it threw Harper against the wall so hard it clean broke his back!'

'Zombies is easy,' Morgan boomed. 'Fire 'em up an' watch 'em buuuuuurn.'

'Yes, Cap'n,' Gullin agreed. 'But not when you're on your own with four dead men facing *both* the zombie and a pirate-wannabe armed with a flintlock. I thought it best to come back here and report to you, Cap'n . . . save not coming back at all.'

Morgan removed his pipe and, clambering to his feet, strode across the cabin. At first, Gullin thought the pirate was preparing to strike him down, but the illusion was quickly dispelled when Morgan moved past him and unhooked a heavy belt from a metal stand beside the door. The belt was adorned with swords, circular blades and various other oddly-shaped weapons of combat or torture. Morgan fastened it around his waist.

'Get 'em ready,' the captain boomed. 'We're goin' zombie 'untin'.'

Gullin jumped up and made for the cabin door, pausing only briefly before he took his leave.

'How many should I—'

'All of 'em,' Morgan growled. 'We're takin' the 'ole crew. I don' wan' this whelp slippin' thro' me fingers agin.'

Davey couldn't seem to get more than the odd word out of Threeday. They'd been travelling for what felt like an age, and the afternoon was pressing on, yet the zombie showed no signs of fatigue as they negotiated the woody beginnings of the peninsula.

He was about to ask Threeday if he knew anything about the donkey that led him into the jungle, when the zombie suddenly stopped and crouched down beside the path.

'A problem?' Davey asked, one hand on his pistol and the other finding the hilt of his sword.

Threeday snatched something from the soggy

ground and, returning to the wary pirate, thrust it into his hands.

'What is this?' Davey asked, trying to make out the words scribbled on it.

'A flyer from the Foolstop Hotel,' explained Threeday, turning the parchment over. 'It was printed in better days, when the hotel – and the island – were inhabited by *decent* people.'

Davey tried to imagine what the flyer *had* been like. Despite being soaked, it was a bit dog-eared at the corners and tattered along the sides, but otherwise *very grand*. It read:

*DOOTOW PAPRIKA PRESENTS*
## THE FOOLSTOP HOTEL
*Benefits Include*
**hot water (some of the time) friendly banter (most of the time) cheap rum (at all times)**
*The above and more, set in a luxurious hilltop residence commanding a stunning view of Cocos Island. Two pieces of eight for a comfortable bed, a tasty breakfast and a scrumptious evening meal.*
**NOW OPEN ALL YEAR ROUND!**

Davey whistled between his teeth.

'Wow,' he said, snatching on to the possibility of an actual conversation with the zombie. 'It sounds like it was *the* place to be.'

'Yes,' Threeday muttered. 'Mister Paprika was a very successful businessman. He made a lot of money, most of it from deals with . . . unwelcome visitors.'

'Mmm?' Davey was gazing intently at the flyer.

'D— do you ever go up there?' he ventured, as Threeday began to walk on.

'No,' said the zombie, determinedly. 'Not any more. No one has been this way in a very long time.'

Again, there was something about the boy's secretive manner that gnawed at Davey's curiosity. He was sure Threeday's anger had a lot to do with his late family, but asking the zombie about himself had thus far proved to be . . . well, a *dead* end.

Davey straightened himself up.

'Well, I really appreciate everything you've done for me,' he said, deciding a change of subject was probably for the best. 'I promise I'll think of some way to repay you just as soon as I've found Morgan's . . . er . . . whatever it is.'

The jungle thinned out for a time, then seemed to

return with a vengeance. The path that wound towards the peninsula to the Foolstop Hotel was completely overgrown, and the late afternoon sun only managed to break through the overhanging trees in thin slivers. Threeday had to snap thin branches and yank down clusters of vines before they could go on.

'Wow,' Davey muttered. 'You weren't joking when you said you hadn't been up here in a long time.'

Threeday nodded. 'I never joke.'

*You're not kidding*, Davey thought. *You'd have to have a personality for that . . .*

They'd been walking along in silence for some time. Even McGuffin, who was usually full of annoyingly abusive conversation, hadn't made a single sound for the best part of an hour.

Eventually, the path widened out and dull light began to seep through the trees more frequently. Threeday seemed to know each new track like the back of his worm-ridden hand, and in no time they emerged from the jungle to an incredible scene.

'Your objective,' said the zombie, his ragged flesh glowing a pale green in the afternoon light. He was pointing east. 'The end of Paragon Peninsula.'

Davey looked out towards a long, snake-like piece of land that extended about half a mile from the island.

It looked as though Cocos had reached out an arm in an effort to pull in some of the sea.

Davey cupped his hands around his forehead and squinted into the distance. There, on a high hill overlooking the peninsula, was a vast and very impressive building.

'Is that the Foolstop Hotel?' he hazarded.

'It is,' said Threeday, with a grim smile.

'What're those funny-shaped trees around the base of the hill?'

'A small forest – the islanders called it Glad's Wood, because they always said they felt glad to be out of it. The hunk of rock a little way down the peninsula is called the Beached Whale. People seemed to name everything, once . . .'

Threeday glanced away into the middle distance, as if awaiting some sort of spiritual instruction.

'Er . . .' Davey swallowed, trying to decide if it was worth actually *telling* this strange creature anything. 'I'm trying to become a pirate.'

'The world doesn't need more pirates.'

'You're wrong,' Davey told him. 'It needs *good* pirates . . . and I was hoping to be one of the first. A man called Frank Corsham promised me a boat if I fetched this parcel for him.'

Threeday's gleaming eyes flickered slightly.

'You were set up,' he muttered. 'And now Henry Morgan and his men will hunt you down and destroy you.'

'They can try,' Davey said, determinedly. 'Morgan already murdered my mother and father, back when I was a baby. I don't know how I escaped then, but now he knows I'm alive he's obviously trying to finish what he started.'

'You are walking into a trap,' said Threeday, suddenly. 'The Foolstop is at the end of the peninsula; if the pirates catch up with you while you are still inside, there will be no escape for you.'

Davey frowned at him. 'What about *you*? You're here with me, after all!'

'Yes,' agreed Threeday. 'But I fear not for myself, not any more. Death – for me – would be a mercy . . .'

Davey clenched his fists and gritted his teeth. The zombie's evident despair somehow made him feel even more determined to fight.

'Guess we'll just see what we'll see, won't we?' he said, tapping the pistol at his belt. 'Either way, you've been a great help. I'm truly sorry about what happened to your home, and I don't expect you to come any further.'

He started off down the hill, but Threeday grabbed his arm and pulled him back.

'I will stay with you,' said the zombie.

For the first time, Davey looked the creature directly in the face. 'Why? I don't understand! What's the point of you coming with me if you're not even going to talk to me! I *know* something happened to your family, and I know that it has something to do with *why* you are . . . as you are. But you have to let me know something about yourself . . . because I've already got one useless pet and I don't want another . . .'

Threeday glared at the young pirate, and his expression seemed to undergo several transformations, through hatred, outrage, annoyance and regret. Eventually, however, the creature just looked wretched.

'I will tell you of my family when there is more time. I travel with you because you brought vandals and murderers into my home.' He paused. 'Because I also hate the name Henry Morgan . . . and because it has been a long time since I've had a friend, even one as unexpected as you.'

Davey found he couldn't look at the zombie as it finished its sentence.

'Thanks,' he said, awkwardly. 'I really need friends at the moment. I guess I just wanted to make sure you were a real friend, and not just travelling with me so that you could somehow get revenge for your home being destroyed.'

Threeday smiled for the first time, a rather unsettling sight to witness.

'If I had wanted revenge,' he muttered, 'I'd have ripped your arms and legs off by now.'

'Arms and legs, arms and legs,' McGuffin squawked mechanically, as he jerked awake. 'Chance'd be a fine thing. Where are we then? Anywhere nice?'

The two companions dropped their conversation, and continued along what remained of the twisty, overgrown path.

The Beached Whale was an awful lot bigger up close than it had looked from the edge of the jungle. In fact, it rose higher than most of the trees surrounding it. Davey wondered what it looked like from the air, and couldn't help imagining an immense bald patch.

'We are almost upon it,' Threeday muttered. The zombie was walking with such lengthy strides that he was almost running. Davey didn't know how the creature even managed to *stand* on legs so rotted, let alone how he moved with such predatory speed.

'Nice spot for a picnic,' said McGuffin,

conversationally. 'Short Jack Plat'num liked his picnics. Always gave me a few crackers 'n' all. Gentleman, he was—'

'Until he hung himself,' Davey finished, with a grin.

They were about two thirds of the way along the only road on the peninsula, at a point where the land began to climb. Soon after passing the Beached Whale, they entered Glad's Wood, and Davey admitted that Threeday had been right about the place; he couldn't wait to get out of it. The trees were banana shaped, and they sprouted from the ground at odd angles. It looked like gravity had temporarily forgotten about the place, but might remember at any moment.

'Wrang Trees,' said Threeday, as if he could read the pirate's thoughts. 'Nobody knows what keeps them standing.'

'Would you lie down if you lived in this dump?' McGuffin squawked, his claws digging into the young pirate's shoulder with renewed vigour. 'I wouldn't.'

Davey pointed up ahead.

'Look, they're blocking the path,' he said. 'We'll have to go around them.'

'It was different once,' Threeday continued, leading the way. 'Paprika used to keep them off the path, in case they stopped treasure-hunters from getting to the hotel and spending more money. Since he . . . *died*, things have fallen into neglect.' Once again, the zombie's voice had an edge to it. 'Everything does, eventually.'

Threeday had taken them on to a smaller path that led unhindered to the summit of the hill. Davey boggled at the Foolstop as they approached it.

'Stone me,' said McGuffin. 'And I thought Short Jack let his place go . . .'

The hotel was quite a sight. An old, rambling structure, it stood about seven storeys high with flaking white walls and far too many broken windows. There was an enormous weather-vane on the top of the Foolstop and several more positioned on a number of smaller roofs all over the building. Davey noticed that the main vane was fashioned into the twin letters 'FH'; it was also rusted, and bowing dangerously. The entire building looked extremely unsafe.

Threeday had already made his way up some weed-strangled steps to an imposing front door. He knocked, first with his skin-peeled knuckles and then again using the heavy brass doorknocker.

'I thought you said Paprika was dead?'

The zombie didn't bother to turn around.

'Oh, he is. Yet some customs must remain observed, out of habit if nothing else. I owe Paprika ... more than I gave him.'

A minute or two passed in silence. There was no answer.

'What're we waiting for, exactly?' chimed McGuffin. 'A written invitation?'

'We may go in, now,' Threeday advised them. 'A path has been cleared for us by the gods of light.'

'Kind of 'em,' the parrot observed.

Davey gave a puzzled nod and then absent-mindedly tried the door handle. The front door swung open with a shivering creak. Threeday stepped over the threshold, allowing Davey to move past him, and the two companions peered into the gloom.

'I'm goin' to 'ave a quick shufty round the back,' McGuffin squawked, flapping into the air and taking off at high speed.

The hallway of the hotel was dusty, musty and very dark.

'I can't believe it's been left in this state,' Davey admitted. 'I mean, you'd have thought someone from town would have—'

'No,' said Threeday, firmly. 'The townsfolk were deathly afraid of Paprika. They never came up here when he was alive . . . and they certainly wouldn't do so now.'

Davey returned his attention to the dereliction around him, and suddenly a thought occurred.

'Is Paprika . . . like you?' he asked, stepping back as Threeday turned towards him. 'The walking dead?'

'No,' the zombie replied, another grim smile on his decaying face. 'Paprika was a voodoo priest, albeit one who betrayed his gods and seemed more interested in money than he was in people.'

'You . . . er . . . you didn't like Paprika very much, did you?'

Threeday smiled, bitterly. 'You could say that,' he muttered. 'Seeing as it was he who made me like this.'

Davey glanced at his new friend for several moments, his interest in the house suddenly taking second place to his fascination with the incredible creature standing beside him.

'I don't understand,' said the young pirate, slowly. 'Why would Paprika bring *you* back from the dead but not himself?'

Threeday shook his foetid skull. 'You talk as though my condition is a gift,' he said, striding over to Davey and glaring at him. 'It is a CURSE, don't you see? An evil, sickening, soul-destroying curse. I'm doomed to watch myself waste away, piece by piece, until

I'm nothing but dust . . . I'll survive another year in my present state, and that's if I'm *lucky*.'

Davey was about to offer a shaky reply when the zombie quickly turned and made off down the hall. About halfway along the last quarter of the corridor, he loped into a doorway on the left. Davey drew his pistol and followed.

The Foolstop was in a terrible state. All the walls were cracked, gnats crowded every room and there were barrels of rum stacked ten high in some places. A family of rats had made a home in the kitchen, and it took Threeday several minutes to coax Davey down from a table when he saw them.

'A *pirate* who's afraid of rats,' the zombie muttered.

'I know, I know,' said Davey, checking the cluttered floor-space for more signs of vermin. 'I admit I'm not your *average* salty sea-dog, but I'm still going to make a fine pirate, I reckon . . .'

Threeday turned his burning eyes towards him. 'You will be famous, certainly. There aren't many pirates with no ships who walk into a patch of quicksand to read a warning sign which says, "Don't walk into this patch of quicksand". You are, indeed, a one-off.'

'Yes, all right. Point taken.' Davey wasn't going to

argue, especially as this was the first time he'd heard Threeday make a joke of any sort. 'I bet rats can't do *you* any damage though, am I right?'

Threeday shrugged. 'They could gnaw one of my feet off. That wouldn't be welcome.'

'Yeah,' said Davey, sarcastically. 'But surely losing a foot wouldn't worry a zom— ... er ... I mean some*body* like you.'

Threeday nodded. 'It would certainly be something to hit you in the face with. Now, do you think we can stop talking about rats. I'm a lot more interested in finding your "item" and getting out of here before those pirates return to put me to the torch.'

'You're right,' Davey agreed. 'Why don't we split up? We can probably search the place a lot quicker that way.'

Davey's search of the first floor of the Foolstop Hotel yielded nothing except dusty bedrooms, broken furniture and an awful lot of dead spiders.

Then, after working his way up a second rickety flight of stairs, past a number of old paintings showing the hotel enjoying better days, he found himself in a lengthy passage with doors leading off either side.

Davey swallowed. There were six dead rats on the

floor outside one of the rooms. Strangely, they had been placed in a circle. He decided to search *this* room first, but he soon wished he hadn't.

There were flies everywhere and, as soon as Davey opened the door, he was hit in the face by a strong odour comprising dead flowers and garlic. He made a face, and tried to peer through the swarm of insects hovering in the air between the door and the bed. Then he put a hand in front of his mouth and edged further into the room.

There was someone or some*thing* asleep on the bed. At least, it looked as if it was asleep. Davey needed to get quite a bit closer before he could see it clearly.

He took another few steps.

The sleeping creature was in fact a very large dog, a bloodhound, unless he was very much mistaken. It appeared to be breathing normally, if a little slowly, and its eyes were rolled right back in its head.

Davey noticed that there was a box wedged between its forepaws, a box with the word 'Morgan' scratched into the side.

*That's it*, he thought. *What should I do now? Try to grab it? What if that dog isn't dead? It's breathing!*

He wanted to run out into the hall and call Threeday, but he definitely *didn't* want to wake the hound. There was a chance, however remote, that it was rabid . . . albeit in a slumber.

Davey crept forward. *Hmm . . . can a dog be rabid and asleep at the same time? Probably. I wonder if I can grab the box without the beast waking up.*

It was a stupid idea that was almost certainly doomed to fail, but Davey had little common sense so he tried to do it anyway. The dog growled a bit as his fingers brushed its maw, but the resulting sound was more dreamy than aggressive.

Against all odds, Davey's plan worked. He lifted the box out from between the hound's giant paws, one flopping sideways like a cut of meat as he moved it, and the dog went on sleeping like a baby.

Davey swallowed, holding his breath for fear of inhaling a dozen or more flies. Then, clutching the box as if it were a water bottle in the desert, he sneaked from the room and ran back downstairs to find Threeday.

As he arrived at the foot of the hotel's creaky, worm-ridden staircase, Davey found McGuffin perched on what remained of one of the banisters.

'You found it, then,' the bird squawked, eyeing the box in the young pirate's arms.

'Yeah, think so. It's got Morgan's moniker scratched into it. I don't really want to open the lid until we're away from here, though. Where's Threeday got to?'

'Dunno – aint seen 'im since I left the pair of you at the front door . . . blimey, what's *this* place supposed to be?'

Davey had stumbled into an ancient-looking glasshouse that appeared to form an extension to the main kitchen.

It was hot, smelly and packed to the roof with twisty tropical plants.

There was also another smell, underneath the odour of heat and leaves. Davey couldn't tell what it was but he knew it was far, far worse. He was just thinking how dreadful the source of the smell must be when, rounding a corner between two giant ferns, he suddenly came face to face with it.

The corpse was sitting in a deck chair amid a small jungle of plants. A straw hat with the words 'Hotel Manager' scrawled across the top in black ink made it clear that the skeleton was that of Paprika, erstwhile owner of the Foolstop Hotel. He was holding an ancient, rather battered cutlass in one hand, and he looked as though he had been dead for a very long time.

'He's seen better days,' McGuffin squawked, flapping on to a thick plant beside the chair. 'Better years, come to that.'

Davey cupped a hand over his mouth and cursed his luck.

'Bad things happen to bad people.' Threeday's voice broke the silence, as the zombie emerged from the shadows behind the corpse. '*He* pretended to be a friend to this island, but he betrayed us all. Henry Morgan was just an evil pirate when he first met Paprika. It was this evil *wretch* who made him . . . who told him about . . . the ostrich.'

Threeday noted Davey's confused expression and shook his rotting skull. 'There's no time to explain, right now. I see you have your box; we need to leave.'

'Yeah,' muttered Davey, finally tearing his gaze away from the spectacle. 'Let's get out of here, shall—'

A very loud thump interrupted the young pirate and almost caused him to leap out of his skin. McGuffin flapped into a mad panic and even Threeday seemed momentarily uneasy.

All eyes turned to the hallway.

'The front door?' Davey hazarded, staring imploringly at the zombie.

'Definitely,' Threeday advised. 'But we should go via

the kitchen and not straight up the hall. You'll need food.'

'Food?' Davey exclaimed. 'But what if that is Mor—'

'You'll still need food,' Threeday snapped. 'Besides, if you go straight up the hall and they *are* out there, you could be painting a target on yourself. Let's move.'

'Fine, but *I'm* going first. It's ME they're after, and you've put yourself in enough danger for one day. Here, take the box.' He handed Corsham's booty over to Threeday, and nodded.

The Foolstop's kitchen was very well stocked, but unfortunately most of the food was mouldy. Davey managed to find some hard bread that he should probably have left alone and a sealed bottle labelled 'Cocoswater', which Threeday quickly explained was the blanket name for any water drawn from the ancient well in the centre of the town.

'Ready?' Threeday said, his eyes molten in the gloom of the room.

'As I'll ever be.' Davey waited for McGuffin to settle on his shoulder, then put a hand on his belt. 'Let's go . . .'

The two friends lowered their heads and began to creep towards the front door. Davey felt as though a terrible fate awaited him on the other side . . .

The front door of the Foolstop Hotel creaked open, and a pistol shaft emerged, very slowly, from within. It was followed by a young and extremely nervous-looking pirate.

'Get off my shoulder,' Davey hissed. 'Just in case . . .'

McGuffin flapped on to the remains of a nearby window ledge, as Davey stared down at the floor of the porch.

There was a boot lying there, obviously thrown from the garden.

Davey looked out into the greenery, but silence and stillness reigned.

'I'm going out,' the young pirate whispered. 'Cover me . . . er . . . well, you know . . .'

Davey tiptoed out to the edge of the steps, under the dark shadow of the hotel porch. The garden of the Foolstop seemed a lot wider when you were coming at it from the hotel itself. There were a large number of suspicious-looking bushes and plenty of gnarled trees to hide behind.

Davey waited a moment, his eyes searching every inch of the garden for signs of unnatural movement. Then he turned back towards the hotel.

'I think we're OK,' he called. 'No sign of anyone.'

Threeday emerged from the giant doorway, and slowly scanned the garden.

'We should have gone out the back way,' he muttered. 'There's only an old cemetery – we could take a trip down there and—'

Suddenly, a deep, booming voice cried out:

'Freeze where ya stand, Swag! I'm thinking ol' 'Enry has ya surrounded. Nobody shoots 'til I've gutted the whelp.'

Davey solidified, with only his twitching pistol hand betraying him as a statue.

The garden had quite literally come alive. Pirates stepped from behind every tree, clambered out of every bush and even emerged from the high grass in some places. There must have been more than twenty of them in total, all with cutlasses drawn, a handful carrying torches; one or two were loading pistols. They weren't attacking, though, and Davey soon learned the reason for this.

A lone figure was heading up the central path, which ran through the garden. He was tall, massively built and disproportionately ugly; a giant of a man. He had a long nose, hardly any chin, and a beard so thick that it looked as though someone had thrown a bucket of ink over him.

Henry Morgan – Davey realized with a terrible clarity that he was looking upon the monster who'd killed his parents.

'Game's up, kid!' he roared, coming to a halt in the middle of the garden and drawing his own deadly cutlass from a belt crammed full of assorted torture instruments. 'You 'scaped me wrath once as a nipper, bu' Mallory made a mistake when he took ya fro' me. Ne'r agin. Now you'll die like yer ol' man an' his wench. Throw down the box and 'cept ya fate. If Mallory's in there wi' ya, tell 'im to get out the shadows an' face ol' 'Enry . . .'

Before Davey had a chance to reply, Threeday pulled him back into the shade of the porch.

'We have to run!' he said. 'We don't stand a chance!'

'Run where? We're on the end of the peninsula! Besides, I reckon they might fall back if I can get a decent shot off . . .'

'Get a shot off? Are you CRAZY?' Threeday's eyes gleamed in the half-dark. 'Davey, listen to me before we *both* die. Henry Morgan is out there with his crew, who are probably all either demented or insane. Some of those pirates have pistols. They'll shoot you dead before you can get a single shot out, and they'll burn me before I can lay a hand on them!'

'But that man killed my parents,' Davey growled, sweat beading on his forehead. 'I've been waiting my whole life for this! I have to do it, Threeday . . . I have to face him for *me*.'

Turning aside the zombie's pleas, Davey thrust the pistol back into his belt, took the box that Threeday had tucked under one arm, and stepped out into the light.

'H— hold your fire!' he cried, advancing.

From all over the garden came shouts of 'dumb scallywag' and 'spawn o' wretches'.

Davey ignored them and focussed his full attention on the imposing shape of Henry Morgan. The man was even more terrifying in the flesh than he had been in Uncle Jake's story of his parents' demise.

'Morgan,' he began, standing his ground at the top of the hotel steps. 'I've waited a long time for this moment . . .'

'O' course you 'ave, whelp, all grown up and seekin' measure. It's revenge you wants, revenge aplenty.'

Morgan's smile bled across his face like a fresh wound.

'You've got your father's flaws, boy,' he boomed. 'Your daddy came towards me when he should 'ave bin runnin' too . . .'

Davey gritted his teeth, but stood his ground nonetheless.

'Will you die like yer ol' man?' Morgan continued, his mocking grin spreading even wider. 'Or 'ave you got Corsham's luck, a' well as 'is stolen bounty?'

Davey looked down at the box in his shaking hands; for a moment, he'd completely forgotten he was holding it.

'Well?' Morgan prompted. 'You wanna die slow or you wannit quick? Make yerself 'eard now, 'fore I take the choice from ya. Throw yersel' on ol' 'Enry's mercy – what little I got left – and you might see in a new moon . . . or you can follow yer parents into the ground where ya standin.'

'I— I hate you . . .' Davey admitted, trying to stop his hands shaking. The sheer stench of the man was breaking his confidence, reminding him of the past. 'I'll m— make you pay for what you did.'

Davey felt ashamed by the sudden fear that consumed him, freezing him almost to the spot. All his courage had left him. Threeday was right; he stood no chance against this mountain of a man, no chance at all. He'd been foolish even to think he could fight an unholy terror like Henry Morgan.

Davey looked back at the hotel, but he couldn't see

Threeday's face at any of the windows. Eventually, he swallowed and returned his attention to the growling captain. Morgan had already advanced halfway up the hotel's front steps.

'H— have mercy,' he stammered, hating himself for his cowardice and knowing it was the wrong thing to say as soon as the words had left his mouth – the pirate had no intention of sparing him. 'I was only doing Mister Corsham a favour. I didn't know . . .'

There followed a few seconds of terrible silence.

'Well,' Morgan boomed. 'That 'bout puts a whole new face on ya problems, don't it, boy?'

Morgan strode forward, taking the steps two at a time, and Davey, in his trembling state, suddenly found himself nose to nose with the man who'd slaughtered his mother and father, arguably the most fearsome pirate ever to ride the waves.

'Open the box.'

It wasn't a request; it was an order that had to be obeyed. Davey flinched under the pirate's terrible glare.

'Open it. Now. Or die like yer mother did: in these arms. Hahahahaha!'

Davey cried with anger, spit forming at the edge of his lips, but he found his hands were moving of their own accord. They made short work of the twine, and the lid of the box lifted with little or no pressure applied to it.

Davey gasped.

Inside was without a doubt the most terrifying thing he had ever laid eyes upon. It was a decapitated head, partly decomposed, with a mop of rotting, jet-black hair and a grotesque length of beard. The mouth was open, its lips wrapped around a scratchy piece of parchment that had been rolled into a tube.

'Do you know what this is?' Morgan smiled, displaying a set of cracked and rotted teeth. 'This,' he snarled, 'is the 'ead of Will Dampier. No' much o' a pirate but he had a fair eye for the treasurin'. Ol' Will bit off more 'an he could chew. This is all we 'cided to save o' him, a trophy o' sorts. The map it 'olds is a key to *ol' 'Enry's own secret treasure*. You're honoured to 'old it, boy ... even if ya won' live long enough ta see inside ...'

Despite his own terror and increasing nausea, Davey found himself snarling at Morgan. He knew that, somewhere in the shadows behind him, Threeday was listening to the pirate and, somehow, he felt the boy's anger welling up along with his own.

Morgan leaned in so close that Davey could feel his malodorous breath.

'Tha' map leads to Charnel Island,' he whispered, the stink of his flesh almost too much to bear. 'A place where somethin' special lies in wait f'r ol' 'Enry. Gi' ya somethin' ta wonder on in the afterlife, kid . . . Gi' ya somethin' ta wonder on . . .'

This was *it*. All became clear in an instant, and suddenly Davey knew that Morgan intended to kill him now, just as he'd killed his mother and father sixteen years previously. A hundred different thoughts ran through his head all at the same time, but the one that kept flashing on and off was 'fight'.

This man couldn't be hurt, though. He was legend. He was . . . invincible.

Davey's train of thought was blown to the four winds when McGuffin appeared, as if by magic, and dropped on to Morgan's face. The parrot screeched, clawed and flapped in an explosion of fury.

Shouts were heard all around the garden as the rough assembly of pirates suddenly rushed forward.

Davey didn't have time to think, so just did the first thing that came into his head. He kicked out, as hard as he could, just as McGuffin took off again.

Morgan was still reeling from the parrot's attack. Caught with the full force of Davey's kick, he tumbled backwards down the stairs and landed with a loud thud on the path below.

Davey glanced down, and remembered the pistol. He'd been holding it beneath the box, so that none of the pirates knew he was armed. In one quick movement, and without quite knowing why, he snatched the map from Dampier's mouth and tossed the box aside. Then he backed into the house, firing off a warning shot that caused several pirates to dive for nearby bushes. Nobody fired back, and when Davey's heel found the door of the Foolstop Hotel, he was quickly pulled inside. Seconds later, the pirates seemed to overcome their hesitation and pistol shots erupted all over the garden. All went wild, smashing windows and spinning several of the strange weather-vanes on their rusty bases.

'McGuffin attacked him!' Davey panted, racing up the Foolstop's central staircase with Threeday practically snapping at his heels. The zombie, who never seemed to look actually afraid, was nevertheless in no mood to hang around and wait for the pirates to arrive. 'He actually attacked *Henry Morgan*.'

'So did you,' Threeday reminded him. 'We don't have much time; they'll be in here in seconds. This way.'

'But McGuffin is still out.'

'There's more to that bird than meets the eye. THIS WAY. NOW.'

Threeday overtook Davey and dashed off down the east passage. The pair then ascended four more flights before arriving beside two doors at the end of a small corridor on the fifth floor. Threeday waited a few seconds for Davey to catch his breath.

'Left one,' said the zombie. 'Quick!'

Davey pulled open the little portal and they scampered up the new flight together, bursting through the attic door and slamming it shut behind them.

Luckily, the attic turned out to be full of broken furniture, and Davey grabbed several bulky chairs to prop against the portal. One of the larger seats was so heavy that, after three attempts at lifting it, he and Threeday had to slide the wretched thing across the floor instead.

'Do you think *Morgan* made a copy of that?' Threeday said, collapsing on the armchair with a weary sigh and pointing toward the map still clutched in the young pirate's hand.

Davey shrugged.

'Who knows? Besides, I'm not interested in the map. I just want us both to get out of this hotel alive.'

Threeday raised himself to his full height. His eyes

were glowing and he looked absolutely furious. Davey already knew that the zombie hated pirates, but he also fancied that he'd heard a particularly nasty growl when Threeday had mentioned Morgan. Could it be possible that they shared a mutual hatred for the same man?

Davey locked eyes with his strange friend. 'I don't suppose you know how we can get out of here?'

A few minutes later, Davey peered down at the garden below. Several of the pirates were still milling around down there. Davey guessed that this remaining rabble were probably the cutlass wielders, as Morgan would undoubtedly have wanted the pistol carriers with him when he entered the hotel. He wondered how long it would take the pirate to realize they'd gone for the attic, but he didn't have to wonder for long – an eruption of lead shot suddenly peppered the attic door.

'GET OUT THERE!' Threeday snapped.

The young pirate dived for the floor as more shots opened small holes in the wood, and scrambled frantically across the floor.

'THE WINDOW, IDIOT!' Threeday screamed. 'THE WINDOW!'

Davey rolled behind a smashed bookcase. 'You're joking, right? The garden's chock full of pirates!'

'And you'll be chock full of holes,' the zombie screamed, as a piece of lead shot removed part of his ear. 'NOW GET OUT THERE BEFORE I KILL YOU MYSELF!'

Davey hung from the attic window of the Foolstop Hotel, legs scrambling for purchase on the cracked walls. Uncle Jake had told him many times of his adventures at Port Gildrake, which included one episode on the roof of the Royal Museum. The trick, when hanging over any precipice, Jake had advised, was never to look down.

Davey looked down.

Far below, in the Foolstop's overgrown garden, a crew of twenty or more pirates stood screaming abuse and angrily waving cutlasses. They looked like a pack of hungry sharks, and Davey felt sure they could do just as much damage if he fell on those cutlasses – he'd be skewered like a pig on a spit. All things considered, there was only one way to go. Up.

Davey clenched his fingers and pulled himself close to the window ledge. Then his feet found a small dent in the stonework and he was away. He climbed through the attic window, then out again and, finally, upwards. The guttering groaned under his weight, creaked dangerously and began to shy away from the roof, but Davey had seized his opportunity. He swung himself up and over the edge of the roof, rolled on to his back and stared, thankfully, up at the sky. It looked a lot nearer.

'Every man for himself,' squawked a familiar voice. McGuffin flapped overhead and landed on the highest part of the Foolstop's multi-layered roofscape.

Davey watched the bird and shook his head in amazement. Then he turned, leaned over the roof and helped to pull Threeday up on to the slates with him; it wasn't a difficult task, as the zombie was all skin and bone. Infuriatingly, he still looked calm . . . even when his foot slipped and he almost plummeted into the garden below.

'Thank you,' Threeday said, as Davey helped his rotted fingers find purchase on the roof tiles. 'You owe me one less.'

'You're too kind.'

Davey struggled to his feet and peered over the edge of the roof. The pirates on the ground were still waving their cutlasses in the air, but there was a new threat and it was a good deal closer. Two mangy pirates, both wearing scarlet bandannas, were leaning out of the attic window. Both were holding pistols.

Davey stepped back from the edge of the roof seconds before two blasts removed part of the Foolstop's complicated drainage system. Then he peered over the edge again.

'Are they climbing up?' Threeday asked, clenching his fists and gritting the few teeth that still clung for survival among his rotting gums.

'No, they're reloading,' said Davey. 'And if their pistols are anything like mine, it might just buy us some time.'

He turned and stared out over the landscape. The view was incredible; most of Cocos Island was visible from the top of the Foolstop Hotel.

'This way,' Threeday instructed. Davey hurried over to him.

There were a number of weather-vanes sprouting from different tiles all over the roof, and a large, unstable-looking chimney pot occupied centre stage. There was also, at the back of the roof, a bucket pulley. The bucket in itself wasn't of any interest, but the rope on which it hung ran all the way from the roof to . . .

'Wow! It goes all the way over to the next peninsula!' Davey gasped, yanking hard on the rope. 'Is that where the cemetery is?'

Threeday nodded.

'Don't hang about, then,' McGuffin advised, taking wing and flapping past them.

Davey took a step sideways, ripped off his shirt and swung it over the rope so the sleeves hung down on either side. Then he gripped the cuffs, winding the sleeves around his fists until he was certain he had a firm hold on the material.

'Come on, Threeday,' he said. 'Put your arms around my neck, and hold on tight.'

'I'm stronger. I should—'

'Come on, will you!'

The zombie did as instructed and threw two foetid arms around Davey's neck. The young pirate held his breath.

'OK, now don't let go, whatever you do,' he finished. Then he jumped into the air, tucked in his legs, and the two companions flew down the rope at a near deadly speed, pistol fire ringing out all around them.

Davey and Threeday came to land atop a tombstone in Cocos Island cemetery. The pirate removed his torn shirt from the rope and pulled it back on, while Threeday took a moment to steady himself. Davey noticed that the zombie tended to walk like someone who was trying to remember the right steps.

He wondered why this was, but his thoughts were swiftly interrupted.

'Move it, lardfoot!' McGuffin screeched, flying for the safety of a nearby tree.

'They're following us down the rope,' Threeday growled. 'We don't have much time. I could fight these for you . . .'

'No! We're *both* getting out of this . . .'

'They don't have fire—'

'I don't care!'

'Fine. In here quickly!'

Davey looked to where Threeday was pointing.

'That's a crypt!' he exclaimed, suddenly backing away. 'I'm not hiding in there. I'd rather make a run for it!'

'THERE'S NO TIME! THEY CAN'T SEE US YET - QUICKLY!'

'No! It's dark and full of dead people . . . er . . . no offence intended.'

Threeday gritted his teeth.

'Look,' he snapped. 'You can either go in now as a guest or you can wait around and end up as a resident. The choice is yours . . .'

Davey muttered under his breath and hurried inside the crypt. Threeday pulled the heavy door closed behind them. Then darkness descended. The three friends found a deep flight of stone steps and, negotiating them carefully, found themselves in a dank, dark room containing an ancient-looking tomb. Threeday waited at the top of the steps for a time.

'Can you hear them?' Davey prompted, after several minutes had elapsed.

'Just about,' Threeday answered. 'I can hear echoes. They're definitely in the cemetery, but I think a few have headed for the path. They won't hang around long in this place – pirates can be a superstitious bunch. Either way, we need to stay in here for a bit.'

Davey peered around him, then put his head in his hands and sighed.

'I can't believe Morgan remembered me,' he whinged. 'And he mentioned a name . . . Mallory . . . *that* must be the name of the person who rescued me. And speaking of rescue, I can't believe you attacked Morgan like that! I tell you, McGuffin, I was REALLY impressed. Why did you do tha—'

'Forget Mallory,' McGuffin squawked. The interruption was so sudden that Davey started. 'You've got enough problems without going off in search of old ghosts.'

Davey grimaced. 'I'll bet Morgan despised him for

saving my life. I wonder what happened to him? He must still be alive if Morgan . . .'

'Something terrible happened to Mallory,' said Threeday, arriving at the foot of the steps as Davey began to wipe crypt-dust from his arms. 'Something really, unspeakably terrible . . .'

'You think?'

'I don't think, Davey, I *know*. I was . . . involved.'

Davey's attention was suddenly focussed on the skulking shadow cast by the zombie. 'Wait a minute – how do you mean *involved*?'

Threeday seemed to hesitate before he spoke again.

'I supplied ingredients for Paprika's voodoo enchantments . . . and I know he did *something* to a cabin boy called Mallory. Paprika—'

'You did what?' Davey's shock was made evident when he leapt up and banged his head on the ceiling. 'Why would you do something like that? I thought you DESPISED Paprika?'

Threeday sighed, and the glow in his eyes seemed to fade noticeably for the first time.

'Isn't it about time you started telling me *something* about your past?' Davey hazarded. 'I mean, we've both been through a *lot* today and—'

'Both?' McGuffin squawked. 'Don't you mean *all*?

Besides, let's not go delving into—'

'I will tell you some things,' muttered Threeday, reluctantly. His voice, which suddenly seemed very menacing, echoed in the darkness. 'But I warn you that my story is a dark one . . . and it will most likely shock you. Are you certain you want to know the truths that lurk behind *these* eyes?'

As if to demonstrate, Threeday's ruby pupils shone in the shadows.

'Tell me,' pleaded Davey. 'We're stuck here anyway, and I *really* want to know what happened to you . . .'

Threeday released a second sigh, and tried to clear his dusty throat. 'I told you Paprika betrayed the people of this island, but his deception went far deeper than that. The reason this place is always a haven for pirates is that Henry Morgan *made* it so. He came here once, long ago, and slaughtered the council of governors. Mister Paprika had always hated the council because they thought he and his magic were an abomination and, although my parents worked for Paprika at the hotel, they were fiercely loyal to the governors.

'One night, they chanced upon some scrolls Paprika had written *communicating* with Morgan, betraying secrets and weaknesses in the island's defence in exchange for certain *promises*. They realized a terrible attack upon Cocos was imminent. Unfortunately, they were too late to warn anyone about it – Morgan's men attacked the island that very night. Typically, the attack was ferocious and the pirates left only a handful of islanders alive. Paprika then took over Cocos Island. Paprika killed both my parents – burned them along with several others while Morgan and his men stood by and cheered.'

Threeday paused, as if fighting to keep control of his feelings. 'Then Paprika clapped me in irons and made me his slave. I was instructed to fetch ingredients for his various evil incantations: chicken blood, monkey paws, you name it. I had to watch him do some horrific things, all the while knowing that I desired nothing more than to see him suffer as my parents had suffered. It was while I worked for Paprika that I began to discover things about him, like the fact that he had obtained a vial of strange blood that would make him immortal for many years. He kept it in a special case, hidden away until he was ready to test its power. Morgan stole this blood, which was said to originate from the carcass of a magical creature called the Voodoo Ostrich, and became even more evil and merciless than he had been before.'

Davey didn't know what to say ... but he was suddenly glad of the crypt's darkness and of the fact that he could not see Threeday's face.

'Morgan was ecstatic,' the zombie went on. 'He took more and more risks, testing his immortality to the limits by having members of his crew stab him and set him on fire ... or so it was said. Then he became paranoid about losing his gift, especially when Paprika told him in a fit of rage that the vial's contents would only last for twenty or so years. Morgan didn't like the news. He came to Paprika demanding more of the creature's blood as a sort of safeguard. That's when things started to go wrong between them, and the lucrative partnership dissolved. Paprika didn't have any more of the blood. The old man had become so sure of his own magical *abilities* that he had decided he didn't need it; he was wrong.

'Morgan demanded to know where he could find the Ostrich itself, putting a blade to the voodoo priest's throat and threatening to test whether Paprika's own gift of immortality had "expired". Paprika told Morgan that the Ostrich was on a secret island that could only be found with a special map, and he gave him directions on how to find it.'

Threeday's voice cracked a little, and a great deal of

menace seemed to creep into it. 'I knew Morgan wouldn't kill Paprika until he'd located the map,' he muttered. 'But it was *my* right for revenge, and I decided to get there first. One night, as Morgan's men threw a rowdy party on the beach, I made my move. I didn't just take care of Paprika, who turned out to be *very* mortal, I also drank *every* potion and swallowed every pouch of dust the evil wretch had in his possession. I wanted to erase him and his fell work from the world, and I think I'd actually lost the will to live at that point. When Morgan's men found out and hunted me down, it was almost a relief to feel their blades sink into my flesh. *Then* I woke up . . .'

Threeday sighed. 'I don't know which potion did it, or whether Paprika himself uttered a curse as I throttled him, but the old man certainly got the last laugh on me. Now I'm stuck in this rotting, limbo-state until someone puts me to the torch. I'm sooooo tired.'

Threeday's eyes dimmed once again . . .

'Rough luck,' admitted McGuffin, but his scratchy voice lacked even an ounce of sympathy.

'D— do you think this is the map to the Voodoo Ostrich?' Davey asked, tightening his grip on the scroll and wishing he could see it.

Threeday's eyes glowed suddenly. 'I'd put money on that fact,' he said. 'Morgan arrived at the inn too quickly for it not to be important.'

The two companions sat in silence for a time.

'What about Mallory?' Davey said, eventually. 'Did you really get the ingredients Paprika needed to curse him?'

'I had to do everything Paprika asked, at least, while Morgan's men were around. I didn't know anything about Mallory until Morgan came back here one night in a terrible rage, screaming his name and swearing black revenge upon him. Then, a few weeks later, they caught him . . . I remember a group of pirates dragging him up the beach and throwing him face first before Morgan. I was hiding nearby, so I couldn't make out the exact conversation, but I know Mallory wouldn't beg for mercy. He didn't make a sound.'

Davey frowned. 'And Morgan didn't just kill him there and then?'

'Oh, he was going to . . . but before he brought his sword down he told the assembled pirates that death was too good for a thief like Mallory. That was when Paprika stepped in and told him he knew of something worse. I had to fetch some ingredients, and I remember Paprika tying him down to the floor in one of the rooms at the Foolstop, and sprinkling something that looked like salt into his eyes. Then I was dragged away by Morgan's men. I never saw him ag— OWW!'

There was much flapping in the darkness, and Threeday let out a sharp cry of pain.

'Sorry,' McGuffin squawked, from the opposite end of the room. 'Your eyes went funny for a minute, there – I thought you'd gone feral or something . . .'

Davey sighed.

'Can we get out of here, please?' he said.

At length, Threeday knelt beside the crypt door and listened very carefully. It felt like they'd been in this subterranean cell for hours.

'Anything?' McGuffin prompted.

The zombie shook his head. 'They *must* have gone by now. Shall we chance it?'

'I reckon so; it'd be well into darkness out there . . .'

The door of the crypt creaked open and they emerged, bleary-eyed, from within. Night had drawn in, and eerie clouds drifted over the island.

'What should we do?' Davey ventured, glancing from the parrot to the zombie and back. 'We need to get off the island, but the only way to do *that* is to find a boat . . . which means going into town . . .'

'Yeah,' Threeday added. 'And Morgan is bound to be looking for us there. He's probably got men running all over the island searching for his accursed map!'

'I'll go,' McGuffin chirped. 'I've got a better chance of avoiding the crew.'

Davey shook his head. 'Nah, if you go we'll be limited to the kind of boat owners who would make a deal with a parrot . . .'

'Beggars can't be choosers,' Threeday reminded him.

Davey sighed.

'I need to think straight,' he muttered, taking a moment to glance at his surroundings. As cemeteries went, Cocos Island's little contribution was rather pleasant. It basically consisted of a small collection of gravestones, miniature crypts and decrepit little tombs nestling on the side of a low hill that overlooked the sea. Davey could certainly think of worse places to be buried. The cemetery's main gate was wedged between two large trees and the path beyond looked as though it might lead back on to the Shortwalk. There was a signpost visible in the middle distance, but it was too dark to see what was written on it.

'Let's take a look at this thing.' Davey quickly unfurled the map and carefully studied the ancient yet detailed illustration within.

'Charnel Island,' Threeday muttered, peering over the young pirate's shoulder. 'It marks Charnel Island as the home of the Ostrich. I've never even *heard* of Charnel Island . . . but it must be there . . . look, hidden in those – whatever they are – mists?'

'They are . . . I've heard of Charnel Island. Uncle Jake used to talk about it – most pirates think it doesn't actually exist.' Davey grinned. 'We could actually GO there, and hit Morgan where it hurts the most.'

'Steal his immortality,' said Threeday, his eyes ablaze once more. 'Hey – do you think if I drank some of that blood, it might, well, you know . . .'

Davey nodded. 'Right – first things first – we should find somewhere to sleep, and make a camp, preferably in this part of the forest. I doubt they'd search the same stretch twice.'

'That way, then.' Threeday pointed off to the north. 'I know of a useable clearing.'

'Great,' McGuffin chimed. 'What about my plan to get us a boat? Anyone come up with anything better?'

'Not yet,' said Davey. 'But give me time . . .'

The young pirate breathed in some good old sea air, and made off towards the gate. It was difficult to budge at first, but soon came away when he yanked at the handle. The signpost had been driven into the ground pretty hard; the top of it was at Davey's eye level, and he wasn't tall for a pirate. The post sprouted four different boards pointing in four different directions: Shortwalk, Shortwalk, Cemetery, Shortwalk. It was a good job Threeday was directing them – otherwise who knew where they might end up?

'I think McGuffin's right,' Threeday muttered. 'We both avoid the town.'

'Yeah, but like I said, who in their right mind is going to listen to a parrot?' Davey eyed the bird with a mixture of doubt and concern. 'Besides, we don't have any *money* for McGuffin to bargain with.'

'You don't need money to hire a boat,' said Threeday, wincing as he scratched a layer of skin from his tattered neck. 'You just need to be able to make a lot of false promises . . . Either that or find someone so desperate that they'll do whatever you ask for practically nothing in return. However, the chances of that are minimal.'

'I'm not going 'til the morning,' McGuffin squawked. 'So let's all get some sleep, shall we?'


Henry Morgan slammed open the door of his cabin and marched inside, followed by Gullin and another senior pirate called Reik. Clearing the contents of his table with a great arm-sweep that sent tankards and various scroll boxes clattering to the floor, he threw down a relatively new but very bloodstained map of Cocos Island; there was a severed hand clamped on to one of the corners.

'What—' Reik began, before Gullin threw him a warning look.

'Map seller,' Morgan confirmed, following the pirate's gaze. 'Didn' wanna 'and it over f'r the price I offered 'im.'

Terrified at the thought of the conversation drifting to the crew's failure to capture Davey Swag, Gullin decided to plough straight in; he slapped both hands on the map and cleared his throat.

'Cocos isn't that big,' he said. 'But, because of the jungles and the odd layout, it's a difficult place to find someone who's hiding.' Gullin licked his lips and, realizing Morgan had nothing to add, continued, 'The boy and his zombie escaped off the roof of the Foolstop and on to *this* peninsula. They must have landed in the graveyard; a few of our boys followed them, but they'd already high-tailed it by the time they arrived. That means they'll either head into the jungle . . .'

'Most likely,' Reik added, just to show that he was paying attention.

'. . . into Cocostown, back to the Foolstop Hotel or

to one of the secluded coves. Swag will need to get off the island and, as far as we know, he—'

'Put ten inna town,' Morgan boomed. ''Ave five lookin' aroun' the island and sen' two back to the 'otel. They won' move until firs' light, but I aint takin' no chances.'

Gullin swallowed a few times, but it was Reik who found the courage to speak up.

'Is that wise, Cap'n? Do you really think we should put most of the crew in Cocostown? You reckon he'll come back after—'

'Swag won' come back 'ere. Mallory'll make damn sure o' that. He'll come in by 'imself and when 'e does, I wan' 'im caught. He'll give us Swag soon enough.'

'Mallory?' Gullin repeated, his voice now little more than a tremor. 'Isn't that the boy who . . . when . . . what makes you think he's around? I mean, we didn't see him at the hotel, and the chances are—'

'Just 'cause you didn' see 'im, don' mean he aint there.' Morgan straightened up and put a hand to the fresh scratches on his forehead. 'You didn' see Mallory 'cause you was lookin' for a man' and Mallory ain' a man these days . . . He takes the form ol' 'Rika gave him: a parro', all rough an' feathers.'

Gullin and Reik both shared a surprised glance.

'The parrot is Mallory?' Gullin exclaimed. 'But ho—'

'S' right. Now, you ge' down to Cocostown and you bring back tha' bird. You understan' me? I wan' it alive . . .' He slapped a crushing hand on Gullin's shoulder. 'Your las' chance, Gull; don' mess it up.'

# The Escape

Morning yawned over Cocos Island and, despite the early hour, it was obvious that it was going to be a hot one.

McGuffin swooped high over the roof-tops of Cocostown, his wings flapping madly and his beady eyes fixed on the scene below. Pirates were already spreading out through the town in groups, some heading for the Quickly and others bunched up at the mouths of alleyways and on various street corners. This wasn't going to be an easy task.

McGuffin had a lot of personal problems; being a parrot did that to you. He had to admit that he'd grown very fond of his new owner, despite the episode with the hat-cage, and he had a strong feeling that Davey Swag was going to become a pirate to watch . . . like Short Jack Plat'num had been. He supposed that in many ways, he'd contributed to Short Jack's death.

After all, the pirate hadn't been able to stand the sight of him, whereas Davey was very accommodating . . . and oddly familiar. Even though he'd never laid eyes on the young pirate before he'd seen him on Cocos Beach, there was something about him. If only he could remember . . .

McGuffin was still silently cursing his black pit of a memory when he came in for a second pass over the town and, from the corner of his beady eye, spotted the gibbet on the edge of a path leading into the jungle. The structure looked as if it had been recently erected, with haste and enthusiasm but without much care. It supported a large cage containing something that, at first glance, McGuffin had taken to be a corpse. As he flew lower, the parrot reclassified it in his mind variously as *a corpse with a beard, an animated corpse with a beard* and, finally, *a very thin and bedraggled-looking soul.*

McGuffin landed on the top of the cage, partly because he wanted a good look at its raggedy-clothed inhabitant, but mostly because he thought he might get eaten if he landed on one of the horizontal bars.

'Er . . . 'allo?' he chanced, peering at two eyes almost entirely concealed by dirt. 'Anybody . . . er . . . home?'

'Mmfm,' came the reply.

'Can you talk?'

'Food,' managed the starving prisoner. 'Oh, pity. Pity, pity, pity please. Woe is me.'

'Cor blimey – you're not joking, are you?' said McGuffin. 'I've never seen a man in such a state. Are those actual fleas on your eyebrows? They are! Oh, it doesn't bear thinking about . . . let alone looking at. What's your name then, you filthy wretch?'

'Woe is me,' the prisoner spat. 'Oh. Oh. Woe is me.'

'Yeah, I got that,' said McGuffin, beginning to get mildly irritated. 'I know I have a quite incredible vocabulary for a creature of my species, but I must say that yours seems to be lacking. Any chance of your actual name? You know, the word your parents used to call you or, judging by the look of you, the name written on the egg you hatched from . . .'

'Woe is me, featherbrain,' muttered the prisoner, muzzling up to the bars and tapping his mouth. 'Read my lips: Woe. Isme. As in, it's my name . . . and I wasn't hatched, I was born the usual way – my life's just gone a bit downhill in the last few years. Now are you going to give me some food or aren't you?'

'Well, I'll be a monkey's aunt,' McGuffin squawked. 'Your name is Woe? What, really?'

'It is, it was and it always will be,' Woe managed,

coughing several times and slapping a mosquito that had settled on his arm. 'It's actually Woeful Betide Isme, but most folks who know me call me Woe . . . among other things.'

'What did you do to land up in here, Woe?'

The prisoner sagged a little. 'I'm a mental case,' he said, wistfully. 'At least, that's what those stinking sea-dogs on my last ship told me.'

'Yeah?' said McGuffin, eyeing the road out of Cocostown carefully. He thought he'd spotted two *Herring* pirates making their way towards the path. 'Are we talking slightly odd tendencies, here, or full-blown hysteria?'

Woe appeared to reflect on this. 'I have anti-cabin fever,' he admitted.

'Oh yeah? What's that when it's at home?'

Woe attempted a shrug. 'It basically means that I'm OK indoors but a really *bad* companion on the open water. Not great news if you happen to be a pirate by trade.'

McGuffin hopped down on to one of the horizontal bars and treated the prisoner to his most baleful stare.

'You spend a lot of time on the high seas, do you?'

'Aye,' said Woe, regretfully. 'I did; worked on my own for a bit, then with a crew. They soon got tired of me, though – I think I might have driven the captain to drink.'

'Ah,' said McGuffin, ignoring him. The two distant specks were definitely headed their way. 'Got a ship, by any chance?'

'Eh?' Woe looked up with an incredulous expression on his sunken face. 'You think I'd be locked up in here if I had a ship to call my own? Ha! I've got a piddly little rowing boat, me, and I can't even remember where I left *that*.'

McGuffin hopped back along the bar, towards the lock.

'Well, Woe, it's like this: I'll wager you a week's service *and* your memory of where you put the boat that I can get this lock open in the next twenty seconds . . .'

Woe's expression suddenly changed.

'Done,' he said . . . and it was; the lock latch released and the cage door swung open.

'Now follow me,' McGuffin advised. 'And quickly. You don't want *those* pirates who're on their way up the path asking you questions about how you managed to escape . . .'

Woe didn't need to be told twice; in fact, he dashed into the jungle *ahead* of McGuffin.

\* \* \*

Three quarters of the *Herring* crew were tramping along the road into Cocostown when an argument erupted between the two leaders. It had started as a mere exchange of harsh words, but now Gullin stormed over to a tree and kicked out at it.

Reik hurried after him, his face a mask of horrified confusion. 'B— but it's not *me* who's stopping you – the captain said . . .'

'I *know* what the captain said,' Gullin snapped, spinning around and snatching hold of the other man's throat. 'But he also said that I'm *dead* unless I find the bird and bring it back to him. So *you* concentrate on posting men to keep a look-out for Swag and *I* will track down the parrot. Got that?'

'B— but,' Reik managed, trying to measure the fear he felt for Morgan against the obvious hiding he would get if he took issue with Gullin right now.

'What's the problem?' the first mate growled, shoving Reik back against a tree. 'If I take *four*, I can scour every inch of this scummy little island and you'll still have enough to post men in *every* place Morgan suggested. Where's the damage?'

Reik glanced back at the pirates, many of whom were standing around pretending to talk amongst themselves while at the same time trying to conceal the fact that they loved nothing more than a good fight between the seniors.

'The problem,' Reik whispered, 'is that he *TOLD* us to put specific numbers of men in each place. I mean, what if he comes to check?'

'He won't. He'll stay on the boat until I return with the bird or until . . . I don't. In the latter case, I'll hand the sword to one o' the boys and get 'em to . . . help.'

Reik caught the first mate's expression, and a look of sudden understanding filled his face. 'You'd really . . . do that?'

'As opposed to returning without the bird?' Gullin nodded. 'Absolutely.'

He leaned towards Reik and added, 'You better hope I do find it, though. Being Morgan's first mate is a job for life . . . and he's been through a few, I can tell you.'

Pirates, Davey knew, were a pretty difficult bunch to recruit, mainly because they made so many outrageous demands. Some wanted a three-quarter share of the loot or a deluxe ship with everything en suite, while others requested six days' shore leave a week or a brand new set of clothes at every other port. Most of the real pirates wanted an arm and a leg before they'd even turn up to *meet* a prospective captain . . . unless he was one of the 'feared names'.

Davey was muttering to Threeday about the hopelessness of their plight when McGuffin arrived back in the jungle clearing where they'd spent the previous night. He was quickly followed by a scruffy, bedraggled-looking creature who seemed to need either a good meal or a decent coffin.

Woe Betide, it turned out, was in his early fifties, with far too grey a beard for someone his age and a very unnerving squint. It appeared that he had once been a deck-hand on one of the Caribbean's most notorious pirate ships, but that several 'incidents' had put pay to his career at sea. Besides, as he'd explained to the parrot, he had anti-cabin fever . . . and no captain in their right mind would hire a man with that sort of mental problem.

'How bad is it, exactly?' Davey asked, eyeing the odd fellow very carefully. 'I mean, will we be in mortal danger?'

Woe frowned. 'From me? No, not at all – you'll just be very irritated. I can do some quite insane things when the fever takes me . . . and that can unsettle people. I mean, I worked in a boatyard once, over on Sky Island, and it got me the sack there.

One day, I was out on the boards and I suddenly decided that I wanted to stand on my head against the boatshed door for three hours. Then I decided that one of the little rowing boats was evil and so I took a shovel to it and . . .'

Davey and Threeday shared a glance; neither looked optimistic. McGuffin seemed to think his job was done, and paid little attention to the conversation that ensued, only interrupting once in order to squawk, 'He's got a boat and some experience; 's all that matters. Let's get going . . . sharpish!'

'I really don't think this is such a good idea,' Threeday whispered into his friend's ear. 'He sounds . . . very odd.'

'Odd?' Davey exclaimed. 'This coming from a jungle boy turned voodoo apprentice turned zombie?'

'I know, but . . .' Threeday lowered his voice even more. 'By his own admission, he's a LUNATIC.'

'Yeah, well . . . it takes all sorts.' Davey returned his attention to Woe, who had a sickly look on his face, and slapped the man companionably on the back. 'Threeday is an expert in jungle survival,' he said. 'So you're going to take us to your boat and we're going to find you some food along the way. Agreed?'

Woe nodded, cheerfully.

'I've always wanted to be part of a small crew,' he said. 'I assume we'll be splitting all the treasure we find three ways?'

'Er . . . yeah,' said Davey, smiling in a half-hearted way. 'Absolutely.'

'I'm your man, then. I'll sail into hell an' high water for a third share of treasure.'

'T'rific,' Davey finished, trying to ignore the zombie's pained expression. 'We need to stay off the path, though. Don't worry – Threeday will lead. With any luck, I can tell you a bit more about our upcoming voyage on the way . . .'

Davey made an effort to explain himself. By the time they'd reached a rough stretch of beach in the far north-east of the island, he'd managed to give Woe a complete rundown of events, up to and including the bits about Threeday, Morgan and Mr Paprika at the Foolstop Hotel. Threeday had found the man some excellent fruit, and eating it evidently did the mangy pirate the world of good.

It was late morning when Davey and Threeday trotted down the winding path to Mottle Cove, a small inlet on the far north-eastern corner of the island. Relief and surprise came in equal measure; relief because the sandy, seaweed-covered wreck was exactly where Woe had said it would be, and surprise because they found the cove completely deserted. McGuffin had flown off several minutes before to check the Shortwalk for pirate activity – at least they'd be warned if Morgan's men approached the cove.

Sunlight played on the water, making it gleam and sparkle. While Davey helped Threeday uncover the boat, Woe dug around in the sand, produced an ancient-looking telescope and pointed it out towards the bay.

'Sharks out there,' he said, twisting the device so that he could find a better focus. 'A lot of slippery rocks near the lowest part of the peninsula. I bet this place is like a five-star restaurant for them. I pity the poor lubber that falls foul in these waters.'

'I use to come up here all the time with my dad,' said Threeday. 'Fin-land – that's what the locals called it. They wanted to put up a sign, but one of the governors said that the name Mottle Cove was more visitor-friendly. I think he was probably ri— Oh my gods, look at this . . .'

Woe pocketed the telescope and wheeled around, just in time to catch Threeday's forlorn expression.

'What's wrong?'

'Is this *it*?' the zombie exclaimed, staring balefully at the little rowing boat. 'This *thing* is your ship?'

'Aye,' said Woe, trying to sound proud despite the zombie's snorting fit. 'I call it the *Floating Dagger*.'

Davey laughed. 'Really? I'd call it the *Floating Penknife*. I've seen bigger ships in bottles.'

'Size doesn't count for everything,' Woe advised. 'Look at you, for instance. You've been through loads of hardships and come out the other side, but to look at you . . . you're just a kid.'

Woe gave the young pirate an appraising glance.

'Thanks,' said Davey, feeling suddenly very grown up. 'At least it's a boat, I suppose. We should be grateful.' *We're going to be stranded together for weeks*, he thought. *We can't start arguing already*.

'What about food supplies?' Woe went on, ignoring Davey and turning his attention back to Threeday.

'What *about* them?' said the zombie, his red eyes reflecting the sunlight.

'Well, you must be in charge of food supplies, being from the jungle and all. Do you have enough? Do you have any? Have you made provisions?'

'Such as?'

Woe sighed.

'Well, look at Ferdinand Magellan, the famous

explorer. When he went on a voyage he took twenty-one thousand pounds of biscuits, one thousand seven hundred pounds of fish, one thousand one hundred and twenty pounds of cheese, five hundred pounds of salted beef, two hundred barrels of sardines, four hundred and eighty pounds of oil and two and a half tons of gunpowder.' He gave Davey a severe glance. 'What've you got? Three mouldy rolls and a bottle of water? Ha! We'll be dead by lunchtime on Sunday!'

'OK,' Threeday conceded. 'You get the boat ready. I'll collect some food. But we can't hang around – Morgan's men will check this place sooner or later – you just better hope it's later . . .'

Gullin had instructed his men to stay off the path. Instead, the group was moving through the fringe of the forest, under a half-decent amount of cover.

Gullin stopped suddenly, unfurled the map he'd been holding and turned it sideways. 'I can't tell where we are,' he snapped, as a second member of the hunting group finished peeing on a nearby tree stump and meandered back to where he was standing. 'If we're on this side of the island, and the blue dot is the town, then we're pretty close to the Foolstop again. I hate this place.'

The pirate, who was skinny and sported a variety of interesting warts, spat on to the floor and held out his hands for the map. 'Can I take a look, boss? I'm good with maps, me. I'm good at skimmers, too – I ain't ever thrown a stone that didn't—'

'READ it, then.'

Gullin thrust the parchment into the man's scarred hands, and marched off to shout at the other three pirates, who had ventured deeper into the woods and were beating around pointlessly at random foliage.

When he returned, the warty pirate was holding the map at a different angle.

'The blue dot *isn't* the town,' he said, with a sniff. 'The town is over *here*, which means we're right on the north-east edge of the island, almost.'

Gullin breathed a sigh of relief. At least they hadn't been going around in circles.

'Anything around here of note?' he demanded.

'Only Mottle Cove, and the townsfolk reckon there's not much there except . . .'

His voice trailed off and he looked into the sky.

'You were saying?' Gullin growled, poking the man when he failed to respond. 'What's wrong with you? Have you seen a ghost?'

The warty pirate suddenly dropped to his knees and

snatched up a heavy-looking stone. Then, very slowly, he raised a hand and pointed upwards. 'Isn't that the parrot we're looking for, boss?' he muttered.

When Threeday returned from his food-finding mission, the *Floating Dagger* supported a very nervous crew. Davey crouched, for want of a better word, at the helm, while Woe sat mid-boat with an oar in each hand.

'What did you get?' Davey started, staring hopefully at the sack the zombie was dragging.

'Basic rations from my secret supply,' said Threeday, heaving the sack into the *Floating Dagger* and clambering in after it. 'There's enough food *and* water to last us a while.'

'Well done, Threeday!' Davey exclaimed. 'This is absolutely brilliant!'

Davey rummaged in his coat and fished out a ragged-looking book, a quill and a tiny bottle of ink.

'I'll use my diary as a captain's log,' he muttered, squinting at the book. 'We need to keep a log because . . . er . . . because it's what pirates do. Where's McGuffin got to, I wonder?'

'He's not back?' Threeday put his head on one side and seemed to study the jungle. 'That's odd . . . I didn't meet him on my hunt. Hope the feathery monster hasn't run into any trouble . . .'

'Either way, we need to move.' Woe suddenly thrust out a finger. 'NOW!'

Several pirates had appeared at the lip of the cove. Three were climbing down the cliff face with incredible, spider-like speed, while another pair looked on.

'McGuffin!' Davey screamed, as Woe put his back into rowing. 'We're going! McGuffin! McGuffin!'

'Row!' Threeday yelled, leaping out of the boat and shoving it through the water with all his undead might. '*ROOOOOWWW!*'

Woe was moving like a man possessed, his wiry frame suddenly showing some amazing strength as the boat was swept along. Threeday splashed after it and dived inside, as the first of the three pirates reached the sand and began to dash towards the ocean.

'Go Woe!' Davey boomed, his shaking hands fiddling madly with the pistol.

Threeday had moved to the end of the boat, intent on delivering a rain of blows to whichever pirate managed to reach the boat first.

Davey suddenly raised the pistol and let off a shot which rang out across the bay, causing the nearest pirate to dive for the sand. His two companions, however, produced their own pistols and fired back.

'Down!' Davey screamed, as he, Threeday and Woe suddenly found themselves in a race for the tiny space at the bottom of the rowing boat. All three of them ended up in an untidy heap, as more shots followed.

'They're reloading!' Woe warned, as Threeday snatched hold of the oars Woe had dropped.

Davey, who was frantically trying to reload his own weapon, suddenly looked up as the pirate who'd dived for the sand now splashed into the water.

'He's coming for the boat!'

Woe moved to sit beside Threeday and snatched one of the oars. Together, they heaved on them as if the gods of the ocean were racing after them. The little boat arced through the water . . . and the pirate quickly gave up his pursuit.

Gullin and his warty companion watched from the top of the cliff.

'Pathetic,' said Gullin, a terrible smile consuming his sharp features. 'Utterly pathetic. We can *stroll* back to the docks and still catch them in the *Herring*.'

The wart-ridden pirate nodded.

'We got the parrot, too,' he snarled, tapping the sack

that hung from his shoulder. 'Told you I was good at throwing . . .'

*And saving my skin*, Gullin thought to himself, but he said, 'You did well. Now let's take this cursed avian to the cap'n.' He peered back toward the ocean, and grinned again. 'Catching that boat will be far too easy . . .' he said.

Threeday's skin looked worse than ever; he was losing entire patches from his back and arms.

'The sun,' he managed, as Davey emptied the food sack and tore it apart to form a cover. 'It's strong . . . and I have too little skin to protect me.'

'Yeah,' Davey muttered, throwing the contrived cloak over his friend and watching Threeday fold up his limbs in order to fit everything inside the shade. 'It's very weird – almost like vampires, you know, the sunlight thing.'

'Vampires don't exist,' muttered Threeday.

Davey shrugged. 'I didn't think zombies did, 'til I met you.' The young pirate glanced back at Cocos Island before turning to Woe, who was still rowing frantically away from the shrinking land mass.

'Why do you look so worried?' he said. 'We got away!'

'Yeah,' Woe managed, doubtfully.

Davey laughed to himself and reached into his coat.

'We've got the map I told you about right here. Do you think it's worth trying to set a course yet?'

'Are you mad?' Woe exclaimed. 'We're in a *rowing* boat, kid. It's going to take us ages to get *anywhere*. Besides, I've got a really bad feeling about this . . .'

Davey glanced at Threeday, but it was difficult to make out the zombie's expression as his head was bowed away from the sun.

'Why? We're doing great!'

Woe shook his head. 'They've got a *ship*. Even if we had an entire *day* as a head start, they'd still catch up with us. Don't you understand anything about sea travel?'

Davey looked suddenly crestfallen.

'Even if they had the slowest ship in the *world*, they'd still—'

'I don't care,' Davey snapped, suddenly. 'Threeday saved my life in the jungle, but luck got us both away from the Foolstop and luck just saved us again. They will NOT catch up with us.' Davey stared up into the sky. 'My parents are watching over me,' he said. 'I just *know* they are . . .'

Woe said nothing. He was suddenly *very* concerned

about the trip . . . not because of the pirates who would inevitably give chase, but because he was beginning to feel . . . slightly peculiar. He continued to put a tremendous amount of effort into rowing the boat, and silently prayed that his anti-cabin fever wasn't about to rear its ugly head . . .

Gullin arrived, out of breath, on the quarterdeck of the *Rogue Herring*.

Morgan dismissed the two pirates who were grovelling for attention on either side of him and turned very slowly to face the first mate.

''M thinkin' you aint stupid 'nough to come back 'ere empty o' hand?'

'The bird is in a cage in your quarters, Cap'n,' Gullin managed, trying to keep the pride out of his voice. 'I also found Swag. He now has *two* companions and they've commandeered a pathetically small rowing boat. They got away from us at Mottle Cove, but we should be able to catch up with them in no time. They were heading north, so if we set sail *now* . . .'

'Up the anchor,' Morgan boomed, as pirates appeared from every part of the ship and immediately set to work. 'We're goin' north, 'alf sail!'

'Half sail?' said Gullin, feeling a little confused.

'But surely if we go *full* sail we'll catch 'em . . .'

'Let the kid an' 'is 'horts take us to Charnel. I'll enjoy killin' 'im a lot more when 'e's done ol' 'Enry's legwork for 'im.'

'But—'

'Fetch up me bes' spyglass, the gold'un.'

Gullin nodded and passed the order on to a lackey. 'Good idea, Cap'n,' he said. 'They don't see us but we see them, right?'

'Righ'.'

Gullin stepped back as Mister Reik joined them on the quarterdeck.

'What should we do with the parrot, Cap'n?' he asked, as much to underline his capture of the bird as to discover its fate.

'Nothin',' Morgan growled. 'You leave tha' bird ta me.'

The *Floating Dagger* progressed over the choppy waters north of Cocos Island. Threeday was curled in one end of the little boat, almost entirely concealed by the cloak he'd made from the food sack. Woe still struggled to force back the oars, while fighting another, very different sort of struggle with his wandering mind.

Oblivious to his navigator's inner demons, Davey

carefully dipped his quill into the tiny ink bottle and, replacing the cap, began to scribble in his diary.

'I hope McGuffin is OK,' he said.

'He's a parrot,' Threeday muttered. 'What's the worst that can happen?'

'Maybe he flew into a tree? Do you think he'll ever find us now?'

Threeday sighed beneath the sacking. 'I'll keep my fingers crossed,' he said. 'What little is left of them.'

Davey grinned – it was good to have a friend, as strange as he might be. Woe was a bit too new to be counted as an actual friend, but he'd certainly saved them at Mottle Cove . . .

Davey looked up and found himself wondering what it would be like to sail under the stars. Even if the *Rogue Herring* did catch up with him, at least he'd have made his first official voyage on the high seas. Ha! Captain of his own crew . . . well, almost.

# Personal diary of
# Davey Swag, aged 16¼

*Captain's Log. Day 1.*

**AM** Our first morning at sea and all is well, though there's no sign of McGuffin. Still, this promises to be an exciting voyage into the unknown ... and the *Rogue Herring* doesn't seem to be following! Woe reckons they must have sailed off in the wrong direction, and he knows about navigation stuff. A pity he's feeling so ill...even Threeday is worried; he says he awoke during the night to find Woe making a strange face and slapping himself on the back of the head. A bit odd, if you ask me. However, he has read the map and reckons he's charted us a course for Charnel Island.

**PM** Woe is being very childish. He insists on rowing, but whenever we give him the oars he sits on them and blows raspberries at us. I'm starting to think that maybe Threeday's instincts about him were right.

*Captain's Log. Day 2.*

**AM** Woe is acting very strangely now. He has refused to eat with us and says he will catch his own food. Threeday and I are worried about him, and about ourselves. No sign of the *Rogue Herring*, though.

**PM** We sailed into a storm, and Woe was struck by lightning. Luckily, we managed to fish him out of the ocean, and Threeday gave him the kiss of life. Now he keeps spitting everywhere, and I think Threeday feels that he is to blame for this.

*Captain's Log. Day 3.*

**AM** Woe dived into the sea for no apparent reason. Threeday and I searched the waters around the boat, but could find no trace of him.

**PM** Woe turned up again. He is now swimming in front of the boat making strange quacking noises. Threeday says that he thinks Woe believes himself to be a duck.

*Captain's Log. Day 4.*

**AM** I'll be honest - I've had better mornings. A sea-gull landed on the boat, which was fine until Woe tried to eat it. Now, all of us are bleeding and there are feathers everywhere.

**PM** I managed to grab a leaf that floated past the boat. Uncle Jake once told me how to make a compass using a leaf and a jug of water. There is a problem; Woe won't give me the jug. He says he is trying to make his own compass. He asked for my leaf. I then tore the leaf up and threw it into the sea. Woe hit me with the jug. Threeday threatened to jump into the water and swim back to Cocos if we keep arguing about which way is north.

Captain's Log. Day 5.
**AM** Sharks came to swim around the boat. Against our advice, Woe dipped his scarred fingers into the water. Shortly after this, a shark surfaced and ate one of the oars.
**PM** I have now stopped hitting Woe with the remaining oar. He is more trouble than he is worth and I have told him this. Threeday hasn't stopped complaining about him since yesterday.

Captain's Log. Day 6.
**AM** Things are getting steadily worse. There is still no sign of the *Herring* or Charnel Island, and I strongly suspect that Woe has gone mad. He has thrown all the remaining fruit into the ocean and is biting his toe-nails off with his teeth. The smell of his mouldy feet is a trial by itself without the barrage of toe-nail clippings, which he has been spitting in our faces for the best part of an hour. Threeday keeps being sick, a horrible sight made worse by the fact that I can see the contents of his stomach moving inside his throat before he brings them up. Urgh.

**PM** Woe has broken the second oar while trying to bludgeon the same sea-gull he failed to catch on Tuesday. I would have hit him across the head, but Threeday kicked him somewhere else instead. He folded up in the middle of the boat and hasn't moved for over an hour.

Captain's Log. Day 7.
**AM** Ship ahoy! Woe sighted a square-rigger through his telescope. They are flying the skull and crossbones but, as Woe says, we are pirates too and should try to hail them. I'm inclined to agree, but Threeday thinks this would be a very bad idea. He says the square-rigger might be the infamous *Black Maggot*, which was lost in these waters many years ago.
**PM** We boarded the ship, which was full of long-dead pirates. There were skeletons on the rigging, skeletons in the cabins and a skeleton at the wheel. There was also a skeleton of a spider monkey perched on its head. Threeday looked away in embarrassment, but Woe said he felt hungry.

Captain's Log. Day 8.
**AM** Woe said he could sail the ship, having sailed square-riggers before. I didn't believe him, but there weren't a lot of options open to us, so we allowed him to try. We have winched up the *Floating Dagger*. Woe couldn't understand why, but I have grown quite attached to his little boat.

**PM** Found the captain of the square-rigger in his quarters. Even measured against Mr Paprika at the Foolstop Hotel, he was a pretty dreadful sight. A skeleton with an eye-patch and one eyeball yet to decompose, he had long, sandy brown hair which flowed from a pilgrim hat sporting the skull and crossbones motif. I suspect that, from this day forth, I will never have a nightmare without him in it.

*Captain's Log. Day 9.*
**AM** We haven't moved an inch. I went below decks to investigate and found Woe hunkered down in the hold. When I asked him what he was doing, he said he was trying to rid himself of anti-cabin fever and was refreshing his memory on how to sail a square-rigger from some notes he'd found on board the ship.

**PM** Threeday and I managed to creep up on Woe when he wasn't looking and discovered that he was, in fact, reading two books by the famous sailor, Captain Sir Walter Stagapple. We were a little disheartened (though not entirely surprised) to learn that the books were *Stagapple's Sailing for the Complete Beginner* and *Oops, I've Spliced a Mainbrace: the Idiot's Guide to Staying Afloat*. Any confidence I had in Woe's ability to sail the ship has now gone.

*Captain's Log. Day 10.*

**AM** I'm very angry, having been forced to write this entry on a piece of parchment found in the ship's hold. This is because Woe has stolen my diary, and is reading it in the crow's-nest. Every time I attempt to climb up and get it, he threatens to set fire to the rope ladder with a tinder-box he's found. I now want to kill Woe almost as much as I want revenge on Henry Morgan.

**PM** There has been a wind change, and Threeday has figured out how to sail the ship. I am helping as best I can, and we are now travelling very fast in what Woe assures us in his few moments of sanity is the right direction for Charnel. Woe himself is still in the crow's-nest, sulking. He says that if anyone ever reads my captain's log, he will never be employed on a ship again. I think that, on reflection, this is probably for the best.

*Captain's Log. Day 11.*

**AM** The good news is that Woe seems to have rid himself of the fever that has dogged our entire trip. The bad news is that a ship has been spotted. It is still a little way behind us but we are sure it is the *Rogue Herring*. Woe believes it has been following us at a distance since we set out for Cocos Island, and that Morgan has decided to attack us because we are close to Charnel Island. Threeday and I have spent the morning loading cannons and searching for weaponry in the hold. **PM** The *Rogue Herring* is practically on top of us. I am trying to stay confident, but Threeday says he does not fancy our chances. Finding no official log on the ship that describes it as the *Black Maggot*, I have re-named her *Davey's Pride*. All the cannons are loaded (Threeday and I will run between them) and we are ready for battle. Reflecting on my life during the last few weeks, I am given to wonder how I blundered in to this terrible state of affairs?

# 7

# Charnel

'This is the gun deck,' said Woe, reading from *The Idiot's Guide to Staying Afloat*. Davey had managed to coax him down from the crow's-nest by promising to burn his diary before they were boarded. Allowing him to take the lead in this last-minute tour of the ship had been a stroke of genius. Woe was in his element, and both Davey and Threeday were learning about the square-rigger's arsenal.

'Unfortunately,' he continued, turning a page, 'the cannon-ball store is on the floor below, so it looks like it might be a case of hauling twenty or thirty up here before our target pulls up alongside us.'

Davey scratched his chin thoughtfully.

'How many cannons have we got?' he asked.

'Seven on the gun deck,' said Woe. 'Another six on the waist.'

'What's that?'

'The open deck above.'

'So how do we operate the cannons?' Threeday asked, eyeing the hunk of iron beside him with wary caution.

'As a matter of fact, there are two different types of cannon on board, Flaky. The one you are standing next to is very much of the older style and requires a minimum of three people to operate.'

'Three people?' Davey echoed. 'Well, that's no good, is it? We'd only be able to fire off one shot at a time!'

'Then we're going to want the ones on the waist,' Woe chirped. He turned and disappeared down the corridor at a dead run. Davey and Threeday hurried after him.

'These,' he said, arriving at the waist deck with the others in hot pursuit, 'are your standard big guns. You'll find these boys easy enough to operate.'

The cannon was supported by a wooden stand on wheels. A restraint rope ran from the stand to the side of the ship, looping through a sturdy-looking iron hoop to hold the cannon in place.

'And it only requires one of us?' Threeday ventured.

'Er . . . yes, I think so,' said Woe, flicking through the book. 'Once we've brought up enough cannon-balls, it's simply a case of aiming the thing, lighting a fuse and standing well back. There's a good stock of gunpowder in those kegs, and they're pretty well placed so we shouldn't have any problems reloading.'

He pulled out the telescope and squinted through it.

'We better put on a fair turn of speed with those cannon-balls, though,' he said. 'Our friends from the *Herring* look as though they're ready to fire.'

The cage was filled with iron spikes, leaving only a narrow space on which McGuffin was able to perch. The bird made only the slightest of sounds, as his capture had left him with a broken beak and partially blind in one eye . . . but at least he was alive.

As the parrot stirred, Morgan leaned towards it and displayed a mouthful of rotting teeth.

'Lon' time no see, youn' Mallory,' he growled. ''Siderin' I aint laid eyes on ya since ya got outta me cage back afore I 'cided ta torch yer feathers.'

'You've got a short memory, Morgan,' squawked the parrot. 'Besides, I call myself McGuffin these days. That was my name when you snatched me from my parents, remember that? Don't do yourself a favour thinking I'm going to tremble with fear at the sight of you, either . . . I was terrified of you for a long time, but you can't do anything to me now. Taking my soul backfired a bit, really – didn't it? I mean, what can you do to me while I'm just a tenant in this mass of feathers? Kill the bird, and I transport into the nearest head . . . and considering that's *yours*, I'd say you're pretty powerless. Maybe you should have killed me when you had the chance, instead of getting your witch-doctor to weep over me . . .'

Morgan didn't flinch. 'Is 'at a fac'?' he growled.

McGuffin staggered a little on the perch, one of the upper spikes scraping the edge of his beak.

'It is. I saved that boy from your evil once, and I found him again. Not by chance, but because the fates wanted me to. I don't *need* to save him now, Morgan – he's eluded you this far and he's grown up with determination and a strong spirit.'

A sudden loud explosion erupted from the bowels of the ship, but Morgan ignored it. The pirate captain had moved over to an ancient-looking locker in the corner of his cabin and was rummaging around inside. At length, he produced a worn-looking scroll from within. Then he returned to the cage.

'You used ta be me favourite,' Morgan boomed, as another explosion erupted outside and the ship shook. 'Always rattin' on yon crew an' givin' up their secrets.' Morgan put his face against the cage door and gritted his teeth. 'You're righ' enough abou' me no' bein' able ta 'urt ya . . . bu' I can gi' ya this.'

'You don't have anything that interests me,' McGuffin squawked.

The pirate captain snorted. 'You ain' interested in gettin' yer body back? Well I'll jus' go an' throw this map in the ocean, shall I?'

The quiet calm of the Caribbean had been shattered by cannon-fire. A line of terrific explosions erupted from the port side of the *Herring*. Surprisingly enough, *Davey's Pride* was returning fire with just as much fury.

Woe and Threeday hurried back and forth between the squat guns, loading cannon-balls, plumbing gunpowder and lighting fuses. Davey stood on the poop deck at the rear of the ship, peering through an eyeglass he'd discovered in the captain's cabin.

Considering that none of them had ever fought a sea battle before, they were doing outstandingly well. The *Rogue Herring* was definitely on the losing end of the battle; it had nosed slightly and, from what he could see through the eyeglass he'd found, Henry Morgan's men were actually a disorganized rabble when it came to sea battles.

Boom! Another cannon-ball thundered from the

waist of the *Rogue Herring*. Boom! The shot was returned.

'My body?' McGuffin's scratchy voice cracked slightly as the words were uttered. 'I thought at least you'd come up with something believable – Paprika burned it, remember?'

Morgan shook his head. 'No, he dun 'chanted on it and I 'ad me ol' crew bury it on an island o' me choosin'.'

'Wh— why?' squawked McGuffin. 'Why would you do that? Why didn't you just—'

'Power,' Morgan growled. ''Sides, I knew you'd lead me ta the whelp one day – I jus' knew it.'

Another explosion shook the ship.

'All you 'ave ta do is fin' yer body an' touch it; yer soul'll be back where it 'arked from. I reckon you'll need a goo' man wi' a shovel, mind.'

McGuffin remained quiet for a long time, while explosions rang out around the cabin like thunderclaps. Finally, he said, 'And what would I have to do, exactly?'

Morgan licked his rancid lips. 'To turn ya tide o' treachery?' he growled. 'Ya gotta 'elp ol' 'Enry kill the whelp ya stole fro' 'im.'

The sea battle raged back and forth, cannon-ball after cannon-ball exploding from the ships' ancient batteries.

Then something extraordinary and very fortunate happened. One of the *Pride*'s cannon-balls smashed across the *Herring*'s decks with breathtaking force.

'Solid hit!' Davey cried. 'This is our chance!' He leaped down from the poop deck and hurried over to the far end of the waist deck, where Threeday was kneeling beside one of the smaller cannons.

'Quick,' he yelled. 'The sails! The wind's behind us. Hurry!'

As Threeday took to his feet, Davey called to Woe to do the same. In no time at all they were off again at a rate of knots, leaving the *Rogue Herring* a sorry-looking sight in the waters behind them.

'We're away! We're away!'

Threeday threw his hands in the air and jumped for joy, but Davey was gazing around as if he'd lost something.

'Where's Woe?' he said.

'Taken the wheel, Cap'n!' said Threeday, with a grin. The zombie was almost unrecognizable from the sullen creature Davey had first encountered in the jungle.

'The *Herring*'s behind us and we're on course for Charnel Island. That was a piece of cake!'

Davey nodded, but he didn't look too sure.

'Maybe so,' he muttered. 'But it won't be if Morgan ever catches up with us.'

A few hours after their battle with the *Rogue Herring*, the crew of *Davey's Pride* sighted land. The sighting came as a blessed relief, especially as the half-destroyed *Herring* was still in pursuit.

Threeday and Woe were already on deck when Davey emerged, blinking, from the captain's cabin. He had an oar under each arm.

'What're they for?' Threeday asked. Davey noticed that the zombie had now lost most of the flesh off the near side of his face. It was almost as if the jungle had been protecting him and the sunlight was now whittling him away.

'These? I found them inside. They'll do for the *Dagger*, until Woe comes across another sea-gull.'

'We're taking the *Dagger*?'

'Yeah.' Davey nodded. 'We can't very well sail the *Pride* right up on to the land.'

He smiled wanly, ignoring a guttural growl from the zombie, and waited for his vision to clear. Then he raised Woe's telescope and stared out at the landmass on the horizon.

As the subject of so many strange and mysterious stories, Charnel Island should have been a hideous blot on the sea. However, it was just the opposite; a lush tropical paradise with a number of small mountains, all surrounded by forest as far as the eye could see. The beach was every pirate's dream, an expanse of golden, sun-baked sand dotted with pretty palms. Oddly, however, there were no mists surrounding it and, at first glance, it appeared to be entirely deserted.

Dropping anchor, Davey rounded up his crew and the three companions used the little rowing boat to get ashore.

'Looks empty,' Threeday commented. He'd snatched the telescope and was using it to scan the beach, his red eyes looking even more alien in the sunlight.

'All islands *look* empty,' Woe muttered miserably. 'Then you get a little way up the sand and things begin to crawl from the jungle.'

Davey boggled at him. 'What *things*?'

'Oh, you name it. Big lizards, lost tribes, pirate crews in secret coves – they're all in there somewhere. Death awaits . . . and it's usually carrying a sword.'

Threeday ignored Woe, and tapped Davey on the shoulder.

'There aren't any mists,' he muttered. 'Are you sure that idiot has guided us to the right island?'

Woe meandered up to them.

'If you're going to talk about me behind my back,' he said, 'at least have the common decency to do so in a quiet voice, Flaky.'

Threeday turned and glared at him.

'This *isn't* Charnel Island,' Woe continued. 'I was going to say something when I first spotted it, but, well, I was a bit confused. And BEFORE you go accusing me of messing up the navigation, I can tell you that I have got you to EXACTLY the right place on your map.' He stormed over to where Davey was standing and snatched the parchment from the young pirate's belt, unfolding it as Threeday strode over to join them. 'See here? Cocos. See here? The five small islands to the east of "Charnel". Now, if you look east you will see them.'

Davey and Threeday followed his gaze; sure enough, there were five small mounds in the far distance.

'I don't get it,' said Davey, studying the map as carefully as he could. 'If this isn't Charnel, why is it *marked* as Charnel?'

'Who knows? Maybe someone changed it.'

Threeday looked back towards the ship, and groaned. The distant shape of the *Rogue Herring* was becoming clearer.

'Can this day get any worse?' he muttered, turning Davey around and pointing at the ocean.

'I think it can,' said Woe, suddenly. He was looking in the opposite direction. 'Tell me, did you ever hear about the Arawaks and the Caribs?'

Davey and Threeday ignored him; both were apparently transfixed by the sight of Morgan's ship gaining on the *Pride*.

'If ever you come across a largely unpopulated island in the Caribbean,' Woe continued, wincing slightly, 'the chances are it's full of Arawaks and Caribs. They're two tribes of natives, very hostile and absolutely sadistic. If I remember my geography lessons right, both tribes are originally from South America. Wherever they're from, it's a well-known fact that they've settled on some of the "quiet" islands. If this turns out to be one of them, we're all in big trouble.'

Woe reached out and tugged at Davey's arm. 'I'd turn round if I were you . . . we've got company.'

Davey managed to rip his gaze from the approaching terror, just in time to see . . . an approaching terror.

'Apparently, this day *can* get worse,' Threeday growled.

'You see them?' said Woe, glancing around for some obvious means of escape that didn't involve getting back in the boat.

Davey nodded. 'Yeah, I see them.'

'You see the pot?'

'That too.'

'OK, now tell me that's not what I think it is inside.'

Threeday put a shading hand to his wrecked forehead, and sighed. Then, as if they were controlled by one mind, all three companions ran down the beach, dived into the water and swam for the temporary safety of the *Floating Dagger*.

Woe clambered aboard last and, seizing both oars, began to row them back towards the ship.

'Hang on,' Davey snapped. 'There's a girl in that pot!'

'We'll get eaten!' Woe screamed.

Threeday glanced back towards the natives, and wondered if he'd give them food poisoning.

Woe had continued to row towards the *Pride*.

'Stop! The girl – we've got to help her.'

'She's beyond help.'

'But—'

'No buts!' Woe yelled. 'You'll have to kill me before I give you back these oars.'

'Woe!'

'NO! I'm going back to the shi—'

A well-aimed punch from a rotting fist knocked Woe out cold. Threeday shoved him aside, seized the oars and began to turn the boat around.

In a matter of minutes, they were back on the sand.

'We're doing the right thing, aren't we?' Davey began, trying not to sound too much like his unconscious navigator as he splashed into the water. 'Perhaps Woe was right. Maybe we should get back to the ship and think about another method of attack.'

'Such as?'

'Well, if we sail the *Pride* closer to the island, we might be able to get off a couple of shots and frighten them back into the jungle.'

'Before the *Herring* arrives and blows us out of the water?' Threeday shook his head, dragging Woe after him. 'Not a chance, Davey. That girl would be medium rare by the time we got to her. She'd end up looking like *me*.'

By the time they reached the middle of the beach, the tribe had grounded the cooking pot and were beginning to gather around it, some of them chanting manically and others propping firewood against the base.

The tribal chief, a white-haired man in a loin cloth at least two heads taller than anyone else, was watching the crew of the *Floating Dagger* as they came ashore and clambered out of the boat. He looked ever so slightly amused.

Davey approached first, wincing when he saw that the chief was wearing a necklace of human teeth. He steeled himself, put one hand on his pistol and drew out his cutlass with the other.

'Let her go, you scurvy lubbers!' he shouted, waving the blade around in the vain hope that it might scare the tribesmen.

A few of them laughed. All of them smirked.

Then the chief spoke. Davey expected him to mumble in a heathen dialect of some sort. Instead, he spoke the Queen's English. He said, 'I'm sorry, is there some sort of problem here?'

Davey's mouth dropped open.

'Er . . . what?' was all the young pirate could manage.

'I said,' the chief repeated, slowly and calmly, 'I'm sorry, but is there some sort of problem, here?'

Davey looked round at Threeday, who was also lost for words.

'Yes, there is!' he snapped. 'I demand that you release the girl, surrender yourselves and retreat back to wherever it is you came from!'

The chief looked bewildered.

'Why would you make such a demand?' he asked.

'Because you're going to cook that girl!' Davey exclaimed.

The chief put his head on one side.

'We most certainly are not,' he said.

'So why is she tied up in that cooking pot?' said Threeday.

'Why? Simply because we are acting out an ancient Arawak rite: the Rite of Making Flesh Soup. In times past, our ancestors performed this ceremony for real. I can assure you that we do no such thing. We are *civilized* Arawaks. We're merely *simulating* the ceremony.'

'Arawaks, eh?' Woe grinned through split lips, shook himself awake and struggled on to his feet. 'I hate to say I told you so, but I *told you so*.'

'What about the girl?' Davey asked, watching as the young lady climbed out of the pot and dusted herself off. She looked annoyed. 'She can't be in on this, surely? Where did you get her from?'

'She is an actress . . . from over the sea.'

Davey gave the girl a cursory look. She was certainly pretty enough to be an actress. He strode over to her.

'Is this true?' he asked. 'Are you not in need of rescuing?'

The girl gave him a blank look. She obviously didn't speak the same language. She *did* look distressed, but that could merely have been her normal expression.

'Now,' the chief continued. 'As leader of the Arawaks, I would like to welcome you to our humble island. What can we be doing for you at this irregular time?'

Davey felt awkward, but that was nothing unusual. However, another glance at the ocean told him that the *Rogue Herring* wasn't quite on top of them yet . . .

'We were here to find . . . something special,' he said. 'B— but we think we might be in the wrong place.'

'On the contrary,' said the chief, in a very matter-of-fact fashion. 'There is something very special here.'

Davey, Threeday and Woe suddenly froze.

'Th— there is?' Davey exclaimed.

'Oh yes. In fac—'

'Wait a minute,' Threeday interrupted. 'This *something special* – is it a creature?'

'Oh yes, we would certainly describe it as one. It breathes but does not grow . . .'

'That's it!' Davey yelled, jumping for joy. Threeday grinned maniacally. Even Woe fired off a quick salute.

'Where is it?' the young pirate shouted. 'Can we see it?'

The chief shrugged.

'If you wish. You will find it buried beneath the egg-shaped rock in a clearing we call Strange Badgers.'

Threeday and Woe exchanged glances.

'Er . . . thanks,' said Davey. 'I don't suppose you could give us directions?'

'Ah yes, certainly. You will take the left-hand path into the trees behind us, then you must go north at the first clearing, west at the second, north again at the third, west at the fourth and north-west at the fifth.'

'Phew,' Davey said, exhausted. 'And that will take us to the clearing of Strange Badgers?'

The chief shook his head, the giant head-dress ruffling in the wind.

'That will take you to the clearing that contains the troll-faced oak. From there, you must proceed west, north-west, north, north again, west and north. After that I'm afraid I cannot remember the way. Sorry.'

Davey made a face.

'Why are you telling us all this?' he asked.

'Good question,' echoed Threeday. 'Don't you want the creature for yourselves?'

The chief shook his head sadly. 'It doesn't interest us,' he muttered. 'Besides, the last time we pursued something mythical it caused us an awful lot of trouble. After the Fountain of You, we're steering clear of buried secrets.'

Davey put a finger in his ear and twisted it around.

'Did you say the Fountain of Youth?' he asked, eyes wide.

'No, I said the Fountain of You,' the chief replied. 'Unfortunately we confused the two and that turned out to be a *big* mistake.'

'But doesn't the Ostr—' Davey said, before Threeday elbowed him in the ribs.

'They might not know!' the zombie whispered.

'Well, thanks for the directions,' Davey said, beginning to back away from the tribe. 'I've no doubt you have a lot to do, and we have . . . er . . . something special to find, so if you'll excuse us.'

He turned and made for the edge of the jungle, Threeday following close behind him.

Woe bowed before the tribal chief, blew a kiss at the actress and hurried after the pair.

'Shouldn't we have taken them prisoner?' said a

cannibal tribe member, staring quizzically at the chief . . . who shook his head.

'Absolutely not,' he muttered. 'Didn't you see the zombie? Besides, anyone who comes here in search of that cor—'

'Sorry to interrupt, boss,' said the inquisitive cannibal, pointing out at the ocean. 'But it looks like our little friends brought some company.'

The rest of the tribe turned to look out at the ocean, and slowly began to retreat towards the safety of the wood.

On the quarterdeck of the *Rogue Herring*, Henry Morgan ripped open the door of McGuffin's cage and cackled evilly as the bird took flight.

Reik heaved on the ship's wheel as Gullin strode up to the captain. He looked particularly shocked to see the bird set free, especially after the tortuous ordeal of catching the thing, but he knew better than to question Morgan's motives.

McGuffin soared on the air for a time, then flapped his wings and flew over the ship towards the island.

'We're within firing range, Cap'n,' he said instead, indicating the black mass of the enemy ship. 'We can sink it, too. It looks like there's no one on board.'

Reik stepped aside to allow one of the deckhands to take the wheel, and lumbered over to join them on the edge of the quarterdeck.

'My money says they've gone on to the island,' he hazarded, producing a telescope and passing it to Gullin. 'You reckon we should let 'em get your treasure and *then* take 'em down?'

'No mist . . .' muttered Gullin.

Morgan glanced over at him, as if distracted. 'You say somethin' ta ol' 'Enry?'

'The mists,' Gullin repeated. 'I don't know a lot about Charnel Island, but I do know it's supposed to be covered in a constant mist. Maybe it's just a fake legend, but I always thought—'

Morgan suddenly snatched the telescope from the first mate and forced it against one bloodshot eye. Then he slapped a hand on to the wooden rail at his waist and crushed it into splinters.

Reik almost fell over himself as he tried to back away. Only Gullin stood his ground, and even he was shaking.

'Cap'n?' he said, weakly. 'What's wrong?'

'This aint Charnel Islan',' Morgan growled, spit flying from his mouth as the rage took him. 'This is Dudley Islan'.'

Now even Gullin stepped back, trying to steady himself on what was left of the rail.

'B— but they're following your map,' he said. 'They have to be! Why would they—'

'I knows it's Dudley 'cause I 'as been 'ere afore,' Morgan boomed. 'This is where I buried tha' runt who did wrong by me. This is where I pu' Mallory in the dirt.'

'But if—'

'The bird must ha' sneaked 'board an' switched it 'fore Corsham 'atched his plan ta steal it fro' me. I'll be' 'e's go' both maps, the feather' wretch. Secon' time ol' Mallory's 'ad one over on me. Secon' an' las'.'

Before Gullin could even raise an eyebrow in confusion, a lower deck-hand cannoned into him.

'Mister Gullin! Mister Reik!' he spat. 'We're under attack!'

Morgan didn't move a muscle, but both the senior mates spun around. Two new pirate ships were closing on the *Herring*.

Davey stopped in the middle of a very familiar clearing, screwed up his fist and drove it into the bark of a nearby tree.

'This place is crazy!' he shouted, his expression

advising Woe not to argue. 'I mean, how many times in the past three hours have we seen that tree?'

He pointed at an oak with a bole so gnarled it actually appeared to be making a face.

'What're we going to do?'

'I think we took a left at the last clearing instead of a right,' the zombie replied, his eyes narrowing to slits. 'Maybe I should lead for a bit. I can remember practically everything the chief said.'

'It could just be a story!' Davey muttered. 'A practical joke for visitors! We could be walking around in circles for days and days.'

'We could,' said Woe, 'but we're not going to.'

Davey and Threeday peered up at him.

'What leads you to that conclusion?' said the zombie.

'The fact that I've just found a clearing with a signpost and the words "Strange Badgers" scrawled on it. Of course, I'm next to useless so I don't suppose that's any help to you at all?'

He got no reply. Davey and Threeday were staring up at him with their mouths wide open.

Davey hurtled into Strange Badgers like a madman, dropped to his knees before the egg-shaped rock and began to claw away the dirt with his finger-nails.

'Davey!'

'Hey, has he gone crazy or what?'

'Stop that!'

Mounds of earth flew in every direction. Occasionally Davey would stop, spit out a mouthful of dust and dive right in again. There didn't seem to be anything Threeday and Woe could say to make him stop. Time, however, did manage to slow him down a little.

'You see that tree?' Woe whispered to Threeday. 'The one with the wide trunk that winds up past the tops of the others?'

'Yes, what of it?'

'I'm going to climb to the top and keep watch. *We'll* want to know when the pirates get closer, even if that lunatic over there doesn't.'

'Good idea. I'll try to talk to him.'

While Woe made for the tree, Threeday got down on his hands and knees next to Davey.

'Stop now, please,' he said, simply.

'I can't,' he said, his voice almost pleading. 'I've come too far! Morgan will be on us before we can even get it out of the ground! I can't believe you're being so calm about this; you must want this thing as badly as I do!'

Threeday nodded. 'I do, but you're acting like a madman. Slow down, and let me help. We'll get through this quicker if we work as a team.'

Davey took a deep breath, and shifted slightly. Threeday moved in beside him, and they began to scrape away the dirt together.

A little under an hour later, they found . . .

'A box!' Davey cried. 'It's a box!'

'It's *huge*,' Threeday added, as he scraped some more dirt further along the hole. 'It's . . . like a coffin. How big *is* this Ostrich?'

'Is it a gold coffin?' Woe called hopefully from the treetop.

'It can't be alive in here, surely,' gasped Davey.

'I woke up in one of these,' Threeday reminded him.

Together, the two companions heaved the coffin up over their heads and deposited it on the ground beside the hole. Then they clambered out.

'No lock,' Davey gasped. 'That's a relief.'

Threeday worked his bony, fleshless fingers into the gap beneath the coffin lid, and wrenched it open. The two friends stepped back, and there was a collective intake of breath. Inside the coffin was . . .

'It's a boy,' Threeday said, turning to Davey. 'He looks a few years older than you.'

The boy did indeed appear to be in his late teenage years, with a shock of blond hair and small, elfin features.

Davey's face was awash with confusion. 'So much for the Voodoo Ostrich,' he said. 'Is . . . he a zombie?'

Threeday knelt beside the coffin and forced open the corpse's eyes; they contained no glow. 'He's certainly breathing . . . but not a zombie, I fear. I'm not sure what he is.'

'I am,' said a voice. At first they thought it had come from Woe, but then Davey spotted a large and familiar-looking parrot perched on the dirt mound beside the hole. 'He's me.'

McGuffin hopped down on to the face of the corpse and pecked gently at its mouth. For a moment, nothing happened. Then, very slowly, the body began to glow with a dark purple fire. As the energy spread out to engulf the frozen youth's frame, it lifted the body out of the coffin and raised it aloft. A dozen sizzling bolts of purple electricity exploded from the corpse and shot into the air as the body floated to land on the ground beside the coffin. As the fiery coating faded, the boy's eyes flicked open . . . and the parrot flew away.

* * *

A cannon-ball ripped into the port side of the *Rogue Herring*.

*Sharks*, Gullin thought, as he commanded the *Herring* crew to prepare for combat. *All pirates were sharks. They'd chanced upon a broken ship and now they were closing in for the kill. Well, not on this day. Wait 'til they realize they've just attacked Henry Morgan's flagship.*

'Fire!' Gullin screamed across the deck, snatching hold of Reik as the man rushed past. 'We can only take another direct hit,' he muttered. 'Then we board. Get it? Tell 'em to get ready to *board.*'

Morgan was brandishing two swords; he had the devil in his eyes.

'I ain' got time fer this,' the dread captain boomed. 'Move inta board 'em – I wants on tha' islan'. *Now.*'

Davey and Threeday sat in silence while Mallory told them a tale. Even Woe climbed down from his tree to listen to the story of how the bird with a soul had escaped from Morgan's clutches and how, many years later, it had learned of the man's new ship and had snuck aboard . . . only to discover a conspiracy in the making. Two of Morgan's own crew were planning to steal the captain's long sought-after and recently-seized map to Charnel Island . . . before the ugly wretch had a chance to use it. However, a quick switch of maps and suddenly Corsham hadn't stolen the pirate's great prize, but a map to the hidden location of a certain burial site that . . .

'You set the whole thing up!' Davey said, thrusting an accusatory finger at Mallory. 'That's amazing! What about the real map, though? Do you have that?'

'You do,' said the boy, massaging his wrists. 'Remember that document of ownership I gave you back at the Quickly on Cocos?'

Davey's eyes widened, and he thrust an exploratory hand down into the intricate lining of his coat. His fingers closing on the scroll, he ripped it out and quickly unfurled it. An ancient-looking map was concealed within.

'Our meeting wasn't by chance,' Mallory went on. 'In fact, I'd been watching you for years. Jake Raskin raised you well, and it seemed only right that you should end up stealing Morgan's most-desired treasure . . .'

Davey smiled. 'But not until I'd found your body and dug you up?'

Mallory returned the young pirate's grin. 'Of course,' he said. 'You did owe me one, after all . . . and it seemed only right that you should be the man to give me back my life.'

'Just as you gave him back his,' Threeday finished. The zombie moved over to Mallory and put a hand on the cabin boy's shoulder. 'Look, I'm really sorry about—'

'Forget it,' Mallory said, taking the zombie's hand and grasping it firmly. 'You went through a lot worse, yourself. Being a bird . . . it's not all that bad. You even get to speak to people . . .'

'Look, I'm sorry to interrupt all this talk,' Woe spluttered, wiping his mouth with the back of his arm. 'But if we've got the right map, shouldn't we be getting back to our ship? You know, if Morgan hasn't blown it out of the water.'

Davey nodded, and realized for the first time that he could hear cannon-fire in the distance.

Davey, Woe, Mallory and Threeday arrived on the beach to an incredible spectacle. It seemed that *Davey's Pride* and the *Rogue Herring* weren't the only ships to sail into Dudley Bay. Three other square-riggers were surrounding them, and there was a terrible battle going on. Cannon-fire had been exchanged on all sides, and it didn't look as though many of the ships would be seaworthy afterwards.

'Who're *they*?' Davey asked Woe, who was using his telescope to scan the bay.

'One has a flag with a skeleton dancing on two skulls,' he said. 'That could be any one of a hundred crews. We're in big trouble, here!'

'Not necessarily,' Davey said, trying to pull his gaze from the war erupting before him. 'They might be all the distraction we need.'

'What's the plan?' Threeday asked, looking around for the Arawak tribe. They'd apparently retreated into the jungle. 'Sneak in with the *Floating Dagger* and try to get back on board the *Pride* without being seen?'

'Exactly.' Davey straightened up and drew his cutlass. 'It's our best shot,' he said. 'The *Herring* is totally surrounded, and the other pirates seem to be ignoring the *Pride* completely. They must think it's been abandoned.'

As Threeday and Woe pushed the boat out into the water, Mallory snatched at Davey's collar and dragged him back.

'What is it?' Davey spluttered. 'We need to move quick! There's no time!'

'I'm going after Morgan,' Mallory muttered, a dark glint in his eye. 'He's under attack, so his men won't be so hell bent on protecting him.'

'What?'

'You heard me. You go after the Ostrich. I'm going

to make Morgan *pay* for what he's done.'

Davey lowered his voice. 'The way to do that *is* to go after the Ostrich. If the legend is true, we can fight him then without fear of being killed! Listen to me, Mallory – fighting Morgan now is madness! MADNESS.'

'The Ostrich is probably just a stupid legend, like everything else in these islands! Morgan can't intimidate me any more – I'm *not* frightened of him.'

'Then you're a fool!' Davey screamed. 'Before you had nothing to lose . . . but NOW you've got your life back. Don't you understand that? He can take it all over again – for good this time!'

'What are you two waiting for?' Woe yelled from the side of the *Floating Dagger*. 'Get on board!'

Davey and Mallory hurried out to join them. As they ran, Mallory shouted: 'You more than anyone should understand why he can't be left alive . . .'

8

# Flames and Fury

Cannon-fire erupted all over Dudley Bay, followed by the sound of grinding masts and collapsing sails. The sky was alight with flame. Pirates threw daggers, tried to strangle each other with rope, and swung hooks in an attempt to inflict as much damage as possible upon their enemies. The noise was deafening, and there seemed to be only a handful of survivors on each of the doomed ships.

Men rushed in every direction, some fighting, some panicking and some fleeing. Only one figure, a veritable giant in the crowd, walked along with a grim purpose.

Henry Morgan didn't fence. He simply used his immense strength to *carve* himself a path, hacking off arms and legs as if he was a deranged child playing with stuffed animals. Screams erupted all around him as the defending pirates came to realize the terrible truth of their situation and began to surrender.

Gullin, on the other hand, was *born* to fencing. He'd already taken several skilled pirates out of play, and he and Reik were now finishing off a captain who'd decided that he'd rather die than lose his ship.

In the midst of all the explosions and the madness, almost invisible because of its size, was a tiny rowing boat. Three of the occupants were taking it in turns to row while the fourth, a scruffy young pirate with a blond coiffure, pointed a pistol at the nearest ship and fired. It had taken Davey the best part of fifteen seconds to load the wretched weapon, so he prayed while he was aiming it.

CRACK! BOOM!

Halfway up the mainsail of the *Rogue Herring*, a very surprised-looking pirate dropped a dagger and crashed through the deck below.

Down in the rowing boat, Mallory suddenly leapt up and prepared to dive into the dark waters. Threeday and Woe were occupied with the rowing, but Davey had a resigned expression on his face.

'Right, here goes nothing!' said the cabin-boy, and dropped off the edge of the boat. There was a huge plume of water, and then he was gone.

'What's going on?' Threeday exclaimed. 'Where's he going?'

Davey grimaced. 'The *Herring*,' he said. 'Mallory's going to try to kill Morgan.'

'That's insane!' snapped the zombie. 'He'll get himself killed for good this time!'

'I'm going too,' said Davey, suddenly, trying not to look Threeday directly in the eyes. 'Get to the *Pride* if you can; I'll try to come after you.'

'But Davey . . .'

'Don't say anything. Just keep rowing.'

Threeday pulled back on the oars, his face a mask of shock. Davey unhooked his belt, and dropped his cutlass and pistol into the boat. 'They'll slow me down,' he explained, pulling a rather bland-looking dagger from his sock instead.

Before Threeday could muster an argument, Davey smiled at him. 'I *will* be back,' he said. Then he turned and plunged into the ocean.

Threeday tried to hold back all his anger and confusion as they continued to forge through the waves.

Cannons and pistols still exploded all around them; the noise was deafening.

Threeday took a deep breath.

'Keep rowing,' he said, getting to his feet.

'No!'

'What?'

Woe threw down the oars.

'You're not going as well!' he exclaimed, but Threeday didn't have time to answer – a piece of lead shot ripped through his stomach and plunged straight into the navigator's chest. Woe gasped, toppled overboard and splashed into the water.

'Wha—'

Threeday looked down at his gaping stomach. Then, as realization dawned, he dropped to his knees and began to run his arms through the waters beside the boat.

'Woe! Woe!' He scrambled over to the other side of the little vessel and repeated the search. 'Woe! Woe!'

Threeday quickly pulled the oars into the *Dagger*, and dived overboard.

'Meet yer new captain, yer scurvy dogs.'

Henry Morgan was atop the forecastle of his new ship, waving a rusty cutlass and screaming over the water for his remaining crew to swing across; fire was now consuming the *Rogue Herring*.

Gullin and Reik hurried over to join him.

'The captain's dead,' said the first mate, triumphantly. 'But the ship isn't ours yet; these jacks are putting up some serious resistance.'

'Stay 'ere,' Morgan boomed. 'An' don' leave any o' 'em alive. I'm goin' onta the islan' ta fin' Swag.'

The giant pirate stormed over to the side of the deck. To the astonishment of his own crew, Morgan leapt from the forecastle and plunged into the ocean far below.

'He's g— going on his own?' Reik stammered. 'He's not going to wait for help?'

Gullin raised an eyebrow. 'You really think he needs it?' he muttered.

Davey swam beneath the waves, a dagger held tight between his teeth. He was just approaching the *Herring* when a great shape dropped into the ocean from another ship. At first, Davey took it for a cast anchor. Then, as the shape began to move through the water, Davey recognized the monstrous head. It was Morgan.

Glancing around frantically, Davey saw to his horror that Mallory was already clambering aboard the flaming mass of the *Herring*. He tried to whistle, but the cabin-boy was suddenly dragged over the side of the ship by enemy pirates.

Davey knew he only had one chance. He needed to get to Morgan while the pirate was still in the water; a surprise attack might give him an edge. Thrusting his legs out behind him, the young pirate shot forward like a torpedo. Chopping through the water, he suddenly dived, moved through a complete loop and cannoned into his foe. Using his momentum to draw the knife, Davey stuck it between the pirate's ribs and twisted it. Then he was thrown back.

Morgan flailed around with frantic arms, turning in the nick of time to stop Davey's second dagger biting into his neck. The two pirates jostled for position under the water. Morgan was much stronger than Davey, but the young pirate was more agile; he managed to lift his feet up to Morgan's chest and kick the big man away. The knife floated freely for a second and then began to sink. Davey snatched it up before it went out of reach.

When he'd retrieved his weapon, he saw to his astonishment that Morgan had surfaced and was swimming towards the nearest ship, cackling manically as he went. Davey managed to put on a burst of energy and pursued him . . . to the remains of the *Rogue Herring*.

A few men, too fearful of the big leap, had lowered a rope ladder over the side of the *Herring*, and Morgan scrambled up it like a rat out of an aqueduct. Not only was his chest wound failing to slow him down, it seemed to be having no detrimental effect whatsoever.

Davey was close behind him. He had just put a foot on the fifth rung when he noticed that his foe had reached the top and was attempting to tip the contents of a miniature tar barrel over his head. Davey swung the rope ladder out wide, flinging his legs aside for leverage, as the boiling hot tar came down in a terrible shower. Morgan screamed a curse at him from above, and tried to knock him off the rope ladder by throwing the barrel down instead. It clipped Davey on the edge of the shoulder and he slipped, but he soon managed to regain his footing and raced up the ladder with renewed speed.

Morgan was waiting for him at the top, and several other pirates were giving them a wide berth. There was no sign of Mallory.

'Drop the dagger, whelp,' he demanded, drawing two cutlasses imbedded in the lower rigging and tossing one across the deck at him. 'You wanna be a man an' figh' ol' 'Enry? Take arms to ya.'

Davey nodded, cast his dagger aside and reached down for the cutlass, but Morgan had other plans. The big pirate bolted forward and, kneeing Davey aside before he could put a hand on the weapon, kicked it out of reach. Then he began to slash at Davey with his own blade, missing by a hair's whisker with each new arc he swung.

Left, right, jump, duck, dodge, dive; Davey was amazed at his own agility. Every time Morgan lunged, he managed to predict the pirate's intended direction, and get out of the way before the blow was struck. Deep down, he knew it was luck keeping him alive, and that it couldn't last, but something drove him on. He began to taunt the pirate, making ugly faces and announcing little 'yo-ho-hos' every time the man missed a strike. It felt fantastic, as if he was watching himself from outside his own body. Then, all at once, his luck gave out.

The crow's-nest, which had been burning steadily throughout the battle, chose that moment to collapse entirely, and Davey and Morgan were hammered with lumps of burning wood. Morgan's size helped *him*; he managed to brush away the flaming assault, as if he were swatting fireflies. Davey wasn't so lucky; one of the larger hunks hit him on the back, and knocked him face down on to the deck.

The *Rogue Herring* echoed with the sound of Morgan's laughter.

Placing both hands flat on the deck, Davey tried to push himself up, but he lacked the strength. Morgan reached down and snatched him by his shirt collar, yanking him up in one swift movement.

'You've been a thorn in my side twice too often, young wretch,' he spat. 'Now you'll learn the hard way. To mess with Henry Morgan is to duel with the fates.'

One hand clasped around Davey's throat, the pirate reached aloft with his cutlass and . . .

'BLACKBEARD! IT'S THE GHOST OF BLACKBEARD!'

The cry came from a bedraggled figure tied to the mast of the ship. It was a hoax, and quite an obvious one, but it was all Mallory could think of under the circumstances. And it worked.

Morgan spun around, momentarily distracted. Davey saw his opportunity; he slipped out of the pirate's grasp, rolled across the deck and snatched up his cutlass. Then he took aim, and hurled the weapon straight at him. The cutlass flew through the air, spinning three hundred and sixty degrees, before it pierced Morgan's chest.

The pirate staggered, took a step back and collapsed *through* the deck. There followed a sickening crash from below.

For a moment Davey just stood there, fires blazing

all around him, his breath coming and going in short bursts. Then he remembered the voice.

'Mallory? Are you OK? Where are you?'

'On the deck; I'm tied to the mast! HELP ME!'

Davey hurried through the smoke, carefully avoiding the hole that Morgan had fallen through.

'Over here. Now right a bit. No, *this* way.'

'Mallory?' Davey whispered, his hand closing around an arm in the smoky gloom. 'Is this your arm?'

There was no reply.

Davey yanked at the arm he had hold of and, to his horror, found himself clutching a severed limb.

'Ugh!' he managed, tossing the limb aside and choking back a gasp.

'What's wrong?'

'I just found a severed arm.'

'Throw it away!'

'I did! Look, I'm doing my best, here. OK?'

Davey groped around in the smog, his probing fingers eventually finding Mallory's shoulder.

'Keep still! I'm going to sever the ropes with my cutlass.'

'Er . . . I'm not sure that's such a good idea.'

'Look, do you want me to get you out of here or not?'

'Yes, of course I—'

'Then keep still!'

There was a rapid swish of air and Mallory felt the ropes fall away.

'Well done,' he said, reluctantly.

Davey tossed the cutlass aside, and ran for the starboard side of the ship. Mallory followed after him, complaining every time the fires spat a rogue spark at him. They were almost across the deck, when Davey heard a loud and terrible crash behind him.

He spun around.

'Mallory!'

A second hole had opened in the deck floor, and the cabin-boy was nowhere to be seen. Davey stepped gingerly toward the edge of the hole. Mallory was nothing more than a tiny figure far below.

'Hang on; I'm coming!'

Threeday clambered back on to the *Floating Dagger* and collapsed with exhaustion. Woe was gone. The poor old fool had sunk without a trace . . . and Threeday had failed to find his body in the water. The zombie felt a deep and sudden sadness overcome him as he reached two withered hands towards the oars . . .

\* \* \*

The *Rogue Herring* was still just afloat, nestled amid a world made entirely from smoke and wild explosions. The ship had become a floating fire-ball. The sails and deck were firmly alight, with tar barrels and rum racks blazing merrily in the background.

Deep in the bowels of the vessel, a large red and blue parrot flew down a collapsed corridor that once led to the ship's galley, and came to land on the good end of a half-collapsed shelf. The view from the shelf wasn't great; there was a lot of smoke, a few shadowy cupboards, some water leaking in through a small gap in the hull, and an injured, semi-conscious boy.

The parrot eyed him suspiciously.

'Me aunt's me uncle,' it said.

Mallory stared at it in disbelief. 'Ha! What are you doing here? How does it feel to be free of my mind, you old featherball?'

'Me aunt's me uncle,' said the parrot.

'Look, get out of here, will you? The air in here is getting bad. Go on! Shoo! I kept you alive for years. Don't stuff it all up just to come and watch me die.'

The bird put its head on one side.

'Me aunt's me uncle,' it said.

'Nice,' Mallory admitted. 'I used to have a family like that.'

'Me aunt's me uncle.'

'So you said. I'm thrilled for you, really I am.'

'Me aunt's me uncle.'

'Oh, SHUT UP!'

'Give us an order.'

'What?'

'Give us an order.'

'Will you go away if I do?'

'Me aunt's me uncle.'

Davey pushed his foot forward and tentatively felt the edge of the giant deck-hole. Then, tugging on a sail rope that hung loose from the devastated mast, he began to lower himself into the darkness.

'I still can't see anything! Where are you?'

'Down here!' Mallory cried. 'Left a little.'

'OK.'

Davey reached out a hand and found Mallory's fingers.

'Right, now hold on tight!'

'What?'

Davey heaved on the rope and began to pull the cabin-boy to safety.

'Agghh! You weigh a ton! Is your leg stuck under a plank or something?'

'DAVEY! Is that you?'

Davey froze, his arm still weighed down by what he thought was Mallory. However, the voice had come from elsewhere.

'Mall?'

'Yes! Help me! I'm over here.'

Davey choked out a lungful of smoke.

'But if you're over there, who have I got heaaaaaaarrgh!'

A blade edge bit into Davey's leg, and Henry Morgan climbed the young pirate like a giant monkey, clambering over him with a terrible cackle and rolling on to the deck above.

'Mallory 'ndeed,' he spat, struggling to his feet and working free the cutlass that was still wedged firmly in his chest. The wound stitched itself together. 'If it aint me ol' cabin-boy all 'formed up an' returned to us? An' look who 'e's teamin' with? Once I finished wi' you, Swag, I'll get me revenge on that backstabbin' swine. He'll pay a darker price even 'n you.'

Releasing the blade, he began to take frantic swipes at the sail rope that supported the now swinging form of Davey Swag.

'Mall!' Davey called. 'Help me out here!'

'I'm trapped under a beam, here! You're supposed to be helping me!'

Davey scrambled up the last few feet of rope just as it was severed from above. For a few seconds, he plummeted downwards, managing at the last instant to snatch hold of a wrecked board that stuck out on one of the lower decks.

'Agghhh!'

'What's wrong?' Mallory cried from the foggy depths of the hole. 'Has he got you?'

'No! I'm hanging three decks down, and I've just got a load of splinters jammed in my hand!'

Some of the smoke was clearing. Davey would have been glad of this, had it not been for the fact that Morgan was now visible, climbing down the deck towards him with a dagger pressed between his lips.

It was at this time, with the pirate almost upon him, that Davey made a split-second decision he soon came to regret: he let go of the plank.

'Arrrgghhh!'

Mallory heard rather than saw the sickening crash nearby.

'Great!' the cabin-boy exclaimed. 'Just great! Now we're both trapped down here.'

There was no reply.

Mallory rolled his eyes.

'Are you dead, Swag?' he called.

Still nothing.

'Wake up! Morgan's coming down here to kill us both!'

'Give us an order,' squawked the parrot, significantly.

Henry Morgan was halfway down to the last deck level when the bird flew in his face. The flapping, squawking explosion of feathers took the pirate captain completely by surprise, and he fell back, tumbling down a broken companionway step and badly jarring his shoulder. The arrival of this sudden pain did little to dim the bite of the already agonizing wound in his chest, but Morgan was a fighter to the last, and he struggled back to his feet, spitting blood and cursing with every breath in his body. After snatching up the knife that had slipped from his mouth in the fall, he began stamping and kicking his way across the lower deck.

The parrot wasn't done yet, however. It circled the deck a few times and then came in for a second dive at the pirate, something that turned out to be a big mistake.

This time, Morgan saw the bird coming. He snatched a burning board from the companionway and hurled it through the air. In doing so, he managed to spike and torch the bird at the same time.

'Me aunt's me unc—' it managed, before falling to its smokey doom in the ruins of the ship.

Morgan narrowed his eyes and stared around him. There, a few feet away to his left, was a figure sprawled beneath two heavy wooden beams.

'Davey Swag, whelp o' whelps,' he said, spitting out the words as if they tasted foul to him. 'You should 'a' known better 'an ta cross ol' 'Enry. Now ya can face yer doom.'

'I'm not Davey Swag,' Mallory blurted, a sick smile on his face. 'But you can kill me and be done with it, Morgan, you scum-sucking mutt.'

Morgan took a moment to peer around him. Then, sighting a crumpled body through the swathes of smoke, he nodded approvingly and returned his attention to the cabin-boy.

'No' a bad idea,' he said, dropping to his knees and driving the dagger towards Mallory's throat. 'No' a bad idea at all.'

The pirate threw his weight behind the blade, but before he could pierce the cabin-boy's throat, a large grappling iron hooked his arm and wrenched his entire body skyward.

'Don't like that much, do you?' Threeday Leyonger

cried. The zombie had rigged the grappling rope around the shortest sail mast and was using his own tattered body as a counterweight.

Morgan screamed with rage and struggled with frantic fury, but his advantage was lost . . . and his troubles were just beginning.

Davey Swag emerged from the smoke before him, his consciousness regained and his determination doubled. Moving with lightning speed, the young pirate reached down and grabbed the still-burning parrot-stake. Then he darted forward and thrust the wood into Morgan's stomach.

The pirate went up like a Roman candle, flames licking his tattered coats and melting the flesh from his face.

'That was for Governor Jordel Swag,' Davey screamed, smashing his skull into Morgan's chin. 'And this is for my mother . . . you wretch.'

Morgan's flesh began to peel away. It was a sight Davey found difficult to watch, so he turned away and busied himself freeing the trapped cabin-boy instead.

'YOU, WHELP!' Morgan screamed after the boy, as his body was engulfed in flame.

Davey blocked out the pirate's dreadful noise, and knelt down beside his friend. Threeday hurried over to join him and together they wrenched up the beam that had constricted Mallory's chest.

'Let's get out of here,' Threeday cried. 'Only, this ship IS sinking, you know ... and the *Pride* looks manageable.'

Davey peered up at his friend, and managed to share the zombie's victorious smile. Mallory passed out from shock.

The trio emerged from the smoking wreckage of the *Rogue Herring* in the formidable *Floating Dagger*. Explosions still rang out all around them, as fire was exchanged on every side. One other ship had almost disappeared between the waves, and of the two vessels that *were* still afloat, only the *Pride* looked serene – an horrific battle was taking place on the ship that sat just across the water.

Davey found it very hard not to shed a tear for Woe ... the spindly prisoner *had* stuck by them through thick and thin. Even Threeday was bitterly upset, and he'd been the first to admit that he hadn't trusted the man.

'Do you think *he's* OK?' Davey asked, prodding Mallory with a finger.

Threeday nodded and pointed out that the cabin-boy's breathing was steady.

'He's probably just exhausted,' he said. 'Let him sleep.'

Threeday put his head on one side.

'Davey,' he ventured, 'are *you* OK? Only, that was quite a battle back there . . . and you, unlike me, are not an animated corpse.'

'Tell me about it.'

'Do you think Morgan's really dead?'

'I don't know,' Davey admitted. 'I hope so – don't reckon I could go through all that again if he isn't.' He yawned, and produced a straight-edged blade from his belt. 'I found another good sword at least.'

'Where did you get that from?'

'It fell on me as I made for the boat.'

'Pfft, ha! Some luck at last!'

Davey smiled wanly . . . and leaned over, letting his head rest against the side of the boat. 'Morgan *is* dead,' he concluded, his voice lowering. 'He has to be; no one burns like that and survives.'

'I know, but Davey . . . Davey?'

Threeday hooked the oars and lifted his friend's arm; Davey was snoring like a baby. Oh well, it *had* been a long day.

'Well, as usual it looks like I'm the one left with all

the hard work,' Threeday gasped, resisting the urge to shake the young pirate's shoulders in an effort to wake him. He rowed for the *Pride* instead.

'Arghghghgh!' Reik screamed a battle cry as he drove his sword into the stomach of a fallen pirate.

Gullin knocked out the ship's first mate and threw the man overboard.

'Right!' he screamed. 'Let's find Cap'n Morgan and get this dump moving! Men to the sails! Man to the wheel! Let's finish this thing!'

'I'm taking a crew below decks,' Reik muttered. 'There's still some o' the bleeders holding out down there.'

Gullin nodded.

'I'll come with you,' he said. 'We want to get this over and done with as quickly as possible.'

The *Davey's Pride*, wedged amid the circle of half-destroyed pirate ships like a maypole surrounded by dancers, was being largely ignored. Davey couldn't believe his luck; he thought at the very least that it would have been hit by cannon-fire or boarded. Having scrambled up the port side of the boat and on to the waist deck, the three companions made straight for the sails.

Gullin clambered up the last few steps and almost fell on to the deck, Reik collapsing beside him in sympathetic exhaustion.

'Got 'em,' Gullin panted. 'Got 'em all.'

Reik nodded. 'Cap'n Morgan will be pleased. There's practically no damage to the ship, either.'

Gullin rolled on to his stomach, but when he finally managed to get to his feet again, a look of absolute terror filled his eyes.

'Qu— quick!' he yelled at the *Herring* crew who now surrounded him, pointing towards the receding shadow of *Davey's Pride*. 'The ship! It's moving! Get after it! GET AFTER IT!'

Reik scrambled up with the help of several deckhands.

'What about Cap'n Morgan?' he said. 'We can't leave him behind!'

'Morgan will slaughter us ALL if that is Swag sailing that ship,' he growled. 'Now get the men moving . . . or I'll kill you myself.'

Reik gulped back his fear, and began screaming commands at the bewildered crewmen. The ship began to move out of the smoke.

* * *

The fractured, half-destroyed remains of the *Rogue Herring* blazed merrily on the ocean. As the several remaining crew members fought valiantly (and, it had to be said, pointlessly) to dowse the blaze, others crammed into rowing boats and made to pursue the new ship their colleagues had commandeered.

The last boat to leave contained two junior crewmen and an elderly, ragged-looking dog, which yelped and dived into the water when Henry Morgan rose from the depths like a dark spirit made flesh.

One crewman was so shocked that he also dived into the water and tried to out-paddle the dog in order to reach the shore first.

'It— it's— it's the captain!'

Charred fingers gripped the side of the boat as the pirate emerged from the ocean, his face burnt almost beyond recognition. Morgan hauled the last of his great bulk into the tiny vessel and growled like a man possessed.

'Y— you survived, Cap'n!' said the terrified oarsman. 'Y— you survived!'

Morgan spat a jet of salty water over the side of the boat.

'O'course I did,' he growled. ''Mortal, ol' 'Enry is; one o' a kind.'

'B— but your face—'

'It'll righ' itself in time, ya dogs.' His eyes took on an eerie glow. 'I bin burnt up worse 'an this in me days and no mistake. 'Old still.'

The oarsman frantically wrestled against the tide, and managed to still the boat.

'C— C— Cap'n?'

'Where's the crew?'

'There, Cap'n!' The oarsman pointed at the back of the ship. 'Looks like they're goin' after the other ship what the boy had control of!'

'Swag, Mallory, an' 'at zombie o' theirs don' ge' away from ol' 'Enry twice. Ge' rowin'. I wan' back on me new ship.'

*Davey's Pride* caught on the wind and sailed away, as Davey and Threeday whooped and cheered victorious cries from the deck.

Mallory disappeared into the captain's cabin and returned with a compass. Dropping down on to his knees, he unfolded Davey's map and knelt on top of it.

'Right,' he yelled. 'Now do exactly what I say, when I say it! We're off to Charnel Island!'

'You can navigate?' Threeday exclaimed, casting Davey a surprise glance.

'Does Morgan have bad breath? Of course I can navigate! Besides, I was a parrot, remember? I've been everywhere in the world! Twice.'

'Yeahay!' Davey screamed. 'Voodoo Ostrich, here we come!'

For the first time in many years, Threeday found himself laughing hysterically.

# Personal diary of
# Davey Swag, aged 16¼

*Captain's Log. Day 12.*

Woe wanted me to destroy this diary, and I feel like I've
betrayed him by returning to it. But he was a good man and I
am thankful for his sacrifice and our brief friendship.

The black ship dogs us night and day, though with Mallory's help
we are managing to stay ahead of it. He says the *Pride* is the
fastest ship he has ever seen, and he believes it might even
have belonged to Blackbeard once. Mallory is great; he seems
much nicer as a person than he was as a bird. I only hope I
can repay my debt to him.

Food is in short supply, though Mallory found a fishing rod and has
proved himself very skilful with it.

Captain's Log. Day 13.

Bizarrely, I have started to miss Woe's unpredictable behaviour on board ship. The threat of our pursuers remains ever present, though I spent a nice afternoon playing chess with an old set Threeday found in the captain's cabin.

Threeday seems to have changed a lot since I first met him. He's looking more like a skeleton everyday, but he talks more and more of the Voodoo Ostrich, and how he believes the creature's blood will return him to life. I hope he's right. From what he has told me about his past and from my own experience, Threeday is a kind and unselfish person who never deliberately caused harm to anybody. He deserves to regain the life that he lost.

Captain's Log. Day 14.

AM A great mist is upon us, and the waters here have become almost impossible to navigate. Mallory thinks we are very close to Charnel Island.

I can feel my heart beating in my chest. Threeday says that by killing Morgan I am now a true hero, but I think there must be more to being a hero than bloody conflict. Otherwise, I'm just another monster on the high seas. I certainly don't feel like a hero ... and plunging a knife into the monster's chest didn't quite give me the satisfaction that I always hoped it would. My parents are gone, and putting an end to Henry Morgan didn't bring them back.

**PM** A jut of rock has been spotted. Mallory believes the mist around Charnel is protective and magical, and that it would be sensible to lower one of the *Pride*'s rowing boats and approach the island that way.

# Legends

The mists around Charnel lifted without warning, as if the gods had suddenly removed a great blanket from the island and gone, 'Ta-daa!'

Davey gazed out at a small but impressive landmass with a large volcano in the centre and several small hills surrounding it. A forest covered nearly all the intervening space.

Mallory and Threeday had taken it in turns to row, and now both of them were staring at the island with expectant and gleeful expressions.

'Charnel,' Davey said, beginning to row again. 'Well done, Mall – you're one hell of a navigator.'

'Sometimes, I surprise even myself!' Mallory shouted.

'I hope it's real,' Threeday muttered, and Davey noticed the zombie crossing his crumbling fingers. 'Do *you* think it exists?'

'The Ostrich?' Davey gave a large grin. 'Absolutely.'

Mallory gritted his teeth, and started to row again. However, after a few minutes, it was apparent that the little boat wasn't getting any closer to the island.

'What's happening?' Davey asked, leaning over the side of the boat. 'Are we stuck on something?'

'No,' Mallory said, sternly. 'It feels like there's something stopping us!'

Threeday reached out for the oars. 'Let me have a go.'

Mallory moved aside, but Threeday had no more luck in moving the vessel. It was like rowing in glue.

'Weird,' said the zombie. 'It's like a magical barrier or something . . .'

Mallory nodded.

'Exactly like that.'

Davey peered at the distant island, and then into the water. 'Maybe it only blocks boats from coming in,' he muttered. 'Do you think it would let us swim ashore?'

'I don't know,' Mallory admitted. 'It might. Maybe it would be better to try to swim ashore *anyway*.'

Davey and Threeday frowned at him.

'Why's that?' Davey asked.

'Well, we don't know what's *on* this island; there

might be natives or something. We don't want to get seen from the trees ... they'll probably take the boat! Far better to leave it out here on the edge of the bay. That way we can always come back for it.' He reached down into the depths of the rowing boat and produced a thick rope that was curled up under the middle seat. 'We could tie the oars round this and use them as anchors. We wouldn't be seen from out here, we could swim in, and the boat would be safe.'

'If we *can* swim in, that is,' Davey pointed out. 'We still don't know if the barrier will stop *us* as well.'

'That's settled then,' said Mallory and, after helping the others to tie up the oars and drop them into the ocean, he dived straight over the side of the boat and began swimming purposefully towards the island.

When he'd gone a little way out, Davey turned to Threeday with a dark expression on his face.

'You think he'll get through?' he whispered. 'I've suddenly got a very bad feeling about this place.'

'I agree, Davey,' the zombie muttered. 'But we don't seem to have much of a choice. We can't row the boat any further.'

'But what if the oars come loose? The rope might

break or slip off, and then we've lost the boat! I can't just abandon ship out here! We'll never get off the darn island and, considering that we don't even know *what's* waiting for us there, I don't like the thought of being trapped!'

Threeday shrugged. 'We really *need* to find the Ostrich,' he admitted, 'and at least we'll be safely on dry land!'

'Yeah . . .' Davey muttered. 'Stuffed, cooked over a fire or hung from a tree! Those cannibals we met on Dudley might have been friendly and sociable, but I don't think we'll get lucky like that again! Someone should stay with the boat . . .'

Threeday seemed to pause for a second, and patted his friend companionably on the shoulder. Then he dived into the water and began to swim after Mallory. The cabin-boy had already progressed quite a long way; the barrier had evidently not blocked his progress.

Davey muttered under his breath and sulked for a few minutes, trying to decide whether to follow them or not. He'd *got* his revenge on Morgan, after all. On the other hand, the Ostrich *could* be real . . . and if it was, it would be guarded. Could he really let his friends head for danger? Alone?

Davey deliberated over his predicament, before he

saw something that helped him make up his mind very quickly: a fin.

'Shark!' Davey screamed, leaping up and almost toppling the boat. 'Shaaaaark!'

Either Mallory and Threeday had swum too far to hear him, or the magical barrier was swallowing sound, for both of them swam on.

'Oi!' Davey screamed. 'Sharrrk! There's a shark coming!'

He spun round and looked for the fin which, worryingly, had disappeared beneath the waves. Davey had a terrible vision of the great fish eating *both* his friends alive. Then again, he thought, it might attack the *Floating Dagger*.

Davey looked down, and realized with sudden panic that he was probably a lot nearer.

No treasure was worth dying for.

There was another considerable splash as the young pirate hit the water and swam as if every shark in the world was after him.

Gullin was exhausted. It felt like he hadn't had any sleep for days, especially since Morgan had caught up with the ship. The giant pirate didn't seem to need rest himself, and he paced back and forth on the quarterdeck, looking like something out of a horror story and making the entire crew feel that they had to collapse in order to earn any time in the bunks. Moreover, watching Morgan's wounds slowly stitch themselves together and heal up was a very difficult thing for the most hardened pirate to do. Even the captain's horrific burns were lightening up and becoming more patchy.

Gullin rubbed his red-rimmed eyes and peered into the mists.

'We're almost upon them, I reckon,' he said. 'Shouldn't be much longer.'

'If the legends are true,' said Reik, yawning widely, 'there's a magical barrier protecting this place. We might have to swim ashore. I'll get the men armed up.'

Morgan turned a charred eye on the pair.

'If Swag an' Mallory get to the bird, I'll kill every jack o' this ship,' he said, and strode away.

Gullin bowed his head; suddenly, he was too tired even to fear the incredible wrath of his master.

'Keep awake, boss,' Reik muttered. 'I've a feeling we're goin' to need you on this one . . .'

Mallory waded up the beach, breathing like a man five times his age, and collapsed on to the sand.

A few minutes later, Threeday crawled ashore.

'I . . . hate . . . the sea,' he managed, rolling over and staring up at the sky.

Mallory sat up.

'Bet Davey hates it even more,' he said.

'Why do you say that?'

'Because there's a shark after him.'

'Oh, yes, well that would certainly explain . . . WHAT?'

Threeday scrambled to his feet and squinted to block out the blinding rays of sunlight.

'Davey! Swim! SWIM!'

'I wouldn't worry,' Mallory muttered. 'He's got nine lives, that boy.'

Threeday didn't hear him, for he'd already dashed down the beach and was wading in to the water. 'Faster, Davey! Swim faster! It's going to catch you!'

The scene that followed caused Threeday to slap a hand over his eyes and pray to the fates. The shark had caught up with Davey and dived under the water.

The zombie mouthed a silent oath to every god he could think of, and a few merciful-sounding ones that he made up on the spot but who, he decided, should definitely exist if they didn't already. Fortunately, it seemed that Skinteeth, the god of narrow escapes, not only existed, but was paying attention.

When he opened his eyes, Threeday couldn't conceal his surprise; Davey Swag was still swimming madly to shore, but the fin had overtaken him and was even closer.

Mallory, who'd watched the scene with a strangely detached amusement, wandered down to where Threeday was standing and patted the boy on the shoulder.

'See? I told you he'd be all right.'

'But what . . . how . . . *why* didn't it attack him?'

'Who knows? Maybe it's a vegetarian shark. Maybe it's . . . hang on . . . look at that!'

The fin rose from the waves and floated up the sand. There was a native underneath it; a little bald man of indeterminate origin, wrapped in a loincloth and covered from head to foot with strange symbols that appeared to be scratched on to his skin.

'Evening,' he said, stomping past the two companions and nodding politely. 'Turned out to be a nice one, hasn't it?' He glanced back at them briefly, but didn't stop moving.

As Davey dived, spluttered and flapped ashore, Threeday and Mallory watched the little man drop the spear he'd been carrying and disappear into the trees at the edge of the beach.

'W— was it far behind me?' Davey yelled, scrambling to his feet and checking himself to make sure he hadn't had a leg bitten off without noticing. 'D— did you get a good look at it?'

Eventually, realizing he was unharmed, Davey spun around, cupped both hands over his brow and studied the ocean. 'It must have thought it couldn't catch me. Boy, was I ever lucky there! Ha! Good job I'm a really fast swimmer!' He turned back to face the others when nobody answered.

Mallory and Threeday were both facing away from him, their eyes fixed on the jungle.

'Er . . . HELLO?' Davey spat. 'I've almost been *eaten* by a shark, here – could you two at least *pretend* you're impressed?'

As if swatting away an annoying mosquito, Mallory waved down Davey's protest.

'It wasn't a shark,' he said. 'It was a little bald man wearing a hat with a fin stuck to the top.'

'What?' Davey looked from the water to Mallory and back again. 'How do you know?'

'Because he swam past you, then waded up the beach and disappeared into the jungle.'

'Are you serious?'

'Deadly.'

'He is,' Threeday confirmed, still squinting at the jungle fringe. 'In fact, I think he might have a camp here.'

Davey muttered something under his breath and followed his two friends as they made for the trees, Mallory striding determinedly over the sand while Threeday moved more cautiously, ever conscious of the dangers a jungle could contain.

'Well, well, well,' said a voice, before they'd gone further than a few yards. 'How extraordinary. We hardly get any visitors here, these days.'

The little man they'd seen earlier stepped out from behind a mango tree. He'd removed the shark fin, and was grinning manically.

'Er . . . hello,' Mallory said, turning towards the islander with an uneasy expression on his face. 'Er . . . sorry about the confusion earlier . . .'

The little man frowned. 'What confusion?'

'My friend thought you were a shark.'

'Did he? Oh good. That's the desired effect.'

'I'm Davey Swag,' said Davey, glaring at the stranger with definite apprehension. 'These are my friends, Threeday Leyonger – please try not to stare at him, he's a zombie – and Mallory. We're pirates – sort of. We've been in a great sea battle and now we're here . . . er . . . looking for—'

'Food,' Mallory interrupted.

'Oh.' The little man again glanced at them all and smiled wanly before turning his attention to Davey. 'Tough battle, was it?'

Davey nodded. 'The worst.'

'Of course, pirates can be very . . . aggressive people.'

Threeday held the islander's gaze; he was still a little unsure of him.

'Actually,' he said. 'We were in a battle with a pirate called Henry Morgan.'

'Henry Morgan?' The little man nodded sagely. 'A terrible pirate, by all accounts . . . an unholy legend upon the high seas.' He leaned towards Davey and confided, 'You are probably lucky to have escaped with your lives.'

'Actually,' Davey muttered. 'We were a bit luckier than that. I . . . sort of managed to kill him.'

Both Mallory and Threeday were staring at the little man with quizzical expressions.

'Are you a witch-doctor of some sort?' said the zombie, who recognized the signs.

'I am . . . a guardian of sorts,' said the stranger. 'Though I was once a pirate, much like yourselves.'

'And you live here, do you?' Mallory pressed him.

'Indeed, I have very little choice in the matter. I am currently the only person not born on Charnel to live here. Everyone else comes for something called the Voodoo Ostrich . . . though few ever find it.'

'REALLY?' exclaimed Threeday, but Mallory shoved him in the ribs and gave him a warning look.

Davey licked his lips, and tried to talk nonchalantly.

'Do you mean ostrich as in a big, weird-looking bird?' the young pirate ventured.

'Don't they come from Africa?' said Mallory, doubtfully. 'I've never even *seen* one.'

The little man stared at them for a few moments longer.

'Hmm . . . you mean you found your way here *without* stumbling across the legend or the map required to find us? How extraordinary.'

'What *is* a Voodoo Ostrich anyway?' Davey spluttered, ignoring the comment and ploughing on.

'The Voodoo Ostrich is a long-dead creature that lies in a secret cavern chamber beneath yonder mountain. It is a wicked thing, cursed to bleed for all eternity . . . And it is known by few and suspected by many that drinking the foul creature's blood grants the drinker an immortality . . . of sorts.'

The series of gulps and gasps that followed apparently did a lot to please the little man, who obviously delighted in telling people about the legend. Still, there was a sad and even reluctant edge to his voice.

'Does it really grant immortality?' Threeday managed, trying to keep the pleading edge out of his voice. 'I mean, just by drinking its blood you get to live for ever? How amazing is that!'

The islander shook his head.

'There is a price,' he said. 'There is *always* a price. You see, I believe the Ostrich grants eternal life to people of a certain evil disposition. People, frankly, who tend to have dark souls. If its blood is swallowed *here* on the island, the drinker is granted a long life . . . but is trapped on Charnel for the duration of that life. If its blood is taken away from the island and consumed elsewhere, the gift is said to be a certain immunity to death in combat.'

Threeday's face fell. He looked as though he had just been punched in the stomach. Even Mallory sighed.

'Has anyone good ever drunk it?' said Davey, staring doubtfully at the distant mountain.

'No,' said the little man. 'The only person ever to drink from the Ostrich itself was me . . . and, sadly, I will never be known as a good person. As you can see, I am trapped here. My companion, a man called Paprika, was more sensible.' He ignored the surprised looks the trio were giving him, and went on, 'Now, please follow me . . . we can talk on the way to my camp.'

A group of more than ten pirates began to surface in the balmy waters of Charnel Bay. Knives clenched between teeth and cutlasses dangling from belts, Henry Morgan and his crew emerged from the deep, wading up the beach toward the higher sands. Gullin had a sword in each fist, while Reik was carrying a vicious-looking pike. The rest of the group comprised the pick of the crew; all looked murderous and unafraid.

'Do we spread out, Cap'n?' said Gullin, indicating to Reik that some sort of special formation might be necessary.

'We stay 'gether,' Morgan boomed. 'I ain' spreadin' thin jus' to 'ave Swag and his brood slip through me fingers agin.'

'Right you are, boss,' said Reik, averting his eyes when Gullin glared at him.

'We show 'em no mercy,' Morgan growled on. 'An' I wan' tha' Ostrich in me 'ands afore Swag gets to it.'

The crew moved on up the beach, as a dark cloud began to form over the island.

'You said you drank from the Ostrich?' Davey asked the energetic little man, as the group moved through the forest. They had picked up the pace, and were now almost running through the trees. 'How old are you, exactly?'

'I am . . . quite ancient. However—'

'Then it works!' Threeday exclaimed, suddenly forgetting himself.

'Though, as I explained, I am *not* a good person. Paprika wasn't either, but he was less greedy than I . . . and was able to escape.'

'Nobody THINKS they're a saint,' Davey muttered. 'But I'm a good judge of character, and I can tell you're OK. In fac—'

'You said this island was terrible,' Threeday cut in, 'but you didn't say why.'

The little man smiled.

'There are many reasons. Firstly, Charnel is a terrible place because of the natives who crawl over it and under it in search of sacrifices. Practically nothing can satiate their lust for bloodshed, so visitors to our humble shores *never* last long. Most people who are brought here, well, either the treacherous mountain paths kill them or else they get savagely slaughtered.'

Davey and Mallory shared a worried glance. 'Savagely, you say?'

'Oh yes. The natives are almost definitely insane and they're fiercely protective of Ostrich Mountain . . . and so they should be. Some dark enchantments *do* exist, regardless of what the sceptics tell you. This island has been my home for a looong time.'

'So how come the natives have never killed you?' Threeday asked.

'Oh, they leave me alone because they have great respect for me. In fact, they tend to leave me little gifts like fruit and trinkets every now and then. I know not to push my luck, of course. The natives guard the Ostrich well. If they didn't, I would have got in and—'

'They leave you gifts?' Davey gawped at the islander. 'If it's not a rude question, do you mind if I ask why?'

The little man smiled.

'Not at all. I was quite a legend in my day, you see. I sailed the seas, robbing the rich and giving to the poor. When I finally gave up all the heroics, I retired here and donated a certain amount of riches to the tribe. Then I built a tree-house and started to live the quiet life, away from piracy.'

'You were a pirate?' Davey exclaimed. 'No way! What were you called?'

The little man shuffled to a halt and sniffed the air distractedly.

'My name is Edward Teach,' he said, with a sudden grin. 'But I was once known on the high seas as Blackbeard.'

Davey and Threeday had both frozen on the spot and were staring at the little islander in shock, as if he'd just clicked his fingers and turned into a chicken.

'Y— you're Blackbeard?' Mallory ventured. 'As in, you're named after the famous pirate?'

The islander grinned.

'As in I *am* the famous pirate,' he said, quietly. 'And though I only ever attacked pirates who were a threat to my ships, I was certainly merciless . . . in my day.'

'B— b— b—' Threeday was suddenly having trouble getting his words out. 'But you're nothing like him. I mean you're . . . *absolutely* nothing like him.'

'You can't be Blackbeard!' Davey yelled. 'Blackbeard . . . Blackbeard is . . . er . . .' He seemed to struggle to find the right words to say, and eventually settled on, 'Blackbeard was a giant!'

'Oh, they made me out to be all sorts of things, I know. The fact is, I *did* win a lot of sea battles, but I certainly never plundered the islands in quite the way the stories say. These days, I'm a devoted pacifist.'

'A pacifist? But you're Blackbeard! If you're not an evil despot, then . . .'

'Other pirates took your fame,' Threeday interrupted, a grim and knowing look in his eyes, 'and turned it to their own dark purposes – pirates like Henry Morgan, I'll bet. *He* was the real terror on the sea . . .'

'Yeah,' Davey agreed. 'But the Ostrich's blood didn't do much for him . . .'

Blackbeard's face froze.

'Morgan drank from the Ostrich?' he exclaimed. 'But how? He has never been here!'

Threeday suddenly decided that their pretence was useless. 'Your old friend Paprika gave him a vial,' he muttered. 'To our knowledge, Morgan consumed it far from here . . . so I take it that means he's unstoppable?'

A dark glint flickered in Blackbeard's eyes. 'Your battle with Morgan was not on these sands, then, in these forests?'

'No,' Davey confirmed.

'Then Morgan remains alive.'

Davey, Threeday and Mallory exchanged a terrified glance.

'Then it's MORGAN who was following us in the black ship!' Davey gasped. 'I thought it was another crew!'

'Do you think he—'

'Listen to me!' Blackbeard straightened up, and fixed the group with a penetrating stare. 'For I have waited a *long* time for ones such as you. The only place Morgan can be killed is *here*, on the shores where the fell creature who gives him his arcane gift was hatched. You *must* go into the mountain and bring out the Ostrich. Once it is taken off this island, it can be destroyed. If you succeed in doing so, Morgan will become a mortal man . . . and I will be able to leave this place.'

Davey was too overwhelmed to speak. Even Mallory took a step back and leaned against a tree.

'You mentioned that the Voodoo Ostrich was inside the volcano,' Threeday said. 'Will it be difficult to find?'

Blackbeard shook his head.

'No, but if the natives catch you they'll stop you getting to the Ostrich and will most likely sacrifice you to their infernal gods . . .'

The little man observed the boys' terrified expressions. Only Threeday seemed unafraid and especially determined.

'I should tell *you* one more truth about the Ostrich,' Blackbeard went on, addressing the zombie. 'I am afraid it cannot return life where there is none . . .'

Threeday's face fell, and for a moment Davey and Mallory both felt sure he would collapse with despair.

'Take heart, though.' The old man smiled. 'Your animation could be sustained for many, many years by a particularly talented witch-doctor . . . and I did once know just such a lady. If you do what I ask and help me escape Charnel, I will find her and see that she helps you.'

Threeday brightened slightly, as Blackbeard declared, 'Now prepare yourselves; we're almost *there*.'

At length, the group stopped beside a large wall of rock that Mallory practically walked into.

Blackbeard moved along the rock, paused at a cave and ripped down a strangled net of vines. 'There's a torch just inside the door. It shouldn't take long to light. Follow me.'

Morgan, Gullin and Reik were hacking through the forest with their cutlasses, as the rest of the *Herring* crew spread out around them.

'Keep 'em peeled,' Morgan boomed. 'I don' wan' any mistakes.'

Gullin nodded. 'We'll get him this time, Cap'n.'

'Yeah,' echoed Reik. 'We'll get 'em all.'

The crew made their way towards the forbidding gloom of the jungle.

# The Voodoo Ostrich

'There are spiders in this cave,' Davey mumbled. 'Biiig spiders.'

'Oh?' said Blackbeard, trying to keep the torch flame burning enough for them to see the way ahead. 'Why do you say that?'

'I can feel something crawling on my back,' the young pirate admitted.

'Me too,' said Mallory. 'But right now I'm too frightened to investigate.'

'In my case,' said Threeday, 'they'll only bite something that would have dropped off anyway.' The zombie's eyes were glowing almost as brightly as the torch.

The group proceeded through the dark tunnel, which seemed to wind downhill for quite a way before branching right and starting into a steep climb.

'Do you know every cave on the island?' Threeday

asked, reflecting on his own encyclopaedic knowledge of the woods on Cocos Island.

'Oh yes,' said Blackbeard, with a hint of regret. 'Actually, they're mostly all connected. There's a big lake under the mountain. Many years ago, it saved my life.'

'I don't see that,' Davey commented, finally plucking up the courage to shake himself free of the stowaways he'd collected. 'How can a lake save your life?'

Blackbeard yawned in the dusty half-light of the tunnel.

'Because I fell from a very high place,' he explained. 'And if the lake hadn't been there, I would have become part of the ground instead. Any more questions? Do you want to know what I had for breakfast this morning, or where I was when the Raid on Kerral Cove took place?'

'No,' Davey whispered. 'No more questions.'

'Sorry to have brought it up,' said Threeday. 'I was just curious, that's all. I know what it's like to live in the same, small place for a very long time.'

The little man suddenly took a right turn and walked into what – to all intents and purposes – looked exactly like a section of the rock wall.

Blackbeard pushed against it, and they emerged into

another stretch of dense jungle. Davey, Threeday and Mallory shared a worried glance; the place was a veritable maze.

They followed the ancient pirate along five, six, seven different paths, before he emerged on to a small walkway that seemed to terminate in another section of dull grey rock.

'You are going with us all the way, right?' Davey hazarded.

Threeday and Mallory looked at the old man expectantly.

'No,' Blackbeard concluded. 'But I will draw you a map.' He produced a scrap of parchment from a sack around his waist and began scratching on it with what looked like a black stub of hard ash.

'But—'

'Why can't—'

'Shh! Listen.'

The three companions were immediately silenced. Despite their clash with Morgan, none of them fancied disobeying a direct order from Blackbeard himself . . . however unlikely a fellow he had turned out to be.

'You just need to go through the little cave down there on the right, take a left and then the lines I'm putting down here should see you through the rest of the complex. I know *all* the shortcuts; I'll get you there in double quick time. Do you think you'll be able to follow my scratches?'

Mallory squinted at the parchment. 'I think so,' he muttered. 'Looks fairly straightforward, I suppose.'

'Good job,' Blackbeard muttered. 'Watch the pits and traps in there – one or two have survived the ravages of time. Hmm . . . and I'd move quickly if I were you, because I think we've got company . . .' The little man started to hurry away. 'Leave the torch – there's no time! I'll be fine! Just go! Now!'

As Davey, Mallory and Threeday glanced around the clearing, several odd-looking bushes began to take on alarming shapes.

A native tribe were emerging from the undergrowth . . . and they looked a lot less friendly than the inhabitants of Dudley Island.

Davey drew his cutlass as he and Threeday began to edge back towards the cave mouth. Moving carefully and quietly, they slipped inside and were gone.

Blackbeard took a deep breath and silently prayed that the Ostrich natives hadn't caught sight of them.


'Left, not right! He said left inside the tunnel!'

Mallory waved his arms angrily at Davey, who

quickly realized his mistake and increased his pace in order to keep up with the zombie.

'We go straight along now for a while,' Threeday gasped, pounding along the dank tunnel, which seemed to be cooler with each new section. 'Then it goes . . . er . . . left again!'

'Is *that* the map he drew?' said Davey, staring over Mallory's shoulder as they ran. 'It's an absolute nightmare – it'll take us hours to find our way!'

'Stop! Stop!'

Davey panted to a halt and staggered back to his companions. Threeday and Mallory were staring intently at the map. 'I can't tell if the path up ahead and to the left is a shortcut or not . . .' said the cabin-boy.

'Great map,' Davey muttered. 'Let me see . . . hmm . . . is that cross where the Ostrich is?'

Threeday shook his head. 'No, I think that's an arrow trap of some kind.'

'What about the circle, Mall?'

'Um . . . that might be the Ostrich?'

'You don't know?'

'No!' Mallory snapped. 'We didn't exactly have time to ask, did we?'

'Good point,' said Threeday. 'Let's just head for the circle *any* way we can get to it.'

'Fine,' Mallory agreed, 'But what I'm *trying* to say is that I don't know whether the tunnel up ahead and to the left—'

'Oh shut up about the tunnel and let's just run through it! They're probably right behind us! Come on!'

Davey snatched the map from Mallory and bolted ahead. Threeday and the cabin-boy quickly caught up with him, both making numerous attempts to snatch the map back. All of them failed.

'Back off, Gongsolo,' Blackbeard growled, as the natives surrounded him and their chief stepped forward. 'I'm serious; go back to your village and leave me be. We have an understanding, remember?'

Gongsolo stepped forward and raised his hand; the natives quickly lowered their spears.

'*Malai,*' said the chief. '*Aos reai daiad.*'

Blackbeard kept his eyes on the warrior.

'I was just passing through and I wanted to say thank you for the gifts you left me,' he said, describing the fruits by moving his finger in the air. 'Now, if you'll just turn around and—'

'You bring strangers.'

'No, you're mistaken.'

'We TAKE.'

'NO.'

Gongsolo's expression had hardened and suddenly Blackbeard didn't like the look in his eyes.

'I came here alone,' the old man lied. 'D'you understand? I came here *alone* . . . I was talking to myself, just now.'

'Not alone,' Gongsolo contradicted, tapping his jaw and glaring over Blackbeard's head. 'Others in cave. We see; we *see.*'

'We seeeee,' echoed the tribe, once again raising their spears in a threatening manner.

'There's no need for conflict, here,' Blackbeard growled, clenching one fist around his own spear and gritting his teeth. 'Let's just talk about this.'

'No talk.' Gongsolo sniggered nastily. 'You bring strangers. Try take Ostrich.'

The fire went out of Blackbeard's voice as he spoke, but his determined expression remained. 'That thing isn't the god you people worship it as! I NEED to get off this island. D'you understand? I HAVE to. There is a pirate coming here who is *immortal* – he will kill you all.'

There wa a hesitation in Gongsolo's eyes, and Blackbeard quickly seized the initiative.

'I tell you the truth,' the old man spat. 'An evil pirate approaches, even now!'

'*Racha*!' Gongsolo roared, raising his spear once more and moving towards Blackbeard.

'Just listen to me, please!' the old man screamed, thrusting the spearhead forward in a defensive manoeuvre. 'The Ostrich is a curse, but the curse affects the whole island! You know that; it's *your* legend! If the Ostrich is destroyed, the curse will be lifted and the island will be free. I will be free, and you can live here undisturbed by legend hunters!'

Gongsolo grinned, baring his needle-sharp teeth, and Blackbeard knew that his words were falling on deaf ears. Enraged by the greed of the natives, the old man raised his spear and charged at their leader. Evidently, Gongsolo had had the same idea.

As the two ancient warriors clashed, a detachment of several natives worked their way around the pair and disappeared into the caves.

The hunt was on.


'At least the natives don't seem to be following us,' Threeday whispered, as he and Davey felt their way blindly along the tunnel. 'Maybe Blackbeard held them off.'

'Yeah,' Mallory muttered. 'That's something, at least.'

Davey yelped as his knee glanced off a jut in the rock wall. 'Ow! Are you sure this was the way?'

'No, Davey, I'm not sure,' Mallory snapped. 'And please don't start blaming *me* for not *being* sure. I'm OK at navigating the ocean, but NOT an underground cave system. OK?'

'Davey! Mallory! Get down!'

The three companions dived for the floor as something erupted from the opposite wall.

Whooosh . . . thud.

Whoosh, whoosh, whoosh . . . thud, thud, thud.

Silence.

'Threeday?' Davey called, his voice ringing with urgency. 'Mallory? Are you both OK?'

'Yeah,' whispered the zombie.

'I think so,' Mallory echoed.

'What *was* that?'

'An arrow just flew out of the wall. I managed to duck it, and three more went by. I think this stretch of corridor is booby trapped.'

'Is it marked as trapped on Blackbeard's map?' Davey moaned as he dragged himself along.

Mallory took up the parchment and tried to study

the lines in the half-dark of the tunnel. He couldn't see a thing.

'It's too dark,' the cabin-boy admitted. 'But if it *is* a trap, we could be in more trouble than I thought.'

'Why's that?'

'Because it probably means the *circle* we've been heading towards is the trap, and the *cross* at the other end of the complex is the Ostrich.'

'Tell me you're joking,' Threeday muttered.

'Afraid not; sorry. I think I've been reading it wrong.'

Davey cursed under his breath, and the three friends began to crawl on their hands and knees back along the tunnel.

Blackbeard fought tooth and nail to defend himself from the insane attack now visited upon him by the native chief. Evidently, a new threat to the Ostrich was considered more important than old alliances; the old pirate was fighting for his life.

Gongsolo lunged once more and Blackbeard just managed to glance the strike aside with his own custom-built spear.

The rest of the tribe had backed away and formed a perfect circle, waving their arms and screaming like banshees as their leader demonstrated his adept skills in the combative arts.

Gongsolo was very good with the spear; he was moving fast, striking hard and backing off with surprising speed for a man his age.

For his part, Blackbeard was defending well. Despite the fact that most of his counter-strikes had failed, there was still enough movement in his limbs to enable him to get into a variety of his favourite defensive positions. When it came down to it, spear-fighting really wasn't all that different from sword-fighting . . . and sword-fighting was Blackbeard's favourite thing in the world.

If this was to be his last fight, Blackbeard was going to make sure it was a good one.

Threeday poked his head around a corner and scanned the tunnel for any signs of native activity.

'Are they out there?' Davey asked.

'No. At least, I can't see anyone moving.'

'Can you see anything at all?' Mallory prompted.

'No.'

'Well, then, we might as well take a chance and move.'

'Agreed.'

Threeday, clasping a pair of heavy rocks he'd found

three tunnels back, tiptoed a little way along the wall and listened.

'All clear,' he whispered, prompting Davey and Mallory to hurry past him to the next junction.

The young pirate did a quick check of his own. 'Clear here, too!' he concluded, waiting for Threeday to advance.

The three companions performed this little pantomime until they'd retraced their steps to the tunnel that, according to Mallory's interpretation of the map, *had* contained a deadly trap.

Sure enough, the tunnel sloped upwards.

Davey gulped. 'I've got a feeling this might be it,' he said.


The spear fight in the jungle had unexpectedly turned in to an out and out brawl. Both weapons had broken in the heat of the battle, leaving Blackbeard and Gongsolo in what amounted to a boxing match to the death.

Here, the old pirate was undoubtedly outmatched. Despite his ducking and diving routine, Gongsolo had managed to deliver two well-judged right hooks and an uppercut that would've left a mountain gorilla looking for its teeth. To make matters worse, the natives had begun to spit at the circling pair, presumably for the purposes of some ritualistic practice. Consequently, every time Blackbeard managed to dodge a punch, he was inevitably hit by a random wad of thick phlegm. He'd have seen the funny side of it all if he hadn't been getting the beating of his life.

Blackbeard sighed with fatigue. Then he ducked a particularly substantial spit-ball and threw a desperate sucker punch at his opponent . . . but the native chief was wise to the move.

Gongsolo hopped to one side, grabbed the old pirate's arm and delivered a jaw punch which staggered him. He also seized the opportunity to kick Blackbeard in the vitals, chop savagely at his neck and then round the whole attack off with a head-butt to the *back* of the old man's head.

Blackbeard gave in to the cries of agony from his tired body and collapsed. To his horror, Gongsolo snatched him up again and set him on his feet.

'Fight,' the native chanted, an evil smirk on his face.

'Fight!' echoed the assembled tribe. 'Fight! Fight! Fight!'

Davey was getting worried. He'd sent Threeday on ahead to scout out the top-end of the passage, and the zombie had yet to return.

'Do you think he's OK?' Mallory whispered.

'I don't know.'

Davey was sure they'd been nearing their goal, as the last tunnel had climbed for what seemed like an age before veering off sharply to the right. One thing was certain; this place was a maze. Davey had actually lost count of the various side tunnels and small access ways that seemed to branch off in every direction. Without Blackbeard's map, they would have been lost inside five minutes!

'We've got trouble,' the zombie whispered, hurrying up to Davey and Mallory and crouching beside them. 'I can't tell whether they were already on sentry duty or whether they came in the same way as us and took all the *right* turns, but there's a group of natives standing guard at the end of the next passage.'

Davey rolled his eyes. 'Terrific. Did they see you?'

'I don't think so. I got down on all fours and peered around the bend. I was really quiet.'

'How many of them are there?'

'Four, I think, but there might be twice that number!' Threeday scowled at the cabin-boy. 'If you're so interested in the details, why don't *you* go and look for yourself.'

'OK, OK. I'm just trying to work out how we can take them out.'

Threeday grimaced. 'I can probably take a couple,' he said.

'No,' Davey whispered. 'I think I might have a decent plan.' The young pirate drew his sword and handed it to Threeday. 'Can you scratch a drawing of the tunnel into the floor, here?'

The zombie nodded and put down his rocks. Then he took the sword and began to carve an outline into the dust.

'The group is here, here, here and . . . er . . . here, I think,' he muttered, not sounding all that sure of himself.

Davey stared at him for a moment, and then shook his head. 'Right. So—' He bit his lip, nervously. 'So they're all bunched up in front of *that* archway at the back. That means all *you* need to do is take two of them out and arrange a distraction for the other two so that Mall and I can lie in wait at our end of the passage to take care of *them*.'

Threeday nodded, muttered something under his breath and handed the sword back to Davey. Then the three companions began to make their way up the sloping tunnel, Threeday hefting the rocks experimentally in his hands.

'I've got a bad feeling about this,' Davey whispered.

'I've always got a bad feeling about everything,' admitted Mallory. 'Having your soul taken does that to you.'

They reached the archway at the top of the passage and Davey and Mallory quickly put their backs to the first part of the bend.

'Are you ready?' Davey hissed.

Threeday nodded. 'As I'll ever be.'

'Right. One, two, three, GO!'

Afterwards, Davey wished he'd been able to see exactly what happened in that corridor. All he *did* see was Threeday put on a burst of speed and charge around the corner, screaming as if an entire army were chasing him. Then he heard a loud thud, followed by Threeday swearing, followed by a second loud thud and a second, more definitive curse. Then the zombie reappeared and ran past him waving his arms.

'Did you get any of them?' Mallory cried after him, totally forgetting that he and Davey were supposed to be keeping their own presence a secret.

Davey leaped around the bend, swinging his sword with every ounce of strength he could muster.

His courage was rewarded well by the fates, as the

blade edge felled not one but two of the oncoming natives, slashing ugly gashes across their chests and causing their companions to shriek out and adopt defensive modes.

Realizing that Davey had gone in for the kill, Threeday had skidded to a halt and vaulted back up the passage. Rounding the bend in the corridor, he leaped into the air and cannoned into one of the remaining natives, narrowly avoiding the spearheads that were thrust out too late to impale him. Mallory took care of the other, leaping on to the man's back and pulling his head-dress over his eyes before booting him viciously in the stomach and driving a fist into the back of his neck. Unfortunately, the native blocked him.

Davey moved quickly to disarm the first native, who managed to get on to his feet. The young pirate swept his sword in a narrow arc and severed the warrior's spearhead from the wooden stem supporting it. The native let out a startled yelp and threw up an arm to defend himself, but before he could move back, Davey delivered a targeted kick to his shin and caught him a vicious blow on the side of the head with his sword pommel. The man dropped like a sack of potatoes.

In his own conflict, Mallory had resorted to

punching and kicking like a lunatic. His limbs flew in all directions, raining a series of wild punches on his opponent, who was evidently new to the tribe and hadn't yet been taught how to properly defend himself.

All hell was breaking loose.

To make matters worse, Davey fancied that he heard, far off in the tunnel complex, the patter of many bare feet; trouble on the grand scale. More natives were going to arrive at any moment. They *had* to move.

'Get out of here!' Davey yelled, leaping forward and straightening into a dash as he made for the arch at the end of the passage. 'Try to cause a diversion or something – I'm going for the Ostrich!'

'Wai—'

'Just GO! I'll follow you!'

Mallory wailed something unintelligible in reply as Threeday saved him from two new enemies, but the young pirate was out of earshot. He had already vanished into the darkness beyond the arch.

Davey wasn't sure what he had expected to see in the chamber beyond the arch, but it would have been fair to say that he *hadn't* expected an enormous rope bridge yawning across a wide chasm, several of its planks missing and the rest gone to rot. A dark and sickly feeling gripped his stomach and he suddenly felt distinctly light-headed. Tentatively, he placed one foot on the first decrepit plank, to the accompaniment of an alarmingly loud and terrifying creak.

Davey counted to ten under his breath and prayed to the god of pirates, which included a prayer hoping that there *was* one. Then he did something he wouldn't have done in any other circumstance, at any other time – he closed his eyes and ran.

Davey stopped in his tracks and gasped, half relieved to have made it across the rope bridge and half stunned into silence. He had emerged into a circular hall illuminated by more than twenty torches that blazed merrily around the walls. Most of the intervening space was shadowy and cavernous, but an altogether more powerful source of light threw a blue glow over the middle of the hall.

There was a fountain here, though no water plumed out from its centre. Instead, the monument's main pedestal supported the drooping carcass of what was undoubtedly the fabled Voodoo Ostrich. Davey shook his head in amazement as he spotted the creature. It *was* bleeding . . . a steady, impossibly continuous line of blood ran from it and spilled down the side of the fountain. It really was a sight to be seen on no other island in the Caribbean. For a moment, he found himself rooted to the spot and, very briefly, entertained the notion that he might drink from the creature himself. Then he thought of his mother and father . . . and his mind became clear.

Davey Swag walked towards the fountain.

Mallory had been knocked unconscious, and it sounded as though more natives were on the way.

Threeday Leyonger didn't consider himself to be a hero, but even he had to admit that standing in a corridor waiting for an unknown number of enemies to arrive, probably armed with torches, was pretty brave, especially considering that these enemies were savages who paid no attention to his frightening appearance as all looked pretty horrific themselves.

The thought gave him a great idea: he actually didn't look all that different from the natives.

If he were to steal a head-dress from one of the moaning, wounded souls at his feet, grab a spear and run in the direction of the approaching horde, he could probably convince the tribe that he was one of them, at least long enough to sneak past them and back to the cave mouth he'd come in through. All he'd really have to do was wave a bit and point; they just might go for it. They probably wouldn't even notice if Mallory was slung over one of his shoulders.

Threeday moved like lightning, snatching a headdress from one native and a spear from another. Then, pausing only to heave Mallory's unconscious form on to his back, he ran down the corridor as fast as his legs would carry him.

At first, Blackbeard thought it was his own failing vision that made the sky go dark. He didn't truly recognize that the evil-looking storm clouds were real until Gongsolo stopped punching him and suddenly backed away.

The rest of the tribe had fallen to their knees and were looking sheepish, like a class of school children who'd been caught throwing quills at one another.

A fork of lightning arced from the sky and split the clearing. It was followed by several others that struck more or less in the same place, the last hitting the ground dangerously close to Blackbeard's head and forcing the old man to be thankful that his eyes weren't playing him the full show.

*Lightning from the sky, punishment from the gods. The Ostrich had been taken.*

* * *

Davey snatched the straggly remains of the Ostrich and ran, wincing as the cursed creature's never-ending blood stream sprayed over him.

A rock crashed from the roof of the cavern and blocked his path, but he managed to dive aside. He was now saturated with blood from the expired creature, which inexplicably seemed to pulsate with life.

Davey looked up, just as several other great stones came away and followed suit.

The complex was collapsing.

A roar of thunder rumbled over the clearing as Gongsolo and his native tribe peered up at the heavens. As if in reply to their pleading stares, an incredible bolt of white lightning seared out of the sky and split the earth in the centre of their formed circle. Blackbeard tried to focus on the electric ray, but it disappeared, just as a gang of ten or more pirates exploded from the undergrowth and charged into the clearing.

Blackbeard's eyes came to focus on a giant man he had never in his life set eyes upon, but who was, in every sense, completely unmistakable. The old man smiled as he lost consciousness.

Morgan strode forward, the pirates around him

spreading out in preparation for an attack.

'Sto' yer fussin',' Morgan boomed, pulling a jagged cutlass from his belt. 'Sto' yer fussin' an' kill me so' natives.'

The pirate crew readied their weapons, as Morgan locked eyes with Gongsolo.

'You reckon on trying ol' 'Enry on fer size, ol' man,' he muttered. 'C'mon then, I ain' runnin'.'

Gongsolo snatched up what was left of his spear, and quickly tossed it aside. Then he unhooked a makeshift bow from around his neck and swiftly notched up an arrow.

Morgan dodged it at the last second, his eyes filled with the glee of impending bloodshed.

*A diversion*, Davey had said, *try to create some sort of diversion.*

When Threeday reached the first junction, Mallory still slung over one shoulder, he found a group of natives who were quite evidently wondering what their priorities were. They appeared to be torn between saving the island's sacred relic and joining the clearly audible cacophony which had erupted in the clearing below.

Threeday saw that there weren't any spaces between

the men, who were few in number but had still managed to pack out the passageway. Well, he certainly couldn't go around them; his only remaining choice was to go *through* them. He steeled himself, puffed up his chest and ran.

Over the past few days, Threeday had come to realize that you could achieve pretty much anything with the right attitude; even being dead didn't change that. All you had to do, really, was *believe* in yourself. As he ran, Threeday made himself *believe* that he was one of the natives. Having watched the way the group in the tunnel moved when they were panicked, he tried his best to imitate the various attitudes he'd seen them go through. He brought his ragged shoulders up, clenched his tattered fists tightly around the spear, shook his head-dress slightly and ran flat-footed, his bony feet slapping the tunnel floor in a rhythmic, drum-like beat.

Instead of moving quietly through the group and hoping nobody noticed him until he'd moved on, Threeday did completely the opposite, grunting, flapping and pointing in mock desperation as he arrived.

Only two of the natives actually needed to be shoved aside. The rest quickly moved for Threeday and waited to see what he would do. All of them were in a two-

and-eight, talking frantically in their strange and peculiar language. Several assumed Threeday had discovered an intruder in the fountain chamber and had taken him prisoner.

Hurrying on past the group, Threeday suddenly experienced a pang of something he would, looking back on the event, describe as insanity. He stopped dead, peered back along the tunnel and grunted loudly.

The natives watched him with interest, several obviously coming to the conclusion that they couldn't quite place this member of the tribe . . .

'Mff,' Threeday grunted, trying to keep his words as indistinct as possible. He beckoned the group to follow him and thrust an accusatory arm towards the front entrance of the complex. Then he ripped off what he fervently hoped was a frenzied, blood-curdling war-cry, dropped Mallory on to the floor of the passage, and charged.

To his delight, the native group immediately charged after him . . . which was just as well for them, as at that moment the tunnel – which had stood for hundreds of years – suddenly started to collapse.

On the floor of the passage, Mallory groaned himself awake as half a dozen pairs of feet narrowly avoided trampling him into the dust.

*  *  *

At the moment the Voodoo Ostrich was removed, the great mountain had begun to fall apart. Davey worked this out quickly, as rocks twice the size of men crashed into the ground all around him.

Keeping on his toes, Davey squeezed around the first great boulder that had fallen, managing to fit himself through the small space behind it. He had an incredibly grim scene waiting for him on the other side, however – the rope bridge had gone.

Davey was left standing on a small ledge beside a chasm far too large to jump. There was no going forward and no going back.

His luck had just run out.

Gongsolo chased Henry Morgan through the jungle, occasionally pausing in his pursuit to fire off a series of arrows.

The native chief hesitated, his eyes darting frantically from left to right, watching the trees for movement. Wherever the fell pirate had gone, he was hiding well.

Gongsolo notched another arrow and fired it experimentally at one of the three trees in the middle distance. It thwacked into the trunk, causing a large bird to take flight but not, as the native had hoped, flushing a pirate from its shade.

Moving forward cautiously, Gongsolo put a second arrow to the bow and drew back the string, turning from left to right as he tried to decide which of the remaining trees Morgan was crouching behind. It *had* to be one of these two . . . he couldn't have progressed any further without moving into plain sight.

Thwack: a second tree felt the bite of the native's arrow. This time, the strike failed to reveal a bird *or* a pirate.

Only one left, then.

Gongsolo reached back for an arrow, just as Morgan jumped up from the grass directly in front of him.

As the native readied his bow, Morgan reached back with all his might . . . and pitched his cutlass into the air.

Swsh. Hchk.

It hit its intended target square in the chest.

Gongsolo gasped as the blade edge found him, and staggered backwards, dropping his bow to the floor.

Morgan strode up to the wounded native chief, and downed him with a vicious head-butt. Then he yanked out his cutlass, produced a long dagger from his belt and drove it into the old warrior's stomach.

'See ya in 'ell, ol' man,' he boomed.

Gongsolo closed his eyes and the island received another sacrifice.

When Threeday and the native pack he was leading emerged from the caves, an incredible sight greeted them in the clearing below. Pirates and natives fought tooth and claw, spears lancing forward and cutlasses lashing out.

*Where did this lot come from?* he thought, as his own newly acquired troop rushed past him and joined in the fighting.

Threeday looked among those who had fallen and his eyes locked on the prone form of Blackbeard. The old man was badly beaten and he didn't appear to be moving. Threeday hurried over to help him . . .

. . . And ran straight into Gullin and Reik.

The two pirates circled the zombie, Reik raising his sword while the first mate pulled a dagger from his belt.

'I've got a tinder right here in my belt,' Reik muttered. 'Still, if we cut you up really small . . . there won't be enough of you left to burn.'

Reik rushed forward, but Threeday lifted him into the air and tossed him aside like a ragdoll. The man flew through the air and collided with a tree – head first.

Before he could move against Gullin, however, the pirate had charged. He cannoned into Threeday, driving him back and thrusting his sword into the zombie's stomach.

'Ha! You felt *that*, didn't you?'

Threeday brought up a rotting arm and struck the pirate hard under the chin. Then he staggered back and tried to pull the knife from his withered flesh. He'd no sooner removed the blade than Gullin was on him once more, raining blows on his face and chest in a vicious, near maniacal assault.

When Threeday felt his shoulders meet the rough bark of a tree, he kicked out in a frenzy of his own and, catching Gullin off guard, threw himself into the pirate and lifted him bodily from the ground.

The clearing spun in a wild circle as Gullin felt himself hoisted into the air. Then the scene changed with incredible speed ... as the first mate was propelled through the clearing and collided with a low-hanging tree branch. The pain hit him with devastating effect, and he plunged out of the tree and crashed to the ground.

As Threeday strode forward, Gullin rolled over and came face to face with Reik. The ugly pirate was lying against the tree with his eyes rolled back in his head.

Gullin didn't waste a second. He reached instinctively for the man's belt.

Threeday reached down and snatched hold of Gullin's neck, just as the first mate thrust out his colleague's tinder-pistol and pulled the trigger. Threeday went up like a blue inferno.

'Die, you abomination!' Gullin screamed, as the zombie flailed around in the searing heat of the flames. 'Dieeeeeee!'

Threeday felt nothing but pain and rage. Blinded by the flames and deafened by the roar of steel all around him, he charged forward, colliding with Gullin and driving his flame-wreathed fist into the pirate's skull. There was a sickening crack, as the back of Gullin's head hit the tree, and he dropped like a sack of potatoes.

Threeday dived for the floor, rolling around and slapping himself in a wild and frantic attempt to beat out the flames. Eventually, he managed it.

Pain. So much pain.

Threeday's fingers found the edge of a spear and closed around it. Wracked with agony, the zombie tried to lift himself off the jungle floor, but he lacked the strength to move. Just as he felt his will ebbing away from him, a giant hand reached down and pulled him on to his feet.

'If it ain' the whelp's zombie frien',' Morgan boomed. 'An' 'e all bu' ready ta die.'

Davey Swag tried to consider his options, but it was no good; he didn't have any. The chasm yawned out before him, an impossibly wide, impossibly deep hole of darkness with no discernible end.

Davey spat some blood from his mouth. He was still covered in the red liquid from the Ostrich that lay draped over his shoulders.

Up above him, more rocks were falling from the massive cavern. It was like watching a large-scale version of a hailstorm.

*Only one thing for it, really*, he reflected, sheathing his sword and muttering a prayer.

Davey Swag gathered up every ounce of courage he had left . . . and jumped into oblivion.

Charnel Island had descended into a chaotic hell-hole. Boulders the size of houses broke away from the crest of the mountain and rolled inexorably downwards. In the jungle, trees that had stood for a thousand years inexplicably toppled and crashed to the ground. It would have been impossible from the island floor to tell what was happening, but the birds flying high over

Charnel saw it all; the ocean was rising up to claim the land.

Henry Morgan snatched the spear Threeday had attempted to thrust at him, and broke it in half over his knee.

'Where is 'e, ya undead freak,' the pirate boomed, snatching his victim by the neck and lifting him high off the ground. 'Where's youn' Swag?'

'Y— y— you'll never know,' Threeday growled, trying to match the power of the pirate but failing miserably. Morgan's incredible strength was holding him at arm's length while the man's ham-sized hands were attempting to crush his rotted larynx. If only he could . . .

''As 'e go' 'is 'ands on me prize? 'As 'e?'

'Chfjfff,' Threeday choked. 'Djsja! Cjhgf!'

'Tha's righ', zombie. You wishin' you'd died afresh now, ain' ya?'

Threeday fought as hard as he could against the pirate, but it just wasn't enough to break Morgan's elephantine grip. The zombie screamed out in rage, and his eyes began to burn like fire.

Davey had never in his life fallen from a great height. Uncle Jake's orphanage was built quite close to a sheer cliff face and, as a youngster, he'd been dared a number of times to walk right up to the edge and put a foot over. He'd never done so, for heights tended to scare the living daylights out of him, but one of the other boys had actually performed the deed . . . and had fallen. Davey remembered with no small amount of concern that the idiot lad had broken one leg and badly damaged his arm . . . and he hadn't even fallen *that* far. Certainly not as far as Davey was falling right now.

He clamped on to the Ostrich as if his life depended on it.

The air rushed past him and through him, and he practically swallowed his tongue in the onslaught of air. Any second now he would hit the bottom of the chasm . . . and then it was curtains, unless . . .

SPLASH.

The water engulfed Davey as he plunged into the lake like a dart. It felt as though he would never stop sinking. Regaining the use of his limbs, Davey thrust out the arm that wasn't clamped on to the dead bird and began to make for the surface, yet he quickly found himself swept up and away.

*If this is a lake*, he thought, remembering Blackbeard's reported fall, *why exactly is the water moving this fast?*

Davey kicked with all his might, and surfaced strongly. It was then that the reason for his rapid movement became apparent. The former lake was rushing out of the mountain, the side of which had collapsed, leaving a gaping hole. The new river was rushing to join the oceans ... and it was taking Davey with it.

The natives and the pirates had fought each other to a stand-still. The loss and preoccupation of their respective leaders combined with the sudden raging destruction all around them was sapping their desire to die pointlessly in the name of fear.

Instead, the several remaining members of each group had retreated from combat and were surreptitiously peering around for a likely means of escape from the whirlwind of chaos nature had suddenly thrown at them. A few of the natives saw the destruction of the island as a punishment from the gods for their recent lack of sacrifices, but most of the pirates felt it was the perfect opportunity to get as far away from trouble as possible, and *this* handful of sea-dogs had turned and run for their lives, hoping to stumble across something they could use as a raft on the way.

*  *  *

Mallory stumbled into the clearing and practically fell over Blackbeard, who was muttering to himself and trying to move his head.

'C'mon,' the cabin-boy managed, reaching out for the old man's arms and trying to help him on to his feet. 'Let's get you out of here . . . if we can.'

Blackbeard groaned a little . . . and passed out again.

Threeday's eyes bulged grotesquely in his head.

'Chghgh,' he managed, as his limbs stopped kicking at the giant pirate and began to hang loose.

'You like tha', zombie whelp? Feels ba', doesn' it? I'm crushin' the life righ' outta ya.'

Threeday's eyelids flickered a few times, and then opened wider than they had done before, in shock. An immense wall of water was rushing down the mountainside towards them. Morgan, fully focussed on throttling the zombie, had his back to it.

'Wha' tha', freak? Ya tryin' ta beg for mercy?'

'Chh! Chks!'

Threeday's choked reply and loss of consciousness were delayed as the waves cannoned into the two combatants and swept them away like leaves caught in a breeze.

Mallory had just enough time to grab a tree branch before the tide washed through the area, sweeping Blackbeard out of his grasp and promptly taking the branch *and* the tree he was attached to on its rush for the ocean.

Mallory fought to maintain his scant purchase on the floating tree, but he quickly lost his grip and was thrown off course. He could just make out one or two other vague shapes in the drink, but it was impossible to tell if one of them was the old man.

Suddenly, everything went blue . . . as the river tide hit the ocean.

Charnel Island was sinking, slowly but surely, and what remained of its once glorious beach was now half awash with chaos.

Henry Morgan had used his strength to good effect. Once the immense body of water had met with the ocean proper, he'd quickly swum back to the shore, and was wading up the sand in a definite determination to find and destroy the boy who even now was probably stealing his destiny.

A little way along the beach, Threeday had surfaced, spotting Morgan's march quick enough to crawl behind a sand dune and keep out of the big pirate's way. The zombie ached all over. To make matters worse, one of his arms was shattered, his tattered throat was still on fire and he felt distinctly weak. He wondered where Davey and Mallory were, and if his friends had survived the terrible collapse of the mountain.

He could only pray for them, now.

Henry Morgan charged up the beach, his blood boiling and his temper at breaking point.

'You can' hide fro' me, Swag,' he growled. 'I'll fin' ya 'f it takes me an—'

'Are you looking for me, Morgan?'

The pirate stopped in his tracks, and turned his head slightly.

Davey Swag half splashed, half waded ashore, drawing his sword in the process. He thought his rage at Morgan had been satiated, but the sight of the pirate had ignited his fury once again. 'Well? Answer me, you *mortal* wretch.' A terrible grin lit up Davey's young face, as the giant pirate stepped towards him. 'That's right, Morgan, your fabled bird is out *there* now, drowning in the drink . . .' Davey thrust a hand out towards the ocean. 'Its blood has washed away and its island is sinking into the depths. How does it feel to have a life snatched away from you? How does it feel to *you*?'

Morgan screamed with rage and drew his own blade. 'You'll know soon enough, whelp. You won' escape ol' 'Enry. 'Stroyin' tha' bird'll be the las' thin' you e'er did.'

Davey swept the sword in a wild arc and kept on walking straight at the pirate.

'You don't sound sure, Morgan,' he said. 'And you'll *have* to kill me because as far as I'm concerned we're still not even yet. You took my mother *and* my father from me; that's *two* lives. I've only taken *one* of yours . . . so far.'

Swords clashed in the air, and Morgan seemed surprised at the sudden strength and determination inherent in the young pirate's attack.

Davey swung the blade with all his might, then moved to parry, narrowly avoiding a nasty wound when the giant pirate drove his own blade forward.

For his part, Morgan was overstretching himself, expending enormous amounts of energy by repeatedly lunging at Davey with the full force of his incredible bulk. If he connected with a sweep, the young pirate wouldn't stand a chance . . . but he was finding it practically impossible to *hit* Davey; the boy was just too fast.

Reaching a decision, Morgan suddenly pulled back and waved his sword experimentally, as if he was unfamiliar with the blade and had resorted to testing its weight.

'You come ta me, boy,' he growled. 'You come ta me 'f ya go' the guts.'

Davey gritted his teeth . . . and lunged forward.

Mallory had found Blackbeard washed up against a log on the edge of the jungle. Dragging the old man behind him, he staggered, fell, staggered, heaved, staggered and stretched his way across the beach, collapsing on to the small dune that contained a couple of downed tree branches, a pile of soaked foliage . . . and Threeday Leyonger. Impossible as it seemed, the zombie looked close to death.

There was another roll of thunder, and the entire shoreline seemed to lurch. The island was sinking even further into the waves.

'W— what happened to you?' Mallory spat, checking to see if Blackbeard was breathing before turning his attention back to the zombie. 'Did you actually lose a fight? In your condition?'

Threeday smiled, coughed a little . . . and pointed across the beach to a spot where two pirates, one big and one small, were fighting to the death.

# Dark Justice

Davey Swag and Henry Morgan circled each other, both looking for an opening. The giant pirate was red with rage; a torn hole in his shirt revealed a line of blood that spilled from a wound Davey had opened during his first lunge at Morgan's newly-mortal defences.

The chaos around them wasn't helping. Charnel Island had sunk further into the ocean and now both men were up to their knees in water.

'I'll kill ye yet, Davey Swag,' Morgan spat. 'Ye migh' be the son o' a know-nothin' guvnor, whelp, but ye ain' a pirate *yet*.'

'You're wrong, Morgan,' Davey muttered, keeping his eyes firmly on the giant pirate's blade. 'I was a pirate the moment I was born. Now I'm the *man* you made when you orphaned me.'

Morgan smiled, displaying a set of decaying teeth, but he took a step *back*.

'I don't know what you're smiling about, Henry,' Davey said, his voice sounding a lot less shaky than he was feeling. 'Look down at your side. You see that? When was the last time you took a wound and actually *felt* it? Yet I dare say you've probably been dishing out wounds aplenty yourself, haven't you? WHELP.'

Morgan waded towards the young pirate and stabbed out with his sword. Davey leapt back and, as the blade edge missed by mere inches, knocked the sword aside with his own weapon.

'Ya won' be able t' 'void me when the waters lap ya up,' Morgan chided, testing the edge of Davey's blade with a couple of experimental taps.

The young pirate gave a mock gasp. 'You swim that well? I'd have thought a man of your girth would go straight to the bottom like a stone dropped down a deeeeeeeeeeeep well.'

It worked. Morgan threw himself forward in a great rage and swiped at the space where Davey had been, hitting dead air and receiving a vicious slash across the right cheek for his trouble.

'Arghghh! Curse you, Swag. When I ge' hold o' ya, ya'll bleed twice fer ev'ry wound ya scored on ol' 'Enry.'

Davey waded back a little.

'That's – what – four you owe me so far, then?' he

said, suddenly finding an inner confidence that made him feel ten feet tall. Henry Morgan might have led a terrible life and he might have been an immortal legend on the high seas, but when it came right down to it he was just a man, now – flesh and blood like everyone else.

Davey looked down at his sword, and suddenly he *knew* that this was a battle he could win.

Mallory had fetched the rowing boat and had rowed it on to what was left of the beach. He helped Threeday inside, and together they managed to drag Blackbeard in, too.

The old man was very badly beaten, but at least his breathing was now coming and going in loud and very deep breaths.

Mallory wheeled the boat around, hooked up the oars and squinted at the shoreline.

'What's happening?' Threeday managed.

Mallory shook his head.

'It's Davey,' he muttered. 'He's fighting Morgan, and it looks as though he's holding his own, but—'

'B— but what?' Threeday's whole face was wracked with exhaustion.

'He's no match,' said Mallory. 'I just know Morgan

very well . . . and I don't think Davey has what it takes to beat him.'

'He needs help. I'll—'

Threeday struggled up on to his knees, but collapsed back into the boat as one of them snapped beneath him.

'You can' kill me, whelp,' Morgan whispered, his cheek still running with blood. 'You're too eaten up wi' anger an' revenge ta think straight. All ol' 'Enry 'as ta do is wai' fer ya ta make a mistake . . . an' then you're mine.'

Davey tried to wade further up the beach. If the water rose any higher than his waist, he'd lose the mobility edge over his infinitely more experienced adversary . . . and he *definitely* couldn't afford to do that.

'Ya really think ya 'ave what it takes ta kill a legen'?' the pirate growled, wiping his free hand over the face wound and licking the blood from his fingers. 'I bin tearin' 'round 'ese waters fer a lifetime, whelp. I sin things you ain' sin . . . I done things tha'—'

'You're telling me nothing,' Davey replied, finding a few precious feet of clear sand. 'I don't *care* what you've seen and I *know* the things you've done, remember?'

Davey swilled up a mouthful of spit and hoicked it at the pirate's face. 'That's my review of your life.'

'Talkin' me ta death, whelp? Tha' all you got?'

Before Davey could respond, Morgan did something entirely unexpected; he tossed his sword skyward, caught it along the middle and threw the blade at the young pirate as though it were a spear.

It was a reckless and stupid move that would have failed nine times out of ten . . . but Davey simply wasn't ready for it.

He staggered back, the blade buried deep in his shoulder.

Morgan advanced, a look of sheer and unadulterated glee in his eyes. Spitting with hatred, he rushed up to his injured foe and snatched hold of the pommel of his sword.

Davey made a last-ditch effort to strike him with his own blade, but Morgan effortlessly blocked the attempt, forcing his hand down with a strength that felt as though it was coming from ten men.

'You don' look so chirpy now, whelp,' he boomed, driving the sword down and forcing Davey on to his knees. ''Aven' ya 'ny more words o' wisdom fer ol' 'Enry, or 'as the cat caught yer tongue 'n its claws?'

Davey let out a pained gasp, and gripped his sword tighter than ever before, but it was all he could do just to lift it a few inches off the ground.

Morgan's evil eyes flashed with malice.

'Look a' ya now,' he boomed. ''Elpless as yer paren's when I sen' 'em both to *'ell.*'

The ocean was rising to claim Charnel Island for its own. Most of the beach was now under water, and the single remaining patch of sand was currently being occupied by two pirates, both very different in appearance.

Morgan stepped back and withdrew the blade from Davey's shoulder. Then he put a foot in its place and pushed, sending the young pirate tumbling backwards where he splashed into the lapping water and wriggled around in torment.

'Think I'll 'ave time ta kill thee slow an' still ge' off this drownin' islan'?' Morgan spat, stalking the boy as he tried to slide away from him. 'Only, ol' 'Enry 'as ta get 'is fun while 'e can, now he's jus' a mortal man.'

Davey tried to lift himself on to one knee, but Morgan was on him in seconds, kicking him in the small of the back and sending him crashing, face first, in the ocean. Davey took in what felt like a lungful of salty water before he finally managed to force himself upright again.

'No' so easy, is it, whelp?' Morgan chuckled, raising

his sword again. 'Say yer goo'byes ta the light.' Morgan raised his sword to deliver the killing blow . . . and he was hit in the side of the head with a conch.

Morgan staggered slightly, his vision clouding over. When, after a few seconds, it swam back into focus, a rough and oddly familiar face was staring at him with mounting horror.

'Now be honest,' Mallory said, whistling between his teeth. 'That HAD to hurt.'

Morgan waited a moment for his memory to return. When it did, his eyes filled with pure and absolute abhorrence.

'Mallory,' he growled, clutching at his face with one hand and raising his sword with the other. The pirate gritted his teeth so hard that his gums began to bleed. 'I reckon it mus' fair be me lucky day . . .'

Davey Swag had struggled back to his feet and was staggering towards the pair, his shoulder wound sending shockwaves of agony through his body. In spite of this, he managed to keep a tight grip on his sword.

Morgan swung out a fist and struck Mallory across the face, knocking him sideways with such force that his feet actually left the ground for a moment.

'A taster fer ya,' he muttered, clenching and

unclenching the fist that had done the work. 'I'll deal wi' ya prop'ly when I put pay ta the whelp ya stole awa' fro' me.'

Morgan paced over to Davey and brought his sword down again, but the young pirate managed to raise his own blade in time to partially block the strike. Then, Davey moved like forked lightning, striking so fast and with such fury that his arm was a blur.

Morgan looked down at the blade protruding from his stomach, a disbelieving expression on his face. The pirate's pinprick eyes moved from Davey to the sword and back again, and seemed to grow more bulbous with every movement.

'I—' he started, and staggered a little. 'Wha' ya dun to ol' 'Enry,' he growled, blood and spit congealing on his trembling lips. 'Ya li'l maggot . . . wha' ya dun?'

Henry Morgan, arguably the most fearsome and undoubtedly the most evil pirate in the history of the Caribbean, dropped to his knees for the first and last time in his life. His final glance at Davey Swag was a look of shock and sudden admiration as, rocking forwards, the legendary pirate died.

As Mallory rolled over in the sand and scrambled unsteadily to his feet, Davey Swag watched Morgan's body float out of the bay. At length, it disappeared under the water . . . and *that* was when Davey noticed that his own waist was submerged – Charnel Island's journey to the seabed was evidently gaining speed.

'Mall!' Davey called out, as he noticed the cabin-boy now splashing about at a point further along the rising tide. 'Where on earth did you come from?'

'Out there,' Mallory managed, nursing his bruised face and pointing out at the ocean. 'Threeday sent me. He's in a pretty bad way . . . and don't even bother *asking* about Blackbeard.'

Davey turned and saw the zombie waving a spindly arm at him from the small rowing boat. A smile stretched across his lips – both his friends had made it out alive.

'C'mon,' Davey said, sheathing his sword. 'Let's get back to the boat . . .'

Mallory hesitated, and glanced out at the bay. 'You don't think it's worth looking in the shallows for the Ostrich?' he ventured.

The young pirate shook his head.

'You can,' he said. 'But only if you want to nail it to the wall as a memento – wherever that evil thing is, it's all dried up.'

Davey dived into the water and began to swim for the boat. At length, Mallory followed him, wondering if the bird had been taken all the way out into the great ocean or if it would for ever linger on the half sunken mass than now constituted Charnel Rock.

'You did it, then.' Threeday beamed at Davey, as Mallory helped to haul the exhausted pirate into the boat. 'You know, you're a *real* pirate now . . .'

'Yeah.' Davey sighed. 'Whatever that means.'

'A real pirate and a good one,' Mallory added. 'You've destroyed a man responsible for the death of many innocent people. You're a hero and a half.'

'Aye,' the young pirate admitted, with an exhalation of breath. 'But only if *you're* the half, Mall. Thanks for the last-minute help. If it wasn't for you, I might've ended up floating away on the tide *myself.*'

'Trust me,' Threeday muttered, his eyes flickering weakly in the glare of the sun. 'It was the *least* he could do. Now, if it's not too much trouble, can somebody please take off their stuff and help to cover me up? I'm literally burning away here . . .'

Mallory set about removing Blackbeard's various fronds and using them to cover up the zombie's smouldering torso.

They needed to get back to the ship . . . and fast.

Davey grabbed at his shoulder and collapsed into the

corner of the boat, the pain of his wound searing through him.

'We must get you and Blackbeard to a surgeon,' Mallory muttered, staring out to sea with a worried look on his face. 'I don't know *what* Threeday needs, but some ice and a damn good witch-doctor wouldn't go amiss . . .'

Davey clutched a trembling hand to his shoulder.

'We'll find them all in good time,' he said, his lips breaking into a happy grin. 'After all, the *Pride* is the fastest ship in the ocean.'

'You're right,' Mallory muttered. 'You're absolutely right.'

Mallory took up the oars, and began to row them into the mists.

# Epilogue

Mallory became a pirate captain, and sailed the seven seas in search of high adventure. Unfortunately, he caught anti-cabin fever on his first voyage, went completely insane and – to the astonishment of his crew – instructed *himself* to walk the plank. Though his body was never officially recovered, Mallory was sighted many years later at a bar on Tide Island, talking to a parrot about the price of millet seed.

Threeday Leyonger returned to Cocos Island and soon became the first zombie governor in the island's long history. He married a young witch-doctor called Epitee Kaar who managed to keep his body animated until the ripe old age of eighty-seven.

Davey Swag went on many other adventures and made himself a legend on the expansive and tumultuous waters of the Caribbean. When he eventually retired from a life on the high seas, he met a pretty French actress and went to live on a tropical paradise in the balmy heart of the Caribbean. There, he wrote his memoirs in the hope that one day the world would know of his strange and curious adventures. The fates, he said, had smiled upon him.

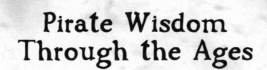

# Pirate Wisdom
# Through the Ages

Shave twice a day 'n' three times a night. That way, you'll never go hungry. *Riebald Perrygonow*

Always talk in your loudest voice; no one ever overheard a man shouting. *Filian Flittershale*

The more you know a man, the less you'll like his sister. *Paolo Sinclair*

When it comes to surgeons, always get a second opinion; the first might not be his last. *Harry Crosspatch*

Never push your luck – always pull it. *Davey Twitcher*

Grow up fast. If you don't, blokes half your height will catch up with you. *Ronnie Muldoon*

Never attempt to steal a man's shoes while he's running after you. *Bill Cogilobly*

Give as good as you get, then go before you're given it back. *Henry Quackers*

Two wrongs don't make a right, but one don't make you even. *Blackbeard*

Kick a fella while's he down; if he's up, it's higher. *Henry Morgan*

Never curse a man for cursing you back. *John Avery*

Throw at least two punches in every fight. If you still can't get to the door, beg for mercy. *Davey Swag*

Never aim low when you're fighting a midget; he's usually got that end covered. *Weedig Rushet*

Break a man's arm in seven places; if he doesn't notice, walk away quietly. *Toby Tannerlingo*

It's rare to find an ambush in your own garden. *Threeday Leyonger*

Run away from people you don't get on with. It ALWAYS surprises them. *Peter Wormy-Woolington*

A pirate's handshake is only valid if it's not the hand he uses to hold his cutlass. *Nellie McGerard*

Never start a fight your friends can't finish. *Portalo Dumpton*

TITANIC 2020

*Colin Bateman*

Everyone said the original Titanic was unsinkable. Shows how much they knew.

Everyone says the new Titanic is unsinkable. But there are worse things than drowning as stowaway Jimmy Armstrong and rich girl Claire quickly find out.

With a mysterious, incurable disease rapidly infecting the population, being at sea seems the safest place to be . . .

## STONEHEART

*Charlie Fletcher*

When George breaks a small dragon carving from the Natural History Museum he finds himself plunged into a world he can't understand; racing for survival in a city where sculptures and stone carvings move and fight, where it's impossible to know who to trust and where nothing is what it seems.

Enter the original and breathtaking world of this epic adventure, the first of an exciting three book sequence, and you'll never see the city the same way again . . .